St. Agatha's Breast

St. Agatha's Breast

T. C. Van Adler

alyson books
los angeles | new york

MANUFACTURED IN THE UNITED STATES OF AMERICA.

THIS TRADE PAPERBACK IS PUBLISHED BY ALYSON BOOKS,
P.O. BOX 4371, LOS ANGELES, CA 90078-4371.
DISTRIBUTION IN THE UNITED KINGDOM BY
TURNAROUND PUBLISHER SERVICES LTD.,
UNIT 3, OLYMPIA TRADING ESTATE, COBURG ROAD, WOOD GREEN,
LONDON N22 6TZ ENGLAND.

FIRST EDITION PUBLISHED BY ST. MARTIN'S PRESS: 1999
FIRST ALYSON BOOKS EDITION: DECEMBER 2001

01 02 03 04 05 **a** 10 9 8 7 6 5 4 3 2 1

ISBN 1-55583-708-5
(PREVIOUSLY PUBLISHED BY ST. MARTIN'S PRESS WITH ISBN 0-312-20019-6.)

LIBRARY OF CONGRESS CATALOGING-IN-PUBLICATION DATA
  VAN ADLER, T.C.
    ST. AGATHA'S BREAST / T.C. VAN ADLER.—1ST ALYSON ED.
    ISBN 1-55583-708-5
    1. POUSSIN, NICOLAS, 1594?–1665—APPRECIATION—FICTION. 2. ROME
(ITALY)—FICTION. 3. MONASTERIES—FICTION. 4. ART THEFTS—FICTION.
  I. TITLE: SAINT AGATHA'S BREAST. II. TITLE.
  PS3572.A4136 S7 2001
  813'.54—DC21   2001045985

COVER DESIGN BY MATT SAMS.
COVER PHOTOGRAPH OF DETAIL OF THE FRESCO OF *THE MARTYRDOM OF
SAINT AGATHA* BY NICOLO CIRCIGNANI FROM THE SAN STEFANO ROTUNDA BY
T.C. VAN ADLER.

Cast of Characters

Community of San Redempto

THE REVEREND FATHERS

Rev. Avertanus Deblaer, Emmeritus Professor of Mystical Theology
Very Rev. Emmanuele Angostini, Prior
Rev. Brocard Curtis, Archivist
Rev. Otger Aarnack
Rev. Berthold (Bertie) Langdon
Rev. Dionysius McGreel
Rev. Pius Poncelet
Rev. Cuthbert Mullins
Rev. Angelus Lennon

THE BROTHERS

Antonio, the Porter
Ephraim, the Launderer
Manolo, the Lay Cook and Economo, brother of Antonio

Others

Professoressa Zinka Pavlic, Art Historian
Professor Charles Mitchum, Art Historian
Madam Camille Blanchierdarie, Directrice of the Biblioteque Française
Dr. Hoop Rhutten, Art Historian
Pino, Hustler
Thius Meyer, Researcher
Sister Apollonia Van Barren
Wilfredo Malouf, Art Dealer

St. Agatha's Breast

Part One

Murder

I

With the light focused on the canvas, all he could see were the cracks which lay just beneath the varnish, spreading weblike around the tortured body. The painting was in lamentable condition, like so many old, anonymous canvases scattered on the mildewed walls of Roman monasteries. For longer than anyone could remember it was one of a series of age-blackened martyrs which had hung so high on the wall of the ambulatory that they were never really noticed, distinguished more by their ornate frames and gloomy presence than for their subject matter. Then with the robbery, this one remaining painting took on great importance, as if it might hold the key to this strange event which had brought an unwanted note of chaos into a world of stultifying order.

In truth, Brocard didn't know what he was supposed to be looking for as he held the light up to the canvas. It seemed part of some ritual without rubrics which he was compelled to perform. With that weighty bravura with which he performed every task, Brother Antonio, the porter, had leaned a ladder to the wall and slowly brought the painting down. In a breath all the monks (except for Father Avertanus who curiously wasn't there) had edged forward, transfixed by the blood-red stain which the painting left behind, surely a sign of life sucked out into the unforgiving walls of San Redempto. Then after placing the canvas on the library table, the brother paced off an arch around it, like a dog marking his territory, so that Brocard alone could get near.

He was after all their archivist, the one set apart to observe and record, to give sense and order to centuries of the order's droppings so that they might be read as history. A tedious job which required the most tedious of monks, an appellation with which he would only take pride. Since leaving Philadelphia nearly thirty years ago, Brocard (né Jimmy Curtis, but who would have believed it) had worked assiduously to remove all sugar from his blood, to rub away that enthusiasm-writ-large which betrayed his New World roots. So complete was his success that any hint of a past, not to mention a personality, was lost. Nor could it possibly rear its head in the world he chose to live in: one circumscribed by a routine devoid of all spontaneity. Balance and order and peace at any price—that was what drove him. Yet as he began to examine the canvas placed on the table before him, when he felt the expectant panting of the community and, for the first time he could remember, smelled the strong mustiness of their bodies pressing down on him, he knew that everything was about to change. How, he could not see, but the sure knowledge that things would change shadowed him with dread.

On closer inspection, the painting was not without interest. Stretched out on a marble slab, commanding the lower third of the canvas, was a young girl, naked except for a strategically draped cloth around her loin. Feet and hands bound, drawn out from her body and held in place by two groups of tormentor voyeurs. He knew enough about classical painting technique to understand the attention which had been given to her skin, the layering of translucent *velaturas* so the flesh seemed alive. Where her breasts should have risen were two gaping cavities. Above her loomed a pagan priest hallowed in white billowing robes. With his left hand he pressed down her arched shoulder while triumphantly waving one of her breasts in a pair of bloodied pliers. The other breast, it seemed to Brocard as he made a fervent search for it, was lost forever in the chiaroscuro. What struck him as most odd, as he made his inspection in full view of his community, was the way in which the girl's head was turned towards his, drawing him alone into her world. Eyes made blank with the darkness of time, head raised slightly, her lips parted as if to sigh some secret. One thing that his years in Rome had taught him was that messages shoot across time and call out from seemingly inanimate objects. The fact that he had chosen to wall himself off from such facts until now was rendered irrelevant. What ever could Santa Agatha, for that is surely who the young girl in the painting was, feel compelled to share with him?

4

As much to break her stare as to continue the charade of expertise, he asked the brother to help him turn the canvas over, intent on inspecting the back. As a stench of mildew filled the air, he dramatically swept a handkerchief from his pocket and held it over his nose. He then leaned forward to inspect the crossbar more closely, and there under the cobwebs and grime, faint but clearly legible, was the marking which began his search in earnest: *Nicolas Poussin, 1629.*

2

*I*mmediately on confirming the archivist's find, those damnable words which only one man could have written, Emmanuele, the prior, felt the pain gathering behind his eyes. Normally his headaches simply appeared for no reason whatsoever. This time, the stress was identifiable. He had, of course, known of the possible attribution of the series of paintings since that Dutchman Hoop had studied them nearly a decade ago. Should he now feign ignorance? And if he owned up to it, would accusations fly that it was his responsibility to let the general curia know? Or at the very least to remove them from a public corridor? Should he have allowed art historians free reign of the monastery to muddle over them, rather than silence Hoop with that gift of a drawing as he had? Now that the possible value of the paintings was generally known, would his leadership be called into question? Would suspicion be cast on him? He had absolutely no idea how he was going to proceed. But being the introvert he was, the dark solitude of his cell was the only remedy for indecision, the only refuge from the coming pain.

He locked the door behind him and drew the drapes, leaving the faint light of his screen saver to hold back total darkness. *Cell*—a silly term, he often thought, for this neat and orderly suite of rooms. Everything in its place, from the book-lined walls to the latest computer hardware, from the tightly made cot and well-scrubbed sink to the end table with yet another posthumous Calvino book. He had neither mirrors nor television (there was after all a mirror in the communal lavatory and a television in the recreation room), but he did have E-mail and it was to that he turned his attention.

Searching his address file, he quickly located the institute in Nijmegen, then the private address of the interim director. For an indeterminate period of time he sat transfixed before the screen, catatonic on the outside alone. Then the following message came tumbling out:

Caro Otger,

How long it has been since you've returned to Rome. Do not forget that this is your community. The monastery seems empty without your expansive presence. We are grateful for the blessing of that visually stunning student you sent our way last year, Thius, I believe his name was, even though he had a predictable northern coldness about him. As you can imagine, many of the brethren, myself not included, found that quality even more captivating. They're so very desperate, poor souls.

I have a practical question. You may remember that nine or ten years ago, you sent down a young art historian from your province. Hoop Rhutten, I believe his name was. As I remember, in his youth he had studied a bit with Blunt at the Courtauld and was fired up by things Baroque. He spent several months with us, a rather flirtatious time as I recall despite his unfortunate face, during which he tore apart our archives with youthful zeal. His project was to catalogue all of our images, mainly the endlesskpkliaseskik on paper. Some quite good period pieces as I recall, some possible Dughets and imitation Carraccis, but most absolutely forgettable. Like so much in this pile of a building.

My problem is simply stated. We have had a little robbery. Six of those seven dreary martyr paintings which hung high above the portraits of the prior generals in the ambulatory-you may not even remember them if your visual memory is as weak as it always was-were removed from their frames last night. By whom and for what reason, we would do well never to know. For this reason I have asked that dullard Brocard to investigate the matter. He is, after all, "archivist" and the one the community would expect would. But his thoroughness, like everything else about him, is colored by such a lack of imagination that this whole matter is bound to fade away as rapidly as it began. We don't need disturbances here and must guard against outside eyes disrupting our contemplative gaze, n'est-ce pas?

So, I want to divert our little man's attention, lead him to the archives which your friend Hoop started to catalogue but ultimately left in a royal mess. There are enough cul-de-sacs there to keep Brocard in the labyrinth until he tires. My concern is that Hoop is unreachable so that our archivist never has to widen his search. I know he left the order many years ago. Will the last address we have for him dead-end? Can you make sure it does? You are a dear. Your willing servant,

E.

He clicked the mouse on Send and felt relief. Damage control done. Now all that remained was to call a community meeting, to encourage Brocard, and to wait for the confusion to set in. His headache too was begining to subside and in celebration of that fact, and the good work he had just done, he decided he could face the day once more. He opened the drapes and then went to push back the shutters. However, without warning, the *tramontana* had started. The incessant dry wind pressed down from the mountains and made some mad. Emmanuele, on the other hand, was not about to fall under its sway. Going over to the medicine cabinet he sprayed himself generously with his favorite fragrance: Escape.

3

It was the season of blood oranges, and so Antonio went directly to the orchard, realizing that Manolo would be there indulging his passion. He caught sight of his brother from a distance, and as he had so often, felt that he was looking at himself. Although Manolo was nearly ten years younger, they both had that squat, rough-featured earthiness which forever identified them as Basque peasants. Their greeting was an expressionless look which they alone knew as intimacy. Antonio plucked an orange from a weighted bough and joined his brother on the ledge of the cistern, ripped off the peel with his teeth, then bit into the fruit, allowing its thick red juice to congeal on his chin and splatter his habit and the ground around him. It was hard to tell what was more satisfying about blood oranges, their sweet young flesh or the messiness with which they met their fate.

"You saw the announcement on the community board?" They spoke in Basque, their private language, unconnected at root from all other languages, from all the others in the community.

"About the house meeting after vespers tomorrow. The prior had to call it."

Then, after he had licked his hands clean, Antonio said what they had both been thinking. "Let's just hope people don't start opening doors."

They had developed quite a system, these two blood brothers. No one knew how extensive it was, but suspicions ran high. Shortly after Antonio arrived in Rome as an illiterate young lay brother he saw the potential. He was too far beneath the priests and the scholars in the house to rouse suspicion. And they were so helpless and gullible. "Let the brother do it," they all said. Answer the door and collect mass stipends, give out scapulars and accept donations, bring shoes to the cobbler and mail to the Vatican post office. No one ever counted the change he put back in the poverty box. As porter, he also had total control over the monastery's communications. Answered and bolted the front door, passed on telephone calls or lost messages as seemed best, sent and collected mail. His was the power of the lowly, and he was quick to point out to his younger brother, who had been searching for ways to get out of his fly-ridden village, where opportunity lay.

When the sisters who ran the kitchen had all either run off with wayward priests or simply expired from old age, Antonio proposed to the prior that his brother, a lay man of great piety who had an uncommon love of cooking, be offered the job. Sight unseen, such was and is the desperation of the time, Manolo was offered the job. And so, armed with whatever recipes he could pick up from villagers and a lust for success which outstripped faith itself, he boarded a train to Rome, never to look back.

In no time at all he learned how to be obsequious, how to volunteer his help, and how to make himself invaluable. Besides establishing total control over the kitchen, he set up a little *bodega*, as he called it, to dispense all that any monk might need, from toothpaste to batteries. There was never a need for them to venture out into the world, should they choose not to. All they had to do was sign a little slip and he would bill their procurators, wherever in the world they might be, at a favorable price. This made life so much easier for the international community who were assigned to San Redempto. Within a heartbeat, Manolo was running the finances of the monastery, and true to the enforced infantilism which was nurtured by this lifestyle, was keeping everyone happily in his place. As community members came and went, he and his brother established themselves as the constant force in the monastery's life. Nothing went on without their notice, and their machinations lay hidden in locked rooms and illegible books. So completely did Manolo fit into the community that he was given a worker's habit to wear, worn and rough like his brother's, so that even without vows he appeared to be one of them. He did indeed become one with the community and, in ways that he was yet to fully understand, they with him.

"I picked up some special porcinis from my friend this morning and have them on the sill."

Antonio realized immediately what he was saying and gave him a wan smile.

"Good. That should disrupt the community's bowels for a day or so. Enough time for a few locks to be changed." The telephone rang, and as he pulled it from his belt, Antonio sank his teeth into the flesh one final time. "Pronto," he answered, red juice flowing from his mouth.

4

The carrel stall at the far end of the biblioteca was his sanctuary, and for half a century—far longer than anyone then living at San Redempto could remember—no one else had ever dared to approach it. There Avertanus was able to speak out loud the mystic words which carried power and was able to stroke the parchment and smell the bindings of his favorite volumes far from the ever-present eye of community. Being staunchly Flemish, he had never adopted the "decadent" practice of taking a siesta. Instead, the long afternoons between *pranzo* and vespers were his time to explore the *disciplina arcana*, the hidden knowledge which modern fools denied existed. He knew it was there: the truth that Bruno was burned for, the heights that the Quietists had reached, the fleshy vision of God which Abelard had known. Now was not the time to reveal his findings, not while he still walked this earth. But soon enough, when he was laid to rest under the conventual chapel floor, as he had gotten extraordinary permission from the general to do, then his life work, his synthesis, could be revealed. Then and only then, the full light would shine from the knowledge which had been hidden and would restore confidence to all those who wanted to give themselves to true wisdom.

His had been a strange and solitary life, although he took it so much for granted that it was a sadly unreflected life as well. At fifteen he had been sent to the monastery by his parents. Too many children; too little money. By sixteen he was sent out to Brazil, along with many other Dutchmen in the order, to help fill the seminaries. The sheer mass of his body, broad shouldered and muscular, belied the frightened child within. And his chiseled face, deep-set eyes and squared jaw made him irresistible to both sexes. At every opportunity he got, he had allowed himself to be worshiped; any mouth would do. Raw approbation of his worth was all that was needed during those years. He stayed in Brazil when his mother died bringing her twelfth child into the world and, not long after, when his father was chopped up by a threshing machine. Distance, time, and money precluded his returning home. A pious notification, combined with a holy card, was all he received in both cases. At twenty he was sent to Rome to complete his studies, having gone as far as he could in Brazil. His Portuguese gave way to Italian and English, the unofficial lingua franca of San Redempto; his mastery of Latin and biblical languages pushed his native Flemish into the far recesses of his mind. Now, when forced to speak it, it was a child's tongue he used, lacking in that grammatical fluidity and rich vocabulary which so marked his normal speech. Belgium was *terra incognita* and so too were the ways of the flesh, which Rome had far less tolerance of than Brazil. At least in his experience.

Today Avertanus had returned to the 1657 edition of the Polyglot Bible, published in London by Walton. Over the years he had studied all six volumes in detail, even to the point of proofing the appendix for errors. But it was the Song of Songs which called out to him again. Because he knew that the scriptures read us, even though we may rashly think that we read them. For well over thirty years, he had made a comparative study of the ways in which the Song of Songs shaped the mystical mind. From anonymous medieval fragments to the Victorines to the glories of John of the Cross. Bits of his research had been used in his rightly famous courses at the Gregorian, where he would relentlessly mine a single word until it revealed its gold. Language was his alchemy and he was brilliant at it.

As he poured over the volume, he ran his hand through his hair, gray now but as full and luxuriant as ever. And as if to verify that he was still among the living, his hand lightly touched his face. The bone structure was still strong but at nearly seventy-five the skin sagged somewhat, pouching under the eyes and cropping up at the jowls. He worked his hand around the back of his neck and felt the tension in his neck. It always went there it seemed, and as he rolled his head slightly to hear the subtle cracks and feel the blood run free, he thanked God that he still stood as erect as ever, no widow's hump for him, no world-wearied slump. He was fit for his age. For any age really.

Returning to the text in Greek and Latin, Hebrew, Syriac, and Aramaic, he wanted to settle his mind about those troubling final verses which began: "Our sister is little and she has no breasts," and ended with her reply, "I am a wall, and my breasts are like towers." Chastity had been the standard hermeneutic. But surely this girl was setting herself up like a fortress which invited scaling? The context had to be considered, because just four verses later, in the very last verse, she invited her lover, the stag, to be swift in coming.

Avertanus's thoughts were broken by the muffled sound of the monks gathering in the chapel below. The bell for vespers would soon be sounded, and he was so pleasurably caught up in his work that, as so often over the past sixty years, he loathed the thought of gathering with community and antiphonally droning praise to God. To savor the remaining moment, he closed the book and inspected the red Morocco binding tooled in gold and slowly lowered his face until it pressed against the leather and breathed it in fully.

Then there was a moan, not his own but from somewhere outside himself, and a thud like the sound of laundry dropping down the chute. How could that be? Still, his heart began to race and he felt the sure knowledge that someone was there. But who? Where? A mind gone crazed with too much silence was all the explanation he could offer.

As the bell sounded for vespers, he prepared to descend to chapel. Then opening the Song of Songs one final time, he read the first words his eyes set upon. A childish practice which he delighted in still. "His lips are red blossoms, they drip choice myrrh."

5

*T*here was a numbing certitude about community prayer which deeply pleased Brocard. Everything was predictable, right down to Father Pius's sneeze just before the final blessing. Each choir stall was assigned, tiered by seniority and rank, and no one would ever think of changing the order. And since the community had diminished these last two decades, from over one hundred to just twelve, the places of those who had died were left empty so that their presence lived on. Those who left the community, those who were "dead to us," were never afforded such respect.

Of course, the way the brothers dressed was distressingly haphazard. Some maintained the full habit, white cape, and cowl, as he had. But the fabric was often polyester and the lengths completely wrong due largely to the fact that they often pilfered habits of dead brothers and didn't have the good sense to hem them. Then there were those who came in work habits, the simple brown tunic and apron scapular. This was understandable for the lay brothers, Antonio and Manolo, who sat off on the side to maintain the division between the educated choir monks and, well, those who weren't. But to Brocard it was completely inexcusable for priests like Father Dionysius, who seemed to be flaunting an air of a lay brother with his newfound interest in gardening. Worse still were those radical few who had abandoned the regular wearing of the habit. To his disgrace, it had started with a young American from his own province just a few years before, and even though that thorn had completed his studies and returned to the States, his legacy lived on. Most flagrant of all in this regard was Father Berthold, who, to add bad to worse, was now insisting on being called

Bertie. His general conviviality and uncontrolled sense of color were totally out of place and worse still, might well be a sign of a groundswell in religious life which could not be held back. Needless to say, the prospect of the latter filled Brocard with dread.

Fortunately the chapel had been spared any major violence these last thirty years. No statues had been removed, no tabernacle relegated to a side altar. A worn, funereal tone draped it all, from the chipped, dark, paneled wood to the faux marble on the pillars and walls, buckling from moisture and retaining the smell of musty incense which spoke not only of an accumulation of rituals but of a decidedly masculine disdain for housekeeping.

As Brocard arranged his ribbons for vespers, he noticed that Pius was not standing, arms propped on his *misericordes*, as was the custom, but had remained seated and seemed to be troubling over his breviary. He had been wasting away for some time now from a malaise which the doctors could not pin down. Senility, for sure, but more than that seemed to be deteriorating his health. From what little anyone could see under his habit and ubiquitous sweaters his legs and arms seemed to be no more than sticks. His once-delicate face and hands appeared cadaverous, as if they longed to be hidden from the light of day, covered in damp and reassuring earth. But this was not a nursing home, and should a monk not be able to take care of himself he was sent back to his province. After a lifetime at San Redempto, though, Father Pius rightfully felt as if he had no other home. Avertanus gently went over to him to help in the arranging of the ribbons, then just as quietly returned to his stall and closed his eyes to center himself before prayer. A man at peace with his God. No such composure marked Bertie, who was sporting a new, aggressively trendy outfit. Far too Italian for Brocard's taste: maroon trousers, teal sweater, and a cream polyester shirt, buttoned to the neck. They were all cheap goods— he never did have a way with money—purchased from carts in Trastevere, but he flaunted them as a sign of his insipient break with community control. Doubtless he would not be in for *cena*, or if the rumors were true, for the better part of the evening. It troubled Brocard that the prior never confronted Bertie about this increasingly cavalier approach to religious life. He was a frail boy, short and nicely formed, of uncommon good looks, and extremely impressionable. Hopefully, it was not too late to save him.

At that moment, as if on cue, Father Emmanuele, the prior, entered the chapel by the hidden door which he alone was in the habit of using and took his place in the third tier on the right. Emmanuele was slightly shorter than Avertanus but still impressive in size. His bearing and forceful yet gentle tone, his impeccably pressed cape, his highly polished shoes, everything spoke of a good religious. He was truly a man of the rule, a leader who balanced tradition with good sense. Someone with whom Brocard thought he could never find fault.

Once the chanting of the psalms began, issues of dress and demeanor receded into the background. Order out of chaos. Pius regained his assurance and Bertie some shred of dignity. But as Emmanuele moved out to the center of the chapel for the final blessing and Pius sneezed, it happened. Avertanus noticed before anyone else but was too dumbfounded to warn the prior. Blood. A few drops at first, warm and thick. Then a steady stream rushed down from the ceiling, splattered his cape, and puddled onto the shield of the order, which was set into the chapel floor. There was no final blessing.

6

$\mathcal{J}$t was late, hours past compline, and Brocard lay bolt awake on his bed, his mind flooded with images. With all the happenings of the last twenty-four hours it struck him as strange that it was his mother's face which loomed largest in his mind. She came to him with that look she had when she first told him of her impending mastectomy during his last visit home nearly three years ago. Her eyes probing his in the hope that he would understand something of her fear. He failed her terribly, although he still had difficulty admitting it, by blocking his fear and trivializing hers with some canned piety. And when she died some months later, he was not there, foolishly thinking that it was an abuse of "poverty" and that a few private masses would help her soul and heal his grief. They may have done some good for the former, but did little or none for the latter.

He also replayed those remarkable moments after the blood started to drench the prior. While the community watched in catatonic silence, Brocard lunged from his choir stall to catch Emmanuele, whose knees were collapsing beneath him. All would have gone well if they both hadn't slipped in the pool of blood and, arm in arm, fallen spread-eagle to the floor. Then in a moment of genius bordering on Grand Guignol, Emmanuele slowly raised himself from the floor and, in that deep baritone of which he was capable when he put his mind to it, intoned the *Salve*, the hymn to the Virgin which ended vespers. On reflex the community responded in chorus and at the words *in hac lacrimarum valle*, in this valley of tears, he signaled to Brocard to follow him. Together, white capes soaked in fresh blood, they entered his door at the far end of the chapel and mounted the stairs to the library above. There Brocard watched as without hesitation he opened the door to the closet nearest Avertanus's carrel and undamned a river of red.

"Who would have thought the young boy had so much blood in him."

"What?" Brocard remembered asking.

To which Emmanuele answered, "Shakespeare, you idiot, or something like it. Oh, nevermind."

The body wedged into the narrow closet was whiter than any human being he had ever seen. Fists clenched, face contorted, and eyes all but hanging from his skull. All inhumanly white except for the area on the right side of his neck which was impaled by one of those many broken pieces of glass which Manolo, incapable as he was of disposing of anything, had stored for possible future use. Despite his undeniable deviousness, it seemed doubtful this was the use he had in mind.

It was only after some time that Brocard recognized the corpse as Thius, the Dutch student who had so knowingly displayed himself throughout the monastery last year. He never wore more than a short towel on his way to the showers and—a fact which was generally known and equally as often put to the test—would parade around the lavatory in less than that at the least sign of company. Death had not treated him kindly.

Taking the briefest of time to assess the situation, Emmanuele instructed Brocard to call Antonio and Manolo, telling Antonio to bring cleaning materials. Likewise, Brocard was to tell Avertanus, who was the subprior, a ceremonial position devoid of real authority, to meet him in his office. The library was to be locked and the community bound to silence in this matter until the house meeting the following evening. As Brocard left, he could not help but turn slightly to see what Emmanuele would do. To his surprise, the prior had bent down near the body and seemed to be talking to it, quietly explaining something to the lifeless form.

But another image came back to him as well, and drew him farther away from sleep. That painted saint, Agatha, the sole survivor of a series of paintings which until so recently had gone unnoticed. Stretched out and bloodied, she seemed more alive than that young boy whose body was crammed into the library closet.

The noise was starting to build outside his window and he knew that all hope of any sleep was over. Brocard, who was usually a sound sleeper and, if vanity would allow him the truth, a little hard of hearing, had one of the few rooms which faced the street. Modern Rome had risen all around the monastery, and while the gardens and cloister kept it at bay on three sides, they could not hold back its relentless seaminess on the fourth. Shutters were flung open, women young and old positioned themselves on balconies, car horns blared, and cafe tables filled up just outside his room. Usually Brocard was impervious to such distractions, but this night, as his mind tried to make sense of chaos within, he found himself peering through his shutters at lives being lived with passion.

7

$\mathcal{B}$y definition, the world was a web of sin and the monastery walls a fortress built to keep all evil out. A hopelessly dated perspective but one which served Emmanuele well as he told the two brothers what had to be done. Standing off to the side, Brocard heard little of their conversation. He could only marvel at their complacency, and the businesslike way in which they handled themselves.

Manolo was to call their contact at Santo Spiritu Hospital, a pestilent place that, were one unfortunate enough to be admitted, one abandoned all hope of ever leaving alive. But healing was not what was needed now. Just expedient secrecy. Given the right amount, Giuseppe, the orderly who had access to the ambulances after dark, was discretion itself. He had helped them before and there was no reason to doubt that he would be able to assist them now, quietly and efficiently.

As Manolo made these arrangements, Emmanuele gave clear instructions to Antonio what he was to do. Then, with great dignity, he removed his blood-stained cape and draped it over the corpse and signaled Brocard to do the same. They left together, in the simple brown tunics of brothers, to meet with Avertanus who was waiting for them in the prior's office. Antonio's long life had taught him that the messy work invariably fell to him, and he took some pride in this fate. With the stone face that shielded him from communicating with anyone, he returned to the chapel with drop cloths to cover the blood and then, armed with mops and pails and a shroud, three things he always kept at hand, he returned to the biblioteca, locked the door behind him, and started his work. He needed no help. Strong and intensely secretive, he threw himself into his task. The body was surprisingly light: a wisp of a boy in life, a shadow of a corpse in death. He had no difficulty rolling it into the shroud and putting it aside. The blood was a different matter, so much of it and so resistant to coming out, but he was a persistent peasant and no stain could withstand his wire brush, nor smudge his scrubbling rags. When he was finished in the library he returned to the chapel, removed the cloths which had already soaked up much of the blood, and attacked it with the same determination. Finally he took all of the rags and cloths and capes out to the incinerator at the far end of the orchard and ate his fill of oranges as he watched them reduced to ashes. Within hours, all evidence of any mishap was lost in the general gloominess of San Redempto, any smell of death incorporated in the mustiness of time, rich in an accord of scents both secular and divine.

Avertanus did not look up as they entered, but kept his eyes transfixed on the beads in his hand. The vision of him, seated with such composure, lost in prayer, seemed to visibly affect Emmanuele far more profoundly than the bloodless corpse they had just left. Brocard was reminded of the pious cliché, one of many that he was steeped in, which placed prayer as the most intimate of activities, far greater than any sexual coupling could ever be. Was it their intrusion into this moment that unsettled Emmanuele, the burning intensity of the old man's devotion to an unseen God, whose very existence the prior increasingly questioned? Taking his clue from the man of prayer, Emmanuele suggested that before considering what they were to do, the three of them pray silently for the Spirit to be with them. After some moments of silence, he was inspired by a perverse desire to begin a litany of martyrs. "San Lorenzo," he chanted recto tono, and Brocard and Avertanus answered, "Ora pro nobis." Then followed San Bartolomeo, Santa Marina, and then, strangely and finally, Santa Agatha. Purified by their blood, he told Brocard and Avertanus the course of action they must take to maintain the honor and dignity of the monastery.

To Brocard, this was one of Emmanuele's finer moments. He told Avertanus of the accident which had transpired and then, always being one to take charge, he outlined what they must do. To Brocard, whose admiration of the prior was undiminished, never before had he sounded so lucid. Never had his actions seemed so determined, nor his intentions for the order, which he so deeply loved, so rightly placed. Avertanus, on the other hand, was somewhat less convinced. The thought that it must have been the dying boy's moan that he had heard and which had gone unanswered distressed him deeply. Could this lad be connected to the disappearance of the paintings in the ambulatory? And was his death something more than just an unfortunate slip on a piece of jagged glass?

The only thing they all were in full agreement about was that the body had to disappear. And that very night.

8

$\mathcal{T}$he screeching of the cats in the cloister took on the air of a Greek chorus, as if they alone knew the full significance of the drama which was being played out before them. In a macabre way, things couldn't have been better. Thick, rain-filled clouds hung low in the night sky blocking out the moon, and a misty fog rose slowly from the ground to shield their activities from prying eyes. No monk would open their shutters to the night air, but one could never be too cautious about the Romani living in the apartments which overlooked the monastery. It was known that they held all things monastic in suspicion.

The ambulance arrived a few minutes past ten. Manolo opened the metal gates and signaled Giuseppe to back slowly all the way in, past the orchard and cistern, then down past the laundry shed and as close as he could to the door of the sacristy. Antonio was waiting for them and together they carried the casket and tools into the chapel and up the far stairs to the library above where Avertanus, Brocard, and Emmanuele had gathered around the body. For Emmanuele, a native Roman, the procedure which followed was normalcy itself. But no matter how often Avertanus or Brocard witnessed it, they realized there was an Italian embracing of death which they could never share, branding them as aliens forever.

The metal coffin was placed next to the shrouded corpse, the lid removed, and then Giuseppe and Antonio positioned themselves at separate ends, neither knowing or caring which was the head, which the feet. Then, as if they were winding up for a pitch—which in a ghoulish way they were—they rapidly crossed themselves, lifted the corpse, and swung it into the metal container. No one skipped a heartbeat when a clenched fist fell. There was plenty of extra shroud to bunch up over it. The lid was placed on, rivets drilled in, and—this was the part that so affected Brocard—a welding torch lit so that the coffin was soldered shut forever. The rapidity and finality of it never ceased to shock him.

It was no small matter to carry the coffin down the steep back staircase to the chapel, but both Giuseppe and Antonio had stocky worker's bodies that were created for just this purpose. When they reached the ground floor their burden became unusually light, as if the boy sealed in the box was helping them rush this whole affair to an end.

While they were maneuvering the casket into the back of the ambulance, a break in the clouds revealed a moon far larger than any of them had ever seen, hanging so low it seemed to join in their conspiracy. And except for a randy stray screaming for raw sex, the cats began to gather around the group in expectant silence. Dozens of them breathlessly purring and stealthily pawing their way towards them like hairy necrophiliacs.

The living followed the dead into the ambulance: Giuseppe driving with Antonio up front, Brocard and Avertanus bracketing the casket in the back, wrapped in black capes to protect them from the night air. Emmanuele was the last to leave the building, pausing to collect the holy water and aspergillum from the sacristy. Manolo handed him an envelope fat with the cash he would need and guided the van out of the drive, bolting the gate behind them. Manolo was greatly relieved not to have had to go to the cemetery with them as he had work to do if he and Antonio were going to keep their own secrets. Something he was fiercely determined to do.

Like all good Romani, Giuseppe could not resist going fast and making noise. Both Avertanus and Brocard, foreign again, did not understand why he felt compelled to blare his siren and weave between cars, waving cheerily at carabinieri along the way. But from the wan smile on Emmanuele's face, he, at least, seemed pleased. If truth be told, the ride did somewhat relieve the unremittingly funereal tone of their outing.

However, blackness descended with a vengeance when they arrived at the gates of San Lorenzo, a cemetery whose sole business was decay. This is where the order had buried their own, and a few others,

25

for the better part of the millennium. They had priority of place, and for the right amount, there was never a problem to open their crypt for immediate interment. Antonio jumped out and opened the front gates, which were unlocked in expectation of their arrival, and then drove back along the main road to the overgrown and unattended crypt in which bodies rotted and bones were stored.

The ceremony was brief. The boy's coffin was placed on one of the shelves on the lower level of the crypt and blessed with holy water. On their way out, Emmanuele paused to arrange several skulls that had fallen and Avertanus distinctly heard him moan.

9

*T*he flatness of the landscape suited him. It held no secrets and stretched out in a vulnerability which demanded control, something he had mastered over the years. Otger recalled how timid he had been to take the reins when he was a young monk. Perhaps some thoughts of the hand of God inhibited him, but it was hard to imagine he had ever honestly given that much credence. No, he had always been a hard-nosed pragmatist, it just took him some time to develop the evil within. When he did, he knew that the much-touted "discernment process" was over, that he had looked deep within himself and truly found God. One who had nothing to do with Christ.

He had decided that it was best to talk things over with Hoop Rhutten in person. So much easier to manipulate him that way. With no explanation to his staff at the institute, he got in his car and drove south from Nijmegen to Maastrich. The roads were clear, well maintained, and boring. A perfect backdrop against which to weave his web.

But before he could focus on Hoop and the nasty business with the bungled theft, his mind went back to how he had made Jan, his latest assistant, act like the dog he was. It amused him to think of how he had so willingly hid himself under Otger's desk, butt naked, and worshiped his feet during the entire staff meeting. Of course, approval of his dissertation methodology was on the line. The prerogative of power as Otger saw it. The thought that he might be discovered down there never troubled Otger for a moment. Needless to say, Jan's feelings were of no consequence to him. The entire exercise was about humiliation and control, which for him was where all true pleasure lay.

No one would have known any of this from looking at him. He was a settled-looking middle-aged man, somewhat prosperous in girth, with that very white look that the Dutch do so well. Petit bourgeois was what came to mind with Otger, and slightly dotty as well. He affected that professorial vagueness about life which belied his meticulous attention to details, no matter how mundane.

Hoop had always been under his thumb and would be easy enough to keep in line now. He would no doubt be distressed about Thius's untimely death, their teacher-student relationship was inordinately intimate in Otger's opinion. It was almost as if Thius had the upper hand, a loathsome thought. Still Hoop had such a low self-esteem, probably because he was so physically unattractive. What attracted students was his mind, a strange amalgam of traditional and New Age thinking. Everything else was a mess. A mouthful of teeth that went in conflicting directions and were stained by years of smoking. A complexion that looked like the dark side of the moon and a twisted frame of a body, puffed up by years of bad eating habits and not a hint of exercise. Long and straggly hair bunched around the ears and tortuously pulled along his balding crown. Not a pretty sight.

But there was no denying how helpful he had been these past few years. Since he first discovered the worth of San Redempto's holdings, he had worked tirelessly, always through graduate assistants, to establish their provenance and authenticity. It was Otger who had encouraged him to leave the order and to work on this covertly so as to avoid prying eyes. He had also found him the position at Maastrich, one which seemed to suit him much better than monastic life. Not that accommodating Hoop's needs was his concern. It just worked out that way.

As he was driving through some indiscriminate village in northern Brabant he saw a young girl, probably not more than fourteen, small suitcase in hand, hitching a ride. From the tentative way in which she held out her hand and the way in which her body trembled, he had no option but to stop. She told him she was going to Maastrich, a favorite haunt of runaways, and he signaled her to get in. This, he knew, was going to be easy. He said nothing to her for some time, his thoughts were still on the work at hand and she would wait. The main thing was to make sure that Hoop never surfaced. He was so remarkably naive and ingenuous that he could slip up and mention the ongoing research they had done, or worse still, the substantial findings they had made. No one must ever get to him, or in case they did, he must be told of the importance of deflecting all questions.

The girl he had picked up had begun to sob. For one brief moment the monk in him thought of handing her a handkerchief. Instead, the man that he had become reached into his wallet and pulled out twenty guilders. He threw them down on her lap and told her to take off her panties. She was afraid and uncertain, so he reached into his wallet and doubled the amount. Slowly she began to lift her dress and ease her trembling hands up her legs.

"For God's sake, just do it," he ordered, refusing to look her in the eye. To look at her at all for that matter. She was, after all, like all the creatures who got entangled in his life, an object to be played with and debased. Nothing more than that.

He no longer heard her crying—although cry she did—as his thoughts had gone out once more to that tedious flat landscape which surrounded him and beckoned to be controlled by man.

10

*T*here was no passageway Manolo didn't know, no nook or cranny he hadn't explored and made his own. He alone was able to negotiate the monastery in complete darkness, with that unerring sense of space and distance usually granted to the blind alone. Or cats. Until and if San Redempto ever began to disclose its secrets, it appeared the most straightforward pile of a building. Essentially it was a vast L-shaped building, indistinguishable from many other sad yet dignified structures which stand in the shadow of the Vatican. Two enormous doors fronted the street. The one to the left, the entrance to the chapel, had been permanently sealed shut as their chapel was strictly conventual. The community had long since excluded outsiders from intruding on their services. When shut, the other door, the only one into the monastery, was as imposing as any castle's: two stories of oak with iron crossbars and studded with pointed spearheads. When bolted shut, as it was during siesta and from ten at night until dawn, it acted as an impenetrable shield against the world. Even when open it was only slightly less off-putting, as the dark and shallow foyer was dominated by three deep marble steps leading up to still another barrier of oak doors. On the right of the foyer was the porter's window, the room where Antonio lived and the seat of his power. No one came or went without his knowing. Most of the commerce with the world was conducted in this awkward space, and entry was only gained when he pressed the buzzer to release the spring lock on the inner doors. Having gained entry, outsiders who had appointments were either shown into the speak room to the left or made to wait in an uncomfortable open space dominated by a statue of Our Lady of Divine

Succor, the patron of the order. Only members of the order were allowed to enter the final set of doors marked *clausura*. Beyond the cloister doors and along the entire length of the building was one wide, vaulted corridor, with windows and French doors opening out into a cloister garden to the left with yet another statue of Our Lady, this one grander still. This smaller garden was for walking and praying only. The larger working cloister garden, where fruit and vegetables were grown, deliveries made, and laundry hung to dry, was out back. Just beyond the monastery, and bearing down on it with threatening proximity was a massive modern apartment block, with balconies draped with laundry. It was impossible for all but the most brazen monks whose rooms faced the cloister to open the shutters in their rooms lest they be seen. To the right of the main corridor were the old classrooms, a sad reminder of a time when the monastery was filled with students. One of these rooms was now used for house meetings, the rest sat empty. Were it not for the muffled sound of traffic, it would have been impossible to know that a bustling city side street lay on the other side of these classroom walls. The barred windows were set up so near the ceiling and were so covered with grime that no light came in.

To the left of the main corridor was the main staircase and the ambulatory which led into the conventual chapel. It was here that Manolo paused briefly before the stretch of wall which had recently been violated to admire the audacity and the brilliance of whomever it was who pulled it off. He had always suspected that the stolen paintings had more than curiosity value but they were far too public for the Basque brothers to touch. Theirs was a more covert enterprise. There was nothing to detain Manolo on the ground floor, so, retrieving his toolbox, he took the grand marble staircase off the interior chapel entrance to the *primo piano*. In the light of day he would never have been so presumptuous to take this route—the service stairs to the kitchen were for the brothers—but in the dead of night he was uncontested master.

Only once before had he taken the precaution to change the locks on the several rooms he and his brother used to stockpile items and bank their savings. They had worked out an ingenious system of building false walls in unused rooms so that, were a room opened, someone would have to remove piles of debris, art, or whatever the room ostensibly held, before ever finding the concealed doors which led back to their storage areas. Even the prior did not know of the existence of these false rooms, but he did have keys to the outer doors and he was notoriously lax with them, especially when he was in the mood to give young men favors, which often seemed the case these days. It was the outer doors, all nine of them, in rooms spread throughout the top three floors, which he had to make secure. A night's work, but in the light of the dust which was surely going to fly should Brocard take his task as seriously as expected, an absolute necessity.

When he checked the lock of the room near the top of the staircase, his heart began to race. The door was open. Had others been tampered with as well? Someone had been in there. Surely neither Emmanuele, who kept keys only for security, or Antonio, who was so conscientious about locking up. But who? Nothing seemed to be disturbed, and the hidden door in the false wall remained locked. Still something had gone amiss.

Poor dotty Father Pius slept soundly next door; but Bertie, who had just gotten in, cracked open his bedroom door to see Manolo at work.

II

*A*vertanus hung his cape on the back of his door and thanked God the ordeal was over. The forces of evil at work in San Redempto were palpable. How deeply rooted and how pervasive he did not care to know because ultimately the workings of evil held little fascination for him. His studies of Patristics had taught him that long before the image of Satan took on hoofs and dragon's tail, the personification of evil was imaged as the most beautiful of men. Not handsome, but ravishingly beautiful as some men can indeed be. True evil attracts like that, luring us in and leading us down the path of self-destruction.

He might be an old academic but he was no one's fool. Little had escaped his notice recently. Bertie's sadly anachronistic adolescence, Dionysius's ruse of gardening to facilitate easy exits, Emmanuele's duplicitous role-playing, the robbery, and the murder (for he had no doubt that it was) were all part of a developing matrix of sin. As he saw it, the foundations of the order, indeed of the faith itself, were being undermined. Tragic, and unstoppable as it all might be, everything would have been bearable had he not lost the "taste of prayer," as the mystics put it. Being a man of consummate discipline, Avertanus maintained the full horarium plus meditation periods, devoting himself daily to oral and contemplative prayer. All to no avail. This surely was the *sequedad* about which Juan de la Cruz so eloquently wrote—that stultifying dryness which parched the soul and deadened the heart. He knew no consolation, could not feel the presence of the God he had devoted his life to and whom he now so desperately needed. The benign tremor in his hand was all that betrayed any emotion as he patted himself tentatively on the forehead as if to verify that he was still there. How strange, he thought, to be so old and be incapable of feeling anything. As if life had washed over his shrinking body and taken all emotions in its wake.

Strange too to think of himself as dumb. Quite simply, the Reverend Doctor Avertanus Deblaer, Emeritus Professor of Mystical Theology at the Pontifical University had run out of answers. This was surely what Aquinas meant when, at the end of his life, he said that "all was straw." Not faith or God—he could never fall into such a deep abyss—but rather the pleasant sensations of religion and the intellectual gratification of the mind had vanished. What was left was a void so complete that it should have been painful. Indeed life might have been bearable if it had, because living in pain would have been infinitely preferable to this. He longed for some sensation that he was alive, some feeling of that humanity which had irrevocably slipped away.

Fortunately he could still lose himself in books, but even there things seemed to be getting skewed. What had always been a healthy interest in books was now becoming something of an obsession. He found himself sneaking incunabula into his room rather than leave them in the biblioteca where others could benefit from them. At first he told himself that it was because they were all dullards who had no need for books in any case, but he soon realized that he had begun smelling them and rubbing his face along their bindings as if they could supply that intimacy which he knew could come from God alone.

Without any expectation but only knowing well that he would not be able to sleep for some hours if at all, he decided to go down to the chapel and silently sit with the Lord. He pulled his cowl up over his head to protect himself from the night air and, quietly closing the door of his claustrophobic cell, stepped out into the madly cavernous hallway. How strange, he thought, the way space is squandered in a monastery. Being, as he always joked, a "child of the light," he pressed the first illuminated light switch he came to, and walked quickly towards the staircase, knowing that the timers had been shortened to give only the briefest tease of light before plunging back into darkness. When he turned the corner he caught sight of Manolo darting into one of his rooms like the night rat Avertanus always knew he was. Surprising to see that he had his toolbox with him, but in the Faydeau comedy world to which San Redempto had succumbed, nothing seemed too bizarre. Predictably, Father Pius was snoring quite audibly as he passed his door, and Bertie—why had he disavowed a name as powerful as Berthold—was up late, if the light flooding out from under his door was any indication. He made his way down the marble staircase just in time to hit the switch at the bottom which controlled all the lights in the ground floor passageway. Before turning to go into the chapel, he saw a figure in secular clothes slipping out the back door into the kitchen garden, presumably to access that service gate through which they had just hours before removed the body of that poor unfortunate boy. Probably just Dionysius going out on a harmless prowl. But in this house of mirrors, who could say?

12

$\mathcal{N}$ot being one to wallow in problems, nor for that matter even face them, the prior immediately went on-line when he got back to his room. Nothing could be done about Thius, the unfortunate boy who had been sealed into the crypt at San Lorenzo. There was never time to find out if he had loved him, not even time enough to build up a healthy obsession. All that could be hoped for now was that no trail led back to him. He had several new messages in E-mail, among which was one from Nijmegen:

> *My dear Emmanuele,*
>
> *You are quite right: I haven't the slightest recollection of those paintings in the ambulatory, but at my advanced age I'm lucky if I remember who I had for breakfast. Yes, I still keep up the practice of going to the* mensa *and mentally consuming some young thing first thing each morning, They all think I'm lost in prayer, of course, as they clash about with their trays and gulp down their coffees. There's that feeble old theology professor wandering off into some interior mansion again. I have never been as gender specific as you of course, just a fresh young thing of any sex, as long as the skin is translucent and clear, is the perfect accompaniment to my cheese and chocolate. Although I still find such a diet as delicious as ever, it seems to go right through me. I find it is getting harder to carry their memory throughout the day as that spiritual nosegay Francis de Salles, in one of his more inspired moments, recommended we do. I still have no doubt, by the way, that my modern take on this classic prayer technique,*

somewhat holistic, so very Incarnational, would delight that long-gone saint to no end.

Now as for our old confrere Hoop Rhutten. Would that he were fully "dead to us." He was and presumably still is such a relentlessly earnest chap. I always found him far too three dimensional for my taste. You never could stick him in a box and sort him out. One of my guiding principles has always been that unless a man is capable of being reified, he will always be dangerous. And should be avoided.

To the best of my knowledge, since leaving us nearly five years ago now, he has become quite well-known in the emerging, but still quite soft, academic discipline of art and spirituality. One of those hybrid fields that students seem to rush to in droves but the academy still has no idea what to do with. It seems a little of this, a little of that, and a lot of nothing to me. But even here in Nijmegen there is movement afoot to add it to the curriculum. Hopefully I will be long since back in Rome before that comes about. Anyway, our long-lost brother has become something of a guru and set up a little art and spirituality dynasty for himself in Maastrich, always a silly step ahead of the rest of the universities here in Holland. Despite his limited fame, it seems unlikely that timid little Brocard will discover his new identity. Should he try to contact him through the university here, I will intercept his message and refer him to a vacant building in Arnhem, have no fear.

There is one possibly strange coincidence to report. I heard just this morning, in one of those professionally convivial coffee breaks which this culture forces on us each morning, that Thius had recently returned to Rome to do some more research. Were you aware that he had become a follower of Rhutten this past year? Quite taken by him, to the extent that he was negotiating to change his thesis topic to something about early modern French art and, dit donc, spirituality. Perhaps by now Thius has looked you up. I know he had more than a professional fancy for you, attracted no doubt by that commanding maturity you do so well. And, if I am not mistaken, you could not have been inured to his considerable charms, aesthete that you are. Do be careful. There may be more to his visit than slipping in the garden door for a look-see, if you know what I mean.

Well, all for now. Regards from the land of moisture and perversity. In the most manly of senses, because I know you prefer it that way, je t'embrasse.

Otger

So this was the reason Thius had been solicitous with visits every night for the past week. Had the worms not gotten to him first, Emmanuele would have thrashed him good.

13

*E*mmanuele always rose to the occasion at house meetings, and despite the unusual events and undeniable stresses of the past couple of days, Brocard had no doubt that the prior would rise to this one. His undisguised model was Benito Mussolini, whose hallowed memory he deeply revered. Although just a child when the fascists held power, as he remembered it, theirs was an Italy that commanded world respect and dispensed swift justice; an Italy, as he delighted in recalling, where the streets were clean and the trains ran on time. The Lombard League aside, there was only the smallest of chances such halcyon days would return on a national level, but that did not mean that they were not possible within the confines of his world, San Redempto. House meetings, at the very least, could be run with Blackshirt determination and dictatorial fervor.

Typically, Brocard was the first to respond to the bell summoning the community to meeting. He took his usual seat at the far side of the Aula and waited for the others, in predictable order, to take theirs. Although he moved the slowest, Father Pius Poncelet was always next to enter. Adjusting his tattered cardigan, which he wore over his habit due more to the thinness of his blood than the dampness of the monastery, he gave a profound bow to Brocard, which those who did not know him well may have mistaken as facetious. Then, in rapid succession Fathers Avertanus, Cuthbert Mullins, and Angelus Lennon—the latter two Irish priests who had arrived within the past year and kept resolutely to themselves. Both seemed to be quite busy with research at the Vatican archives and some undisclosed project for the general of the order, which could not have been too terribly important or it would have been discussed at the last general chapter. Two quiet brothers who seemed more intent on perfecting their Italian than stirring up gossip—a refreshing change, as Brocard saw it.

Brother Ephraim, the final member of the triumvirate of workers, came in with Manolo and Brother Antonio. Simply put, Ephraim was the drone. All communities need them, although most have more than one. His was the Herculean task of laundry and housecleaning. Needless to say, the laundry was invariably late and inadequately done, so that a pungent smell clung to all things conventual, and the public spaces were covered in dust and grime. Thank God for monastic down lighting. Brocard, being more fastidious than the rest, hand washed his own clothes (the laundry shed being off limits to all but Ephraim). Emmanuele sent his out. Secretly, of course, so as not to offend poverty.

After everyone was assembled, the prior entered and took his seat, a baronial armchair, at the far end of the circle of school desks the others were forced to sit in. This, after all, had been a classroom, in those long-forgotten days when young people were flooding into monasteries, and as Emmanuele had persuasively argued, it was fiscally irresponsible not to make use of the furniture that was already there. Of course, the visual metaphor of grown men looking up at him from crammed little desks pleased him greatly.

Pregiamo, he said in the most solemn of tones. As he led them in prayer, his fluid and magisterial Italian, in an international house where it was the poor second language for everyone else, sealed his authority over the community. In many ways, English would have been the most universal of languages. Except for the lay brothers, who always remained silent at such meetings, all of the monks had a working knowledge of English. However Emmanuele's spoken English, by his own admission, was far too heavily accented to command the respect he required at such times. As Wittgenstein so beautifully put it, "The master of the language is the master of us all." The prior's linguistic control was total. Some basic housekeeping announcements were made and then he brought up his major concern, the theft or at least disappearance of the six canvases from the ambulatory. Interestingly, no one knew when exactly they were taken, which showed how much they had been taken for granted. He was formally appointing Father Brocard to research the remaining painting to see if it had significant value. He was also to begin a discreet search for their whereabouts, without drawing any adverse secular attention to the monastery. In other words, no police need know of this. Father Emmanuele then opened the matter up for comments in such a way as to preclude all further discussion. As an afterthought, the prior mentioned that Manolo had been reprimanded for not having stored paints correctly in the biblioteca broom closet. He was assured that the unfortunate mess, presumably caused by a buildup of heat and inadequately stored cans, would never happen again. As the community bowed their heads for the closing prayer, few found peace in their hearts.

14

*F*ather Brocard Curtis, bald as a cue ball and short as Puck, had been cast into the most unlikely of roles, that of avenging angel. He suspected that others might not have taken the clear mandate he had been given by the prior as seriously as it warranted, and that even Emmanuele's expectations for him may have been quite limited. But for Brocard the monastery had been violated, as fully as any rape, and its honor must be restored. Likewise, reasons must be found for the body in the closet. Although he felt confident that the secular world would never find out about it, he was equally sure that until and unless the mystery of that blood-drained body was cleared up, a cloud of suspicion would hang over the community; despite an admirable try, the prior's story could not long survive.

Galvanized by a sense of mission that he had never before known, Brocard put on his good habit, the one with cross-stitching on the cowl and professional hems, pulled together his documentation and writing materials, and prepared himself for the hard work at hand. As he stepped out into the hall, he fervently asked God to give him the strength to persevere in this task. And prayed to Saint Lawrence to intercede for him that he not be made to look like a priggish fool, as he knew all too well he had appeared to be before. This was far more serious than anything that had ever been entrusted to him, and the knowledge of this so filled him with confidence that he appeared transformed to those he passed. To Dionysius, he seemed to storm by with manic determination; Father Pius, who was moving particularly slowly that day, barely had time to recognize him; and Bertie, convinced Brocard had done some strange Abruzzi mushrooms, decided that a trip to the larder might be in order. He gave Antonio a limp papal wave as he passed through the foyer and then, out on the sidewalk, Brocard merged into the crowds of average Romani going about their business. Father Brocard Curtis, archivist at the Gran Monastario di San Redempto, actually seemed at one with the world for the first time that he could ever remember. Despite his medieval outfit and his ghostly pallor, it actually appeared that, remarkable as it may be, he was going to work.

His plan of action was clear. In order to see if there was any truth in the attribution scribbled on the back of the painting, he had to see if there was any mention of Poussin having treated this subject. Although the Vatican library had a substantial holding of art history reference works, the biblioteque of the Academie Française housed in the Palazzo Farnesse was the only complete source of the materials he would need in all of Rome. Which from his perspective, meant the world. Undaunted by the fact that he had not used the Farnesse in years, and was as unknown to them as they to him, he turned his back on the tidy Vatican and crossed the Tiber to the chaotic historic district. The movement all around him was exhilarating: bands of tourists following the lifted umbrellas of their guides, the roar of the *motorini* arrogantly weaving their way through traffic, the smell of slow-roasting chestnuts and fast-moving women. A riotous, giddy backdrop to the terribly serious task at hand. He made his way over the bridge of the angels to the Via del'Orso, than took a shortcut he remembered from years before, past the uncontrollably exuberant little church of the Magdalene. Bejeweled and gilded, it was just as he had remembered it, a celebration of the Magdalene before the fall, the courtesan who one day, but not now thank you, would give it all up for Jesus. So very much like Rome.

When he entered the Campo dei Fiori, with the Renaissance palace of the Farnesse within sight, his mood was dampened by the sheer weight of its sad history. Although merchants had spread out their flowers and set up their fish stalls, he could only smell the burning flesh of all those heretics who had been torched there, surrounded by Romani much the same as these, lusty and loud, glossed with piety yet seething with brutality. In the center of the piazza was that lugubrious statue of Giordano Bruno, whose burning in 1600 marked to many the precise moment when and location where "modern" started. Was Bruno the summation of ancient wisdom, as Avertanus had once argued, or simply the victim of clerical intolerance? The question did not engage Brocard for long, because his path was blocked by two armored vehicles parked just outside the Farnesse. In his rush, he had forgotten the French embassy was housed on the lower floors. Getting in posed a major problem, but nothing would deter him. As he might have suspected, the gendarme at the door presented him with one of those Roman riddles. No one was permitted access to the biblioteque without a card and cards could only be obtained in the biblioteque. Accustomed to such logic, Brocard just waited for the guard to turn his back, slid in with some tourists, and once inside, abandoned himself to the bowels of the building.

There was no mystery about how to find the biblioteque, just take a staircase, any staircase, to the top floor. He moved with stealth and assurance, confident that no one would stop, no less shoot, a monk. Once there, he breathed easily again, like an anxious voyager arriving home. Even the humblest of libraries could work magic on him. But this library above all others, surely one of the most beautiful in the world, filled him with reverential awe. Its sense of order, boundless wisdom, and profound silence held him in thrall. Doubtless this was due largely to Michelangelo, who designed the top floor of the palace. His unfailing sense of proportion, the regular yet never boring spacing of the windows, the unusual height of the ceilings, the spare yet striking paneling were, quite simply, marks of perfection. Strange to see smoke rising from research tables—it had been so long since the Vatican library allowed cigarettes. Brocard reminded himself that this great research institute was after all the patrimony of the French, those self-possessed people who, since the Reign of Terror, have cherished self-destruction as a solemn right.

The librarian at the front desk treated him with reassuring indifference. No questions asked, no disconcerting eye contact made. Just a simple form to fill out which had to be shown to the director for perfunctory approval. Nothing could be easier. In the space supplied for area or reason for research he put: "Possible attribution of Poussin at San Redempto in the Borgo." Then he set about his work.

Well-traveled bibliophile that he was, the French library system, a consequence of an unquestioned allegiance to logic, was as familiar to him as the Roman. However it always took him back to see books of varying sizes inhabiting the same shelves. As if subject alone were enough to bring them together. The Italians, for whom appearance is essence, unfailingly place the smallest volumes on the top shelf, then scale the books down to the quartos on the bottom. Dreadfully inconvenient for finding things, absolutely impossible to browse through categories, but visually much more satisfying.

The card catalogue was of polished wood with brass fixtures, canopied by a wrought-iron catwalk that gave access to a wall of books above. Everything was bathed in the purest of Renaissance light. If it weren't for the hump-backed academic who, wouldn't you know it, was camped out at the *P*s, this would have been paradise found. She shared his love, indeed need, for solitude. As he edged in to find the *Poussin* entries, she pursed her lips, patted her bun, and expelled a puff of air not unlike the dying. But Brocard would not be deterred by the harpy. After all, he had an urgent mission.

For the briefest of moments he lost heart. The entries were endless and he was not, after all, an art historian. Sir Anthony Blunt he had heard of, and there was a *Catalogue Raisonee*, so perhaps there would be some record of the paintings there. He took down the number, then almost randomly gathered names and titles of authors who had published more recent, major works: Uberhuber, Thuillier, and Wright seemed promising. His modus operandi was to concentrate on Poussin's early years in Rome. Both in content and execution, the painting of Saint Agatha did not seem to be a mature work. And the likelihood of the order having commissioned Poussin at the height of his luminous career was as remote then as it would be now. The motto still held. Why buy something of beauty when so much ugliness goes begging for a home?

Feeling every bit the archivist that he was, Brocard took the first volume of Blunt into the nearest reading room, found a suitably dismal corner, and prepared to work his way through the catalogue of paintings, ready for the long haul. However, that was not to be the case. Hardly had he passed the frontispiece when a shadow was cast over the book, garlic breath warmed the hairs of his neck, and he turned to see a rather sinister-looking, decidedly French troll hovering over him.

"Pardon, mon pere. The directrice would like to see you."

It was a command, not an invitation, and Brocard treated it accordingly. He felt innumerable eyes on him as he made his way back into the director's office. Something was amiss, perhaps no more than his having slipped in the back door. Maybe much more.

He was in no way prepared for Madam Blanchierdarie, an improbably feminine creature, Hermes scarf pinned low around her neck, smelling to all the world like a woman with intentions. Nor did he know what to make of her warm greeting.

"Eh bien, mon pere, it is about time you arrived. Whatever has kept you?"

15

By early morning the day after the clandestine burial, Manolo had completed his task. All locks were changed and all secret storage spaces secured. He had worked almost without break with a determination that was rooted in a cluster of cardinal sins. Having long since chosen galvanized evil over prosaic good, he lusted after avarice and gorged himself on concupiscence. Rome's black market was his hunting ground. It held no secrets from him, consummate deceiver that he was. His reward was an unmarked account in Lugano and gold bullion in a vault at the Banco Vaticano. But what he treasured most was the expanding collection of Germanic erotica which he received from Father Otger for favors best left unmentioned. Manolo's particular fondness was for lactating women.

Unfortunately his brother Antonio had some vestiges of piety left, a distressing consequence of a youth wasted with lifeless monks as opposed to one abandoned to barnyard animals. Their lives had been as different then as they were similar now. For several years, they had been single-minded in their determination to cajole the few remaining passengers while stripping the decks of anything worth taking. There was no telling how long the once stately ship of San Redempto would stay afloat. All that could be said with certainty was that when it rolled on its side and pitched bow first into oblivion, the Basque brothers will be in the sole lifeboat, overladen with booty.

As the bell rang for morning prayer, Manolo made his way down to the refectory to meet Antonio. They had the habit, one of many that measured the day, of taking a cafe *ristreto*, not too spiked but nicely enlivened, while the others plodded their way through the

Psalter. This always gave them a chance to compare notes for the day. What money might be skimmed, favors supplied at a price, or hidden treasures plundered. All done with such devious cunning that no one would ever suspect them.

Light had no hope of access to San Redempto, so days were indistinguishable from nights. To most it would have seemed forbidding but Manolo was so used to the musty dampness that clung to his flesh and the tomblike silence punctuated by the mumbling of hollow prayers that he found it all positively comforting. Until, that is, he was accosted.

Antonio saw it differently. He was so agitated by his discovery, so uncertain what they should do, so clear that they must do something, that he slid up behind Manolo as he turned the corner from the service stairs and covered his mouth so he would make no noise. Manolo, who absorbed stress infinitely better, was extremely annoyed by such antics. Still, he allowed himself to be led to the second-floor storage room that was next door to Avertanus's cell. Once there, Antonio used his freshly minted key, threw back the door, and flashed a light into the far corner. Then, in that dumb show of body language of which they both were masters, he asked Manolo if he had seen them before.

No, Manolo assured him, his eyes widening, never. Together they got down on their knees and unrolled the paintings. In his rush to change the locks, he had missed them. How did they get here? Would someone be looking for them or were they in some way connected to the boy's body they had just sealed into the crypt?

Seen up close, striped of their frames and vulnerable in his hands, these paintings compelled him to take them as surely as any middle-age virgin. How many years had they gone unappreciated, longing to share themselves with someone, anyone. There was one painting of a body being pressed to death under a stone, the bones freshly cracking after three centuries, the torturers still reveling. Another of some saintly soul being drawn and quartered and yet another flayed alive. Given the subject matter, it was remarkable how stately, indeed how majestic they all were. A master's hand had clearly left its mark.

There was noise in the hall. Morning prayer was over and the community was wending its separate way back to daily oblivion. Action, not discussion, was what was needed. By some quirk of fate, the paintings were now theirs. Manolo fumbled through his keys, found the one for the hidden storage area, and leaving quickly so as to avoid suspicion, gestured for Antonio to conceal the roll of paintings there and to lock up behind him. As he was closing the inner door, he was troubled to see dotty Father Pius lurking in the hallway. Pius, curious as any child, waited for Antonio to leave and entered the hidden room. He had never recalled seeing this hidden chamber and, curious child that he had become in his advanced age, began to explore it. Then he heard noise outside. Someone was coming. Afraid of being discovered, he closed the door gently behind himself and crouched down in total darkness.

In his haste Antonio had neglected to lock up, but he firmly did so now, unaware that Pius was inside. All he thought was that Manolo would have killed him.

16

*D*eath had come suddenly, decisively, and unforgivingly. Resistance was not an option for Pius Poncelet: he was a good religious, well schooled in suffering. *Cristo confixus sum cruci,* his novice master had taught him and he never forgot it. With Christ I am crucified. No short-term memory loss or vagueness in thinking could ever blur that from his mind. *Cristo confixus sum cruci* was etched in his bones and carved in his flesh.

How few there were who would hear no less understand these words. Brocard, perhaps, in his fastidious, North American way. Avertanus to some extent, but he lived so much in his head. There was a time, Pius recalled as he searched the darkness for a place to lie down, when Emmanuele lived by these words. He had been such an exemplary young monk, using the *flagellum* on himself until he drew blood. No artifice there, no cosmetic penance, but unmasked pain which connected him to the agony of the cross. How he lamented the passing of that practice. Community would gather and each in turn would recite his faults, then whip himself free of sin. How could Emmanuele have abandoned such a discipline, even if the Church itself was so misguided as to abandon such spiritual exercises? It made no sense, he thought as he found a thick roll of canvases to lay his head on, that he would have abandoned all his principles for the constant stream of young boys who scurried down the servants' stairs in the depth of night. Oh, he had seen them and he had heard the telling silence of the abandoned theater in which they all were locked. Self-denial had been selfishly denied. The essence of their life was lost: *Cristo confixus sum cruci.*

Perhaps it was best God called him now. He had his fill of dissolution, could no longer adapt to the changes which ran riot in the
community. Chapel had become a charade, and were it not for the
ghosts which pulsated around him, their gray cowled forms clinging
tentatively to the memory of past lives, there would be nothing to
bring him there. In fact God was nowhere to be found at San Re-
dempo. Except, he thought as he pulled himself up into the fetal
position and pressed his head deep into the paintings, in the airless
confines of this room in which he had been forever locked.

While those around him were propelled into the world, he imploded inwards. In the confusion swirling around him, Pius longed to
be walled up, secure as any immured, inviolate as any virgin hermit.
In that, God had assuredly granted his wish. And yet, it seemed at
times as if this inner world was also spinning out of control. Forces of
evil were breeding chaos, from which there could be no escape.

Cristo confixus sum cruci. Should he have spoken up sooner? Fraternal
correction it had been called, back in those days when there seemed
to be a purpose to religious life. When leaving the world was a goal,
not an illusion. Did it start with Otger, the third Dutchman in the
community, and his liberal thoughts? Was it when he abandoned the
habit for his professorial tweed jacket, and the title *Reverend* for *Doctor*.
But how could he have ever confronted Otger, great expert in things
"spiritual" that he was, the great manipulator of words? Perhaps the
influence started there, but even with him away from Rome these
past few months, situations had still worsened. Now Father Berthold,
Bertie that is, sported those obscenely tight shorts in the cloister and
Dionysius used the pretext of gardening so as to go out whoring.
Whom could he tell? Avertanus would "subsume" the evil into good,
refuse to see these details in the cosmic pattern. No one in authority
would even care when the prior himself had become a major player
in this travesty of virtue.

The combined heat and lack of oxygen began to take its toll on
Pius. His health was weak at best of times. Chimeras floated into his
dreams, clouded his moments of consciousness. A peacock's tail flowered on the naked body of the boy that Emmanuele locked into the
closet in the biblioteca. Too late to tell anyone, too late for anything.
A serpent's tale lashed up and curled itself around him. So hard to
breathe, so very hard. *Cristo confixus sum cruci.* The words pounded in

51

his head and echoed in his heart.

Had that young boy in his closet known what it was to be nailed to the cross with Jesus? Had he experienced such joy? Might he also have been one of the two boys with the ladder in the ambulatory a few nights earlier? So many questions without answers.

Hours that might have been days later the outside door opened and Pius roused himself enough to hear Manolo and his brother Antonio in quiet conversation. *No, the nosy old fool didn't see me and who would believe him anyway.* And then the command that sealed Pius's fate. "I think it best," Manolo said, "if you go to Loretto for the Holy Cards this week. No one needs you here and it's better that we keep scarce just in case someone comes looking for them. No need to arouse suspicion."

Pius knew that Antonio would be away for at least two days; he had never made it across the mountains and back in less time. And as it was presumably Antonio who had locked the door on him, he realized that his fate was sealed, that he was immured forever. *Cristo confixus sum cruci.*

17

❦

"Breasts," the professoressa declaimed, "ample, milk-filled breasts were the Baroque obsession." Then, leaning over him with protuberances as grand as the Abruzzi, she added, "and of our own time, which you may recall my calling the Neo-Baroque in my latest article on Poussin in *Cahier*." As they swung pendulously towards his gaping mouth, he signaled that no, he did not recall.

Events had gotten seriously out of control. If only Brocard had time to assimilate them then maybe, just maybe they would be manageable. As it was, he knew that he had entered the labyrinth with no ball of thread and no way out. Still, if truth be known, this research project was turning into serious fun. More than he had ever imagined possible.

Just the day before, Madam Blanchierdarie, the Circe of the Farnesse biblioteque, had lured him in with the most compelling of information. A young student from Holland had worked on the same project as Brocard's the year before. His study in turn was based on substantial but unfinished research done by still another Dutchman nearly six years earlier. He was attempting to show that these seven paintings were not only Poussins but critically important for understanding his early years in Rome. Something about the perversity underlying all French Classicism. Poussin as a precursor of de Sade, she said with the most effervescent of smiles. To her dismay, the project had been suddenly dropped. In a lapse of professionalism, she admitted writing to the student, whose name she searched out on a file box on her desk, Thius Meyer, and when she received no answer from him, to his adviser at the University of Maastrich, a Dr. Hoop

Rhutten from whom she heard nothing, save a terse acknowledgment of letter received. It troubled her that such momentous work had been dropped. But she was certain that someone would pick up the search. If only, she said in tones of deepest longing, my dear friend Professoressa Pavlic, the real expert in the area, could see them. She has the eye, you know, the one that will be able to see.

But as it was, the professoressa had brought far more than her eyes with her to San Redempto that day and she all but smothered little Brocard with them as they ostensibly studied the painting of Saint Agatha together.

Working her magnifying glass deftly over the surface she muttered periodic *"E stupendos"* in a voice whose huskiness bordered on the obscene. "It is remarkable how much of the original paint surface remains, how terribly exciting. See how only a hint of underpainting shows through." Her pedagogy was so blatantly earthy yet so natural that Brocard could not but wonder if she trained all her students, whole classes of them at a time, by applying pressure to the back of their heads and shoulders with her enormous breasts.

By this stage, Brocard was relaxing into the experience. He even felt a vague stirring in his groin but quickly dismissed it as a bladder problem. Surely Brother Antonio, ever observant, had wondered who this solid-looking woman might be. She certainly didn't look like your common garden professoressa. She was Amazonian in stature, six foot three and just over two hundred solidly packed pounds. In fact, Zinka Pavlic had nurtured her God-given strangeness into man-made uniqueness. Born an undefined man of indiscriminate Serbo-Croatian stock, she had long since decided to finish what nature had left undone. Through a never-ending series of hormone injections and several major operations, she had flowered into a dumbfounding creature who dominated every strada she walked, every library and speak room she entered. As she most definitely did now.

"It is undeniably of the period," she offered. "A curious mixture of the Baroque fascination with pain and ecstasy and the classical need for formal control. The reference is clearly to the Circignana cycle in San Stefano Rotundo. You know it of course?"

After a lifetime in Rome, Brocard sadly confessed that he knew little of the city, but would familiarize himself with the paintings as soon as possible.

"You'll thank me for it, Padre, I assure you. They're absolutely confessable."

Then, the strangest of things, the professoressa fell into a silence as empty as death itself. She pulled herself away from Brocard and moved around to the lower right portion of the canvas. "It must be cleaned, it simply must." Then slowly she began to explain how Poussin often signed his early works in the most prominent of places. "We must find Saint Agatha's other breast, the first one that was ripped off. Without that, we are lost."

While he was showing her out, they passed Father Dionysius coming in from his garden. Zinka Pavlic recognized him immediately but, discreet when she needed to be, only winked.

18

*A*s he penetrated her body, he could not help but think of that other woman. Was the wink because she recognized the only unremittingly straight man at San Redempto? Still, there was something as familiar about her as the Brazilian drags in the Villa Borghese. A blatant characterization of a woman. He knew for sure that he had never slept with her though; big breasts always got in the way. For him, the charm of a woman lay below the waist: wide and ample hips to rest on and a willing port to drive himself into for the long haul.

Dionysius had been blessed with the ability to sustain an erection for hours with little or no effort. Sadly, he had not always considered this a blessing. When he was a scholastic in Scotland, even praying the psalms embarrassed him. At the first mention of "exalting his horn like a mighty bull" or "sucking fully from the breast," he was up like a flag pole. However, when he arrived at San Redempto to study under Avertanus a decade ago, his talent began to be appreciated for the blessing it was. But by then his unqualified love of women made it impossible for him to be satisfied by the longings of celibate men whose sexuality had all too often been arrested at the toilet training stage. So he cast his net over Rome and never looked back. Italian women, he found out, were given rapid servicing by large tools. His more manageable size and infinitely longer staying power assured his popularity.

His woman, this one he had lived with now for nearly five years, slowly moved herself under his weight, and he felt as if she were sucking him in, magically moistening and tightening herself by a will to please. There was a precedent for what he was doing—many perhaps, if the truth be known. Fra Fillipo Lippi snuck out the garden door of his monastery in Florence to share his life with a common-law wife and son. And surely there were countless others, forgotten, as he was destined to be. Anonymous religious who could not disassociate their God, who was fully a man after all, from the flesh.

She began moaning lowly, in that contented cowlike fashion which did little to excite him. Still, the erection was there, no danger of that, and he gave a few mandatory thrusts to simulate enthusiasm. Then she resumed rocking gently beneath him, freeing him up to think once more. He could only make sense of things this way, buried inside her.

What a massive disappointment he had been to those in authority. He was, after all, the golden boy of his province, sent off to Rome to do great, or at the very least, serious things. A well-groomed and tidy-looking Scotsman, nothing offensive to his look, small nose, green eyes, and curly hair. Cute in fact, in a Celtic way. It had started off auspiciously enough. Father Avertanus Deblaer himself, the grand master of spirituality, had taken an interest in him. No one realized that it had nothing to do with the prodigiousness of his mind. Still, he was not without innate intelligence. It was just that somewhere in the maze of academia, after his licentiate but long before his doctorate, he lost interest in conquering arcane lands. What he wanted was the smell and feel of flesh, a life lived with minimum expectations. Simply put, the Vatican lost and Rome won.

It was not that he ever lost his faith, he thought as she slid her hand around his ass and edged him onto his back, it was just that he deepened it to its roots. Christianity as he came to know it in Rome, was at one with its pagan roots. As she positioned herself on top of him and swayed slowly up and down, he smiled to remember how naive he had once been. He knew now that the essence of life was to be, not to do, and the wisdom at the root of his faith was quite simply to love, gently and quietly.

Dionysius loved this woman who was sitting upright on him, mesmerized by this endless penetration. Like Saint Augustine, he was unable to call his mistress by name, his fault perhaps, but he gave her all he had. He never could seem to wean himself off the big tit of San Redempto though. What would he have done anyway, a Scotsman in Rome trained in theology and nothing else? So he lifted duplicate copies of books from the biblioteca, some quite rare, things he was reasonably sure no one would miss, and fenced them at one of the many book dealers in the Campo Marzio. Petty larceny, just like the old days in Glasgow before he found Jesus. And he took up gardening, which meant not only easy access to the back gate, but vegetables to bring over to the flat on Via Flaminia where they had set up house. Finances had been a bit strained when the child came along, but now that she had landed a job as a maid in a new hotel in Parioli, things were looking up.

When she began to sway in that now familiar Dionysian ritual, he knew that after going for so long, sadly, it was time to come.

19

Except for their names, the two Irish monks, Cuthbert and Angelus, were normalcy itself. Or so it seemed. Nothing about the Irish was ever as it seemed. Gregarious and open on the outside, they were more fiercely private than any Slav, more deeply distrustful of "the other" than any Melanesian primitive. But, true to their race, in their brief time at San Redempto, they had won the shriveled heart of the community. And no one, not even the most jaded among them, ever suspected their deadly purpose. Nor for that matter had they taken on unique identities, just "the Irish monks" seemed to suffice, although they were distinctly individual creatures.

Cuthbert Mullins had an uncommonly clever mind, unusual to find among monks these days, vocations being what they were—slim in number and rather inferior in quality at that. Coupled with this was an almost Calvinistic zealousness which bordered on the manic. Right was right, wrong was wrong and there was no place in between for indecision or, worse still, casuistry. He would have made a poor Jesuit but was just the monk his order needed for the task at hand.

His older confrere, Angelus Lennon, had a slower more deliberate mind, more befitting his sixty-plus years, most of which had been spent in the order. Unlike many of the monks at San Redempto, however, Angelus had opened himself up to the changes that the church and religious life had gone through over the past thirty years. He had even gone through therapy to get over an inflated sense of deflation. Never, ever was he worthy of anything, it seemed. And the compunction which plagued his every action had virtually paralyzed him. Most of that was behind him now and he thanked God that he had the courage to seek help and the perseverence to see it through. Knowing that we are always what we were, he realized fully that he was still somewhat severe in his judgements. So when he was asked to take upon the San Redempto project, as the general of the order called it, he prayed seriously about it before accepting the mission.

They were united in their agenda, which, like all things truly Catholic, divided into three parts. First and foremost was to reconnoiter the entire physical plant and holdings. This, in itself, was a daunting task. At one time San Redempto had housed nearly two hundred monks, had stored its own food in underground larders, nurtured minds in one of the largest monastic libraries in Rome, and accumulated nearly eight centuries of holdings in a sealed archive, the extent of which was known by the resident scholar, Father Avertanus and Father Emmanuele, the prior, alone. If, indeed, they were even fully aware. How to get to, no less inventory and appraise the monastery's wealth, was the first serious obstacle they encountered. And to date they had no idea how they might overcome it.

Their second task was to research every aspect of the monastery's dealings which might help them assess its true worth, both financially and artistically. In this, they were more successful as there were substantial resources available both at the Sapientia, the city archives, and the Vatican archives. For the time being they saw no need to penetrate San Redempto's archives, although if the opportunity arose, they would seize it.

Finally, and by no means least important, they had to ingratiate themselves to the community. This had to be done for two distinct reasons. First, to facilitate in the information gathering which would allow them to complete their investigation and then to soften the fatal blow that would end San Redempto forever. They knew clearly that they had been cast as angels of destruction and they were prepared to play their part fully.

In order to facilitate this contrived bonding, they studied the community and divided it between them, realizing that the difference in their personalities would serve them well. Besides them, there were only six priests in the community. Five, not counting Father Otger who was on extended leave in Holland and four, not counting Father Pius, who somehow seemed to have been misplaced lately. No one had expressed the slightest concern that he was not at any community exercises for two days. And were it not for Angelus's insistent questioning, the prior would probably never have thought to check his room. Father Emmanuele only shrugged and said that he would eventually wander back, they all do. Nothing more was, or had been since said about it.

Gaining the confidence of Fathers Brocard and Avertanus, by far the most dour of the lot, fell to Father Angelus, a philosopher by trade and plodder by nature. He had already won their good graces. Father Cuthbert, on the other hand, was the livelier of the two, with a pub-tested tenor voice and a knowing glint of the eye to prove it. Unfortunately he was always in need of a good scrub, disdaining water in anything but his whisky, but this aside, Fathers Emmanuele, Dionysius, and Berthold aka Bertie became his charge. They were proving to be a slippery lot—tough less because of personality than the very practical fact that they were rarely to be found in the cloister.

The three brothers were simply impenetrable. Ephraim, being a certifiable simpleton, was too dumb; and Manolo and Antonio, they suspected, far too smart to let on to anything. No, nothing to be done with them except observe them sulking around the corridors playing at work in the hope that, inadvertently, they might slip up and lead them to something of significance.

Still, Cuthbert and Angelus were in no way discouraged. They had made a good start, were beyond suspicion, and were well placed to succeed. But they both realized, as they stood in the second floor corridor near the bathroom, that they were reaching an impasse. Someone in the community had to be taken into their confidence and it had to be someone who could care less if San Redempto came tumbling down around them.

Just then Bertie came out of his room to shower, glided by them, coyly dropping his towel as he passed. Cuthbert stared a bit too long and Bertie flashed him a smile.

The angels of righteousness knew then that they had found their man.

20

*A*t times like this, Zinka didn't care that her life's savings and most of her psychic energy had been devoted to her breasts. With Camille there, burying her face into them and purring contentedly, the endless string of operations and hormone shots were well worth the price. The doctors attributed their grand success to her well-developed back muscles, without which her forty-two-inch bust would have quickly looked like a sack of potatoes. But here they were, fully alert if not quite perky, a testimony to the wonders of science and the glories of womanhood. Worshiped by not only a woman, but the woman she loved.

Camille Blanchierdarie had a more modest femininity. To compensate for this, she invariably wore high-heel shoes when naked, even to bed (but of course not to sleep). More often than not she also sported one of her ubiquitous Hermes scarves, as she had this afternoon. Zinka, on the other hand, preferred to wear nothing at all except panties, which only came off in the heat of passion. The unspoken truth was that her reconstructed genitals were far too aggressive. Her mound was not of Venus, but of Jupiter.

"Knead them, carissima," she hissed into her lover's ear, "like lumpy dough." Camille would have felt far better if Zinka didn't attempt metaphors at times like this. But with such *mammelle* thrust in her face, honestly, who could complain? Anyway, as she put her mouth to work on more serious matters than grammar, she realized that she was getting rather used to Zinka's incessant babble. In fact, she found it rather comforting.

"That painting, darling, is our ticket to fame. It won't matter at all that I haven't played the silly academic game these past five years. Who gives a damn about whether or not I attended this conference or presented a dreary little paper at that symposium. If I can show that Poussin painted that delightfully deranged canvas, they will all be at my feet, baby. No one would ever dare call me Milorad again, you can count on it!"

As Camille had locked herself onto a nipple she could only give the faintest of grunts. Which was more than Zinka needed to be off and running again.

"My only hope is to have the canvas cleaned. And," she paused for the briefest of moments for her extroverted mind to work it out, "blackmail him. Of course, that's it!"

In her enthusiasm Zinka had popped her breast out of Camille's eager mouth, making the most unladylike of noises. Then, standing Amazon-like above her, she issued an order: "Put on your red shift, baby, and your walking shoes. We have business to do!"

Their destination was the Villa Borghese, and their business was to take an early evening *passeggiata*. This was to be no idle stroll, however, but rather a determined walk with the most serious of intents. As the professoressa, for she had assumed that role once more, explained it, there was another way in which Saint Agatha might reveal her secret.

"Context, *carissima*. See what else they have in that fright house of a monastery. If those sad little monks supported other struggling seventeenth-century artists, preferably French, then an argument can be made through association of provenance. Especially," and here her enthusiasm mounted to a feverish pitch "if there are any Dughets in their collection." When Camille didn't respond in kind, she reminded her, "Poussin's brother-in-law, baby, they shared patrons." After another heartbeat she realized how this might open up a whole area of finds. "Oh, think of it, my moist little melon"—Camille just hated it when she invented endearing names—"Saint Agatha might be just the start!"

When they got to top of the staircase leading down to the Museo di Arte Moderna, where the drags and hustlers set up shop, they rested on one of the few unoccupied benches and waited. Camille still had no idea what Zinka was up to. She only knew that in order to study these paintings, granted they existed at all, her enthusiastic lover would not only have to penetrate the male cloister of San Redempto but also gain access to the treasury. The prospect of which seemed remote at best.

They did not have to wait too long before a rather attractive Scottish man and an indifferent Italian woman, broad hipped and plainly dressed, came towards them with their noisy little child in tow. Camille had seen them often before on their walks. Rome, as any Romani would tell you, encourages, indeed demands, routine.

As they began to pass, Professoressa Zinka Pavlic sprung to her feet and stopped them with her massive bulk. Dionysius was visibly upset, but clearly trapped.

"*Buona serra, caro.*" Then looking him straight in the eye, "We must talk."

21

*I*f there was one thing that summed up perfection to him, and all the grace and beauty of God's creation, it was Pino. Granted his teeth needed a bit of work, but those eyes, those strong muscular arms, those big feet (and we all know what that signifies) were nothing short of divine. Bertie knew that he was no better than an adolescent when he was around his dream hustler, but that didn't trouble him at all. After all, as long as his behavior was arrested, why not just get on with things where they were? Fun is fun.

The problem was that it cost, and he had yet to figure out a way of getting access to substantial funds. His monthly stipend went in a flash, so he had been forced to do some part-time table waiting in a Monte Verde pizzeria, where no one would ever recognize him. He knew, or at least chose to believe, that Pino would go with him for free if he were able to, but he simply wasn't. The job in Foggia was only part time; his parents had thrown him out. And he was gorgeous. So why shouldn't he be a hustler? A small part of Bertie realized that he had seriously lost hold of his Moral Theology, but that greater part of him that was excited simply by being around Pino quickly put all compunction to rest.

Maybe the Irish priest who was after his tail would have a plan which could make him some money. Not a whole lot, just enough to buy some freedom. Cuthbert and his compatriot were surely up to no good. Snooping about, making friends even given the fact that they were Irish—this was aberrant behavior at San Redempto.

Sometimes he walked all the way up Via Nationale to Piazza della Republica but it was an unusually humid night so he took the 64 bus so as not to perspire too much. Not that Pino would probably notice as he himself always smelled like a barnyard animal, of the particularly masculine persuasion. But that was Pino, and he was, after all, Bertie.

His pulse raced as the bus approached the piazza and he was so nervous that he nearly jumped off a stop early. He had first seen it years before, a colonnade of forbidden pleasure, seedy to its very soul. It took him a year to muster up the courage to visit it, another to strip himself of his habit and walk there like he belonged, and still another before he had the courage to talk with one of the men who worked it like a city office. The first person he happened to talk with had been Pino. No one else ever interested him.

The triple X cinemas that provided safe harbor for all activities were only just opening. He knew he was very early. And yet, as he propped himself against a marble column and tried to act nonchalant, he couldn't help being disappointed that Pino wasn't there and ready to go like some well-fingered piece of pornography. There was nothing to do but wait, and think about how wonderful it would be when they were together.

The sun went down, the electric lights came on, and the stage was finally set for *depravation*. Pino arrived like a wild cat, stealthily, in total command of all around him. Bertie tried to keep his composure but ended up fumbling like the little girl he was.

"P-P-P-Pino," he said, long since having gotten over the embarrassment of his stutter. "Padre," Pino whispered into his ear and then flashed him an effervescent smile.

Bertie blushed as he always did when he saw him and then exchanged small talk.

But Pino was, after all, a working boy and with little time wasted, he escorted his little prelate into the blue, not the red, sector of the Cinema Moderna where they would have the most privacy. It cost a few thousand lira more, but there were no usherettes flashing lights at you, no matrons collecting change in the toilets. Privacy had its price.

Not that much would happen, if past experience proved true. Pino remembered their first two times together, at the fast food restaurant in the arcade. Bertie had asked him if he wanted a drink and then realizing that he was eyeing the food-he was always hungry-just sat there and watched while he ate. They talked the next few times and then, presumably after Bertie had built up enough courage, went into the darkened cinema together. Being a pro, Pino unzipped his fly, pulled his pants down over his thighs and stretched himself out. Head back, prepared for anything. He had had them down on the floor at his feet and buried in his crotch, but he had never known anyone as strange as Bertie. Not only did he stutter but he never seemed to get an erection or even try. With the gentlest of sighs Bertie would simply lean his head on Pino's shoulder. As the women on the screen exhibited absurdly athletic behavior, Pino found himself encircling the little priest in his massive arms and, in time, happy to the point of orgasm.

Bertie, for his part, knowing he was finally home, would shed a tear of happiness.

22

*T*he stench was strong enough that even given Avertanus's diminished sense of smell, he could take no more. There was an exercise they did in novitiate, in the days of the giants before religious life had been diluted into a boys club, where you were told to imagine hell as a vile smell, the most distasteful, nauseating of smells. He never had much luck with that exercise as he found most of the commonly abhorred smells to be of some interest. From sweaty feet to armpits. Now, over fifty years later, he had finally found the smell that conjured up hell itself and he had to get out.

When at a loss for what to do, clerics of his generation were always taught to ask the brother to handle it. He made his way down to the front door in the hope that Antonio had arrived back from his annual excursion to the Flying House of Mary in Loretto. He had. Even though Avertanus was still nauseated, he began to breathe a bit easier. Wasting no time he told Antonio about the strange smell coming from his wall, perhaps a dead rat or a host of them. Something was rotting.

Of course Antonio—who had not yet unpacked his satchel—knew right away that it was Pius, or what was left of him. Stupid, stupid old man. Now Manolo was going to be upset with him, even though he too was to blame for not checking the storage room while Antonio was away. Avertanus would have to be told about the false wall and storage room. And the mess. He was furious.

There was nothing to be done. Manolo must be told. He was, after all, the only one who performed well under pressure. As expected, Manolo was not at all pleased, but after fixing a look of unmitigated disdain on his brother, he sprung into action. First he explained to

Avertanus the importance of the secret room for the monastery's well-being. This was where provisions were stored up for the benefit of all. Having asked him, for the good of community, to say nothing about this to anyone, he gathered his keys and led the way to the troublesome room. It was after compline and the monastery was a tomb.

It is unfortunate that the expression "a smell to knock you over" has been worn down by overuse. The smell that rushed out from that airless room when Manolo flung open the door did that and more. It stung their eyes, caused Antonio to mutter profanities, and brought up the better part of Avertanus's dinner into the handkerchief he had tightly held over his mouth. Manolo directed his flashlight towards the corpse, carefully leaving the rest of the room in darkness. Amazingly, given the brief time he had been dead, The flesh had hardened, cracked, and pustulated. Maggots had already begun to feast. Antonio was right: it was a bloody mess.

He was at least prepared. Shroud and shovel, a pair of disposable rubber gloves. While Avertanus tried to regain his composure, Antonio, never one to trouble himself with such delicacies, strained to roll the body into the shroud. Trying as hard as he could to absorb the fate of his gentle old friend, Avertanus made a feeble request that the prior be called, that proper dignity and reverence be accorded one of the senior members of the community. For the Basque brothers, this was out of the question. If an investigation was made, not only might they be blamed for criminal negligence but, more significantly, their secret storage areas might be uncovered and years of diligent work, years of conscientious graft and deception overturned.

No, Manolo explained, there was nothing to be done but to bury poor Father Pius in the cloister garden, under the blood oranges which he loved so dearly. Even though Avertanus reminded Manolo that blood oranges had always given Father Pius diarrhea, he would have none of it. Their course of action was set.

Unfortunately the corpse was oozing too much to carry any great distance, so in one of those bursts of inspiration of which Manolo was capable under severe stress, he decided to dump it down the laundry shoot. God willing it wouldn't get wedged in.

Unexpectedly, and very unfortunately for him as it would turn out, Brother Ephraim, the launderer, had a flare-up of colitis that night and had been unable to sleep. Rather than pamper himself he had decided to get up, hobble around, and do a few loads of laundry for the souls in purgatory. He was very old school. Needless to say, Father Pius's severely decomposed body did nothing to relieve his indigestion.

So the four of them buried Father Pius in a shallow grave in the cloister garden. Antonio continued to curse mildly under his breath while Father Avertanus offered the prayers of final commendation, then sprinkled the earth with holy water.

Forgotten for the time being were the roll of stolen paintings which had pillowed Father Pius in his final hours, soaked forever in the stench of death.

23

It was a night of almost epic bleakness, altogether appropriate for
what he had to do. Driven by confusion and grief, grasping at a final
shred of hope, Avertanus wrapped himself in his black wool cloak,
pulled the massive cowl up over his head, and, clutching the precious
volume close to his chest, disappeared into the streets on the far side
of the Tiber. The cobblestones on the Via Gulia were still slimy from
the afternoon rains and the Renaissance palaces bore down on him
unforgivingly. Their shuttered windows and bolted doors reminded
him, as he smelled the *cenas* being set on table and heard the muffled
laughter of families at play, of a world from which he had been eternally excluded.

However, domestic pleasure—no matter how comforting and al-
luring—held no real attraction for Avertanus. Long before it had become fashionable to dredge up spiritual information, to revel in arcane
information, long before it had become de rigueur to connect ancient
religions one to another, he had understood the links between pagan
cults and early Christian texts and practices. For years his painfully
small writing crammed filing cards and notebooks with exotic information. His great life's work was not only to find the intellectual links
but the channels of spiritual energy, as he would put it, which flowed
inextricably from one religious system to another. And his hope now,
realizing that only such supernatural power could resolve the rampant
evil which swirled around him, was that he could harness this power
to bring about a transformation at San Redempto. Even were this to
mean an implosion of all that he knew, day must be allowed to follow
night. A line from Albertus Magnus, one of the many axioms which

acted as leitmotifs to his life, fixed itself in his mind and would not let go: "Everyone is capable of magic if they fall into a great excess." That was, after all what he needed, what they needed, the whole lot of them at San Redempto, magic. Hopefully of the benign type that Pico della Mirandolo had maintained was possible. It was a late-sixteenth-century-copy of his *Conclusiones Magicae* (one with the Cabalistic incantations included) that he concealed under his cloak. The time had long past for pious prayers and good intentions. Rot had taken hold and nothing short of calling down supernatural powers could stay total ruination. This was the great excess he was prepared to plummet into; this was the magic he so sorely needed to work.

The rows of skulls on the façade of of the Confraternita del Mortii, where paupers are prayed for before being dumped into a pit, cast their shadow down on him in disbelief. Their hollowed sockets followed him as he turned down the side of the Palazzzo Farnesse and made his way through deserted streets to the Campo di Fiori. He could not help but recall those words of Bruno, whose place of execution he was approaching, that we should not think that shadow comes from light but rather that light is brought forth from shadow. It was this hope that drove him, this sense that the adumbration of the moment was not obscuring the light but rather, in some way too strange to realize, introducing it.

As Avertanus approached the brooding statue of Giordano Bruno, whose fully hooded earthly body was lost under yards of fabric like his own, he received the sign he had been looking for-a sign was always needed. In front of a deserted flower stand, a young man, unzipped his trousers, pulled out his rather substantial cock, and, catching the eye of the strange monk, smiled engagingly as he sprayed the piazza with abandon. What to others was a normal act, was understood by Avertanus to have far deeper meaning. Urine had always been used in ancient ritual incantations. The Renaissance alchemist Ficino even asserted that the great Hermes Trismegistus himself, the source of all hermetic knowledge, incorporated it in all his greatest acts. Far from being a sign of waste, urine was a sign of the deeper self, the base material which had been transformed into pure gold. The most efficacious was the urine of a young male, virile and confident, caught as it arced out into the world from the depth of his being. As such it was always considered worthy of drinking, empowering to the point of divinizing all who could break down the human and societal barriers of drinking it freely.

Knowing most assuredly that this was the sign from God he had been looking for, Avertanus walked confidently over to him and stretched out his hand. The young man smiled more broadly and projected the arch of gold, fountainlike towards him. Cupping some in his hand—a small amount was all that was ever needed—he raised it to his lips and drank. Finished, the young man tucked it back in his trousers, laughed openly, and shrugged his shoulders and moved on.

Then Avertanus Deblaer, the Mystical Doctor, took the precious copy of *Conclusiones Magicae* out and began his incantations in earnest. As mountains of clouds rolled ominously overhead, the air congealed like blood at an open wound as he commanded an angel to be raised up, one that would break the curse that had been set on San Redempto or, should that be God's will, bring it final peace. Inconclusiveness was unacceptable, *archangel Deo sacrificantur*, total transformation must be achieved, *archangelum Deo*, by the power given Christ himself.

No lightning accompanied his ranting, and when the chanting was over even the few passersby who had gathered around him quickly dispersed. Sadly, all Avertanus was left with was the all-too-famliar feeling of failure and the musty taste of piss in his mouth.

Exhausted or disheartened, it was so hard to make the distinction at his age, the impotent magus wended his way back along the route he had taken. What was it that he had hoped to conjure up? Was it that unity of heaven and hell, that marriage of the flesh and the spirit which Pico strove for? Or was he a failed and terminally frightened man, asking for a peace devoid of flesh, without confusion, emotion, and need he add, sex?

At the turning by the Confraternita dei Mortii, he nearly ran into his old disciple Dionysius and a statuesque, downright gigantic woman. He pulled the cowl down fully and nodded as he passed but they were too caught up with each other to notice him.

24

Later that night, as the skies opened up and the winds tore down from the mountains, Emmanuele's little game took on a sinister turn. Patience and control had always been part of it. And blood to be sure. But his participation had always been minimal until that night. And once the threshold was crossed, there was no turning back.

It was the skin that he always looked for first. The muscle tone of a sixteen-year-old could never be surpassed. But some young men, as old as twenty-three or-four—as Thius had been—still had the elasticity he required. Then translucency was needed so that the blood could be seen flushing the checks and pooling on their temples. Hairless bodies were preferable although not always available given the influx of southerners to Rome these days. Some body shaving was invariably needed, but not when Otger sent down one of those Nordic beauties to brighten up his palette. Yes, palette was the word, for he was an artist and these bodies that he used were his medium. He, not they, created the art.

He used the deserted old theater in the basement which hadn't been used in over twenty years. This was where he had once played Medea, in the days when boys would be boys and seminarians were more numerous than the stars. Manolo and Antonio were the only other members of the community who knew he was using it. The brothers had a way of knowing everything anyway, and since he needed their help in initially preparing the room and then scrubbing it down after each session, as well as concealing the flow of young men into and then out of the garden gate, it made sense to include them from the start.

To be sure, there was a certain commonality between his enterprise at the end of this century and that of Baron van Gloeden at the end of the last. Both took vulnerable boys and posed them in semierotic situations with vaguely mythic overtones. A dead tree stump here, a ruined column there, a shepherd's staff in their hands. Emmanuele was fortunate in the amount of props and backdrops and the surfeit of invariably short togas that were at his disposal. But the similarity ended there.

Whereas van Gloeden was fascinated by the new medium of photography, Emmanuele Angostini had an aversion, in this aspect of his life at least, to anything modern. Even electric lights would have been intrusive, so the theater was lit with hundreds of votive lights which inexorably burnt themselves out as the night grew long. No, his art was the *tableaux vivants*, that total reification of man which so captivated the Baroque world. Kings and queens, cardinals and bankers had considered it the capstone of civilized entertainment. To fix human beings like objects in a still life and to insist that they stay motionless until all voyeuristic needs were met was indeed a joy unlike any other. Especially when Emmanuele gave it the unique spin that was his alone.

The four boys who had come that night ranged in age from eighteen to twenty. Good specimens, not so muscular that they had lost the flush of puberty nor too soft that they could be mistaken for girls. He told them to strip so he could inspect them fully and then began to pose them like the mindless mannequins they were. A hand on this shoulder, leg up on a log, heads turned towards each other. Sometimes he put sandals on them, but as he had a fondness for feet, he generally avoided using them. Togas were used minimally, and always to advantage. When everything was in place, he took his seat at the back of the theater and waited for the first sign of arousal. Then he flew into a rage.

They were told that erections were not permitted, that was the rule, and that if they broke that rule they must be punished. By now all the boys who sacrificed themselves to Emmanuele's whim were aware of what happened. Some came back out of choice, most out of need. The old prints and manuscript pages he gave them could be sold easily in Trastevere for more than a month's wages. Many of them had gotten worse beatings at home. The barbed leather whip he used, his old *flagellum* which was supposed to have been turned in when the practice of self-discipline was discouraged, drew blood quickly. And it was not long before the boys' bodies were drenched in sweat mixed with rivulets of blood. For some, like Thius, the beating itself caused arousal and fed a vicious circle of pain and pleasure which rapidly could spiral out of control.

What set this night off from all the others was that Emmanuele saw the bleeding body of Thius in every boy before him and it so aroused him that he took the discipline to himself. Overcome by guilt and pleasure, he whipped his shoulders, chest, and groin until he was completely drenched in blood. He knew then that he was doomed.

25

*A*t that very moment Professoressa Pavlic too had nearly lost control. As she probed the wonders of San Redempto's treasury, brimming over with the perversest of riches, Dionysius, ever true to form, was penetrating her. "That which is imaginably implausable cannot be binding" was all that he remembered from moral theology and all that he ever needed. It was indeed totally inconceivable for Dionysius to say no to a woman's kind offer of entry. In consideration of this, he had long since understood his vow of chastity to be less a question of physical deprivation than a clarion call to compassionate service. Which was how he found himself inside the professoressa, hard as a week-old biscotto and happy as a clam. How tight and ringlike a sphincter was. How curiously broad her back and muscular her buttocks. They certainly bred them differently in the Balkans.

Feeling particularly charitable herself, Zinka let him sit throughout, his habit hiked up, her panties down. To facilitate things, she had propped up dozens of canvases against the wall within easy reach. She tried to minimize her movement. Not that it mattered too much as she quickly found out, because were it to pop out she had only to present herself again and in it would go, no harm done, no hardness lost. This man was a marvel.

It had been a relatively easy job for Dionysius to slip into the porter's cell while the community was at dinner and get the keys, which were compulsively ordered and labeled on the back of the closet door. He rarely ate with the community anyway in the evening as he was usually at Via Flaminia, and Antonio never missed a meal. He was confident the pilfered keys wouldn't be missed for one day.

The treasury was rarely visited. Or so he thought.

"Merciful Savior," the professoressa moaned, "could this really be happening." Pressing down deeper and tightening to a lethal knot, she rested the smaller canvas on her knees and examined the painted surface. "Without doubt Le Valentin. I can tell you with certainty, my precious little cucumber, that this is not listed in Benedict Nicolson's *Catalogue Raisonee*. What a stir this will create." Thinking out loud she pieced the puzzle together. "All of the paintings in this lot are French, representative of the whole community of expatriates that lived in Rome in the early years of the seventeenth century. What these canvases seem to lack though is that sweetness one so often associates with them. It is almost as if they were given the theme of bloody death, as if the community or someone in charge almost four hundred years ago had stipulated what they could paint."

"Were they cheap?" Dionysius questioned, his voice muffled by her back.

"Of course, that might be the key, my tasty little squash." Her enthusiasm so far outstripped her command of the language that her metaphors, lame as they were, took on a certain charm. "The Caraccis, Adam Elsheimer, Caravaggio, those were the ones commanding big fees in Rome in the early years of the seventeenth century. The French, ghettoized as they were, went begging. Yes, San Redempto may well have been their redemption."

Her heart racing, she excused herself and got down on her knees to read what seemed to be a signature on the lower left corner of a sinister-looking portrait of Saint Catherine's severed head presented on a pewter salver. "Yes," she said, "yes," bowing to Mecca, "Henri Traivoel, 1623!" As she explained the importance of her find, she hiked up her dress and Dionysius rose to the occasion. "There is ample evidence that Traivoel was one of Vouet's more accomplished disciples, written evidence that is, texts, but only one painting has ever been attributed to him with certainty. God only knows," she said, tears welling in her eyes, "God only knows how many of them have been entombed here for centuries." She hadn't even touched the numerous liasses of drawings. But shockingly someone had plundered the books. There was a razor near several of them, which lay open, stripped bare of their plates.

It was at that precise moment that the professoressa decided that, satisfying as Dionysius was on the entry level, she had used him as much as required. She decided then that she must take Father Brocard into her confidence. Granted he was asexual, what he was above all else was an eminently malleable figure of authority. Who, if she handled things correctly, could help her take her remarkable find to the next level. Unable to contain her joy, she tightened her grip on Dionysius. He, for his part, never realized blackmail could be so pleasant.

Bertie, returning from his rendezvous with Pino, had hidden behind the cistern at the sound of footsteps. He watched as Dionysius, fully habited like the perfect monk, escorted a positively horrific woman out the garden door, giving her an audible pat on the ass as she went. The man obviously had no shame.

26

*T*here is nothing funny about bodies being crushed to death by a gigantic boulder, but, try as he might, Brocard could not stop giggling. In all probability, the stress was getting to him. Robbery, murder, disappearance—for that is how they decided to pray for Father Pius in chapel—and endless subterfuge were piling up one on top of the other. Like the bodies stacked in neat little rows on the fresco he was studying, squashed flat as pancakes like some old cartoon. Each wearing the same insipid smile. It was simply too much.

It was no wonder the frescoes at San Stefano Rotundo figured in none of the popular guides to Rome. They were the most ghastly depictions of early Christian martyrs. Used as study devices for Jesuit novices beginning in the late sixteenth century, they were meant to be prayed over and committed to memory so that should these men meet similar fates, in England, Quebec, or Japan, they could connect their deaths with that of one of the saints of the early church and die confident of their sanctification. Such was the theory.

Brocard saw the sexton signaling him and at first thought his laughter, controlled as it was, might have gotten him in trouble. But he saw that the deformed little man was directing him to a small door near the rear, which as it turned out was the entrance to the *scavi* or archeological digs under the church. As Brocard followed him down the narrow stairs, lit only by infrequent bare light bulbs hanging from wires, he had the distinct impression that these excavations, unlike all others he had been to, were not just historic piles of stone with a story. These floors, freshly scraped clean, these walls, scrubbed back in time, pulsated with the life of the slaughter they had abetted.

"Mithra," the old sexton whispered so as not to raise the dead, "this is still his temple." It had been some time since Brocard studied the early pagan cults, so he did not immediately pick up the reference. But as Brocard leaned over to the altar, the sexton explained the basic ritual of the warrior cult—how the bulls were slaughtered, slowly drained of blood, and how it was only when the initiates washed themselves in the blood of the bull that they were made clean and strengthened for the battle of life. "This is the sacrifice of the new creation," the sexton said with the conviction of a believer. As they made their way from the cool darkness of the *scavi* to the damp bleakness of the Christian church which had been built above, Brocard knew the old man was right. This was the temple of blood rites and expiation, then and now.

Brocard was surprised to see a young couple, obviously very involved with each other, under the painting of the Sorrowful Mother. Aware of his concern, the sexton whispered, so as not to disturb the living, "It is the spirit of the bull." Then smiled.

Working his way around the church, he studied all thirty panels. Most of the frescoes had more than one grisly episode, labeled so that you could find the names and dates on the accompanying list below. Pots of boiling oil shared space with hungry lions and burley hangmen, all vying for the would-be martyr's attention. Some were considered important enough to warrant their very own fresco. Saint Lawrence being grilled was a particularly engaging example. But by far the most riveting was Saint Agatha having her breasts ripped off. There was no doubt that this was the source of their painting. And no doubt as well that their version had a sophistication and assurance that was totally lacking in the crudely worked fresco at San Stefano. The professoressa had been right.

In his mind he could see Saint Agatha's tensed virginal body, her gaze which never dropped, her breast held high above her head, drenched in martyr's blood. Had the stolen paintings been of similar quality? Sadly, he would probably never know. They must be far away by now. He had passed them by for so many years that he had no right to lament their loss. And yet he did. Like so much of life that had gone by, unobserved and unappreciated. He had spent a lifetime in blinders that he had chosen to put on himself.

There were faint moans behind him, the unquenchable moans of lovers. At first he thought best not to turn, but then he realized that he must. The girl caught his eye first, nervous that they had been seen. But the young man stared at him defiantly, then pinned her shoulders to the marble wall and kissed her so desperately that it was hard to imagine how she survived. Looking back at Brocard, who was at a loss as to how to react, the young man gave him the broadest of smiles and then, as if he was inviting him to ravage her with him, ripped open her blouse and grabbed hold of her breasts. As he pulled she moaned even more, and with each moan he became increasingly aroused.

Brocard could hear the young man's laughter as he turned to leave them alone. Miraculously, to the extent that he could, Brocard had shared in their excitement.

27

$\mathcal{B}$less me, Father, for I have sinned. It has been nearly five years since my last confession. Amazing, isn't it? Me, a priest going so long. Maybe that is part of what I need to confess, my indifference to things. And to people and even, hard as it may be to believe, indifference to myself. There seems to be no reason for anything and there is one sin that cuts through all the others and weighs on me so hard that at times it's hard to breathe. It is that greatest sin of all: the loss of hope. I know that there is no way out.

"It may have started with my first taste of power just five years ago. In any case, I will have to start there, as my long-term memory is very weak. A talent I developed after years of hard blocking. After I was elected prior, I realized that for the first time in my life there was no one to answer to any more. Freed of that control, temptations were no longer to be avoided, but embraced as new and exciting experiences."

Brocard had never imagined that Emmanuele, whom he had always looked up to, would be kneeling in front of him. A perfunctory confession, discreetly screened and sanitized was one thing, but this blatant display of emotions was hard for him to deal with.

"I, like you, Father, am a lifer, dropped off at minor seminary by pious parents of limited means with a surfeit of mouths to feed. In all probability, my vows and priesthood are invalid. There was never any other option, never a choice. And despite all the talk to the contrary, no way out. I was never schooled in life, never once encouraged to walk. This is why I asked to confess to you, Father. I knew that if there were anyone here who might understand, anyone who could forgive in their heart as well as on God's part, it was you. I often wonder who sinned more, Father, me or the system that spawned me.

"This does not excuse my sins, of course, or lessen them. They are more numerous than the children of Abraham, Father, and blacker than hell itself. I know this now, because of the face that haunts me. But let me keep my thoughts in order, if possible, in the hope that God at least can make some sense of the mess which I have made of things.

"The first sins were against my vow of poverty. When I found out the wealth of this monastery, the extent of which I still cannot grasp, and realized that there was no one to monitor me, I began to set objects and moneys aside for myself. But accumulating possessions was never a major interest. Controlling boys was. I am sorry if this shocks you, Father, but I need to make a good confession because I know my time is short.

"This brings me to the second cluster of sins. Those against chastity. It started off as no more than a game really. One of the more worldly monks had contacts, access to young students, boys of all sorts. In return for my giving him free access to the treasury and archives, more for research than plunder, although I have no doubt some of the latter took place, he would have young boys smuggled in for me to use in innocent *tableaux vivants*. Like we used to do at Christmas and Easter, you remember. Only mine took place in the dead of night and became increasingly obsessive.

"Then a week ago, that Dutch student Thius appeared on the door. He wanted access to the archives for one day to do some research. Grandly, because that is how I have come to do everything, I told him he could have the keys to the monastery for a day if he would spend one afternoon with me for a private session. He had his day, then I had mine. I confess I beat him more than I have ever beaten anyone, Father. Beat him until the skin was hanging off his back and legs. But the more I beat him, the more aroused he became and the more furious, and I confess aroused, yes, the more aroused I became as well. It had all started off so well. Thius dressed as Medea, my old costume, holding the severed limbs of her children. The doll body parts we used years ago are still there, as are so many props. It was beautifully put together really. But it all went so wrong.

"When it became clear I had to get Thius out of the monastery, I

84

panicked. With the whole community in a state of high anxiety—this was the day after the robbery—there was no way to get him out unnoticed. Someone would surely see. I know now I should have bandaged him and let him just sleep things off there, but I wasn't thinking. So as it was siesta, I risked taking him up the back way into the chapel and then the secret passage I use to the biblioteca. He bled a bit but nothing the brother couldn't readily clean up. He has had such practice. Thius was so weak I nearly had to carry him. But so trusting. I very quietly hid him in the broom closet near Avertanus's carrel, promising to come back and spirit him out after dinner. All I can think of is that he must have collapsed from the heat, the lack of oxygen, or exhaustion. He must have collapsed on that shard of glass that killed him. I didn't do it, Father. But because of my avarice and greed and the immorality of my entire life, I accuse myself, Father, and humbly beg forgiveness of you and God."

Brocard felt his body tremble. Then, with a tenderness that surprised them both, he raised his hand and offered Emmanuele the absolution he so desperately craved.

28

Nijmegen Kempis Instituut

Fax Cover Sheet

DATE: 30 October 1995   TIME: 1:41 PM
TO: Rev. Brocard Curtis   FAX: (06) 969-66-669
        San Redempto, Rome
FROM: Rev. Otger Aarnack   FAX: (080) 221-729
RE: Inquiry re: Rhutten and Meyer
Number of pages including cover sheet: 2

My dear Father Brocard,

We are in receipt of your kind and provocative fax. You
have my assurance that I will assist in whatever small way
I can to aid you in your ongoing investigation. Father Emmanuele and the entire community of San Redempto, myself included despite my time away, are indeed fortunate
to have such diligent help in the untangling of this truly
knotty problem. Although I have never doubted your
competence, I must tell you of my delight in seeing how
thoroughly you have gone into this situation and how
much progress you have already made in the three days
since the unfortunate disappearance of the paintings in the
ambulatory. The whole affair is so shocking I haven't quite
made sense of it yet.

As to Dr. Hoop Rhutten, I will certainly do my best to

track him down. I found it intriguing indeed that this young Dutch student Thius Meyer, whom I confess never having even heard of, had so recently been researching our paintings at the Farnesse. It surprises me that Madam Blanchierdarie, a colleague for more years than she would ever admit to, never mentioned this to me. Like you, I feel it is logical to presume that Rhutten is behind this whole matter. The researching, that is not necessarily the theft. Although, between us, I must say that I never did trust the man. Too much sugar in his blood, if you know what I mean. A man like that can never be trusted.

Regarding the prospect that these paintings which we had all ignored for so long may well be the work of the great Nicolas Poussin, I can only say I am speechless. Given the rich history of the order it does not completely surprise me. After all the great Giotto himself had worked for us and even the sublime Caravaggio. The former works, you our noted archivist will surely recall, were destroyed by fire, the latter lost to Catherine the Great in circumstances that have never been fully clarified. It seems to have had something to do with a prodigiously talented horse she had and we wanted, I believe. My point is that we have not done well with treasures. In fact, we seem to have lost them all.

The only way in which we could have kept them, it seems, is if we didn't know we had them in the first place. Which is why your theory seems quite plausible. However, I shall resist all temptation to celebrate—this is far too momentous and significant a find for the community and the art world—until the experts decide on the matter.

To this end, I have decided to cut short my time in Holland and fly back to Rome on the first flight out tomorrow. Do tell our dear Prior Emmanuele that I will be with you all soon. I am not sure what assistance I can lend, but only know that my place is there with my community at their time of need, and with those of you who are working so tirelessly to resolve this most unfortunate situation.

One final thought. If it is reasonable to presume that Dr. Rhutten in some way masterminded the whole affair, he would still have needed someone on the inside to assist him. San Redempto, as you well know, is a rather forbidding edifice. Without rushing ahead too quickly, I would wonder if the choice of accomplices isn't limited to the two community members with keys, schedules, and the available means. By this last I mean ladders and hammers or whatever one needs to remove paintings from their frames, roll them up, and store them. The prior, who of course is out of the question, and Brother Antonio, the porter. *Je me demande.*

O A

29

*J*t was one of those autumn mornings when the sun refused to rise. Rome has many such days in November, but as October was not yet over it was ominous indeed. The darkness that controlled Manolo embraced such days, wrapping his soul with gloom and tying it up with hopelessness. His brother, on the other hand, never having abandoned the atavistic superstitions of his peasant roots, realized that God in His wisdom was abandoning them and leaving them to their own devices.

Antonio had left a message to meet him after dawn in their spot in the orchard, under the blood oranges. Only now most of them lay underfoot, shriveled up, worm-ridden, and oozing their final dark red drops. But the smell, Manolo thought as he waited impatiently for his brother, was intoxicating. It was no wonder piles of rotting oranges were hidden behind hedges in Baroque gardens. They gave that unexpectedly poignant aroma of the sweetness of death. So different from the stench of that idiot Pius's decaying corpse, which lay hidden in a shallow grave a few feet away. Without doubt, humanity was truly a lower life form. He had only to look at the community, or what was left of it, to confirm that belief. The prior had fallen completely under the brothers' control—for he thought in terms of blood relation, nothing else signified. Were it not for their sneaking in the boys for his sick little games, he would not be alive. The only life Emmanuele had, and it was a sad travesty of one to be sure, came from the life he sucked from innocent creatures, who in their stupidity deserved nothing more. Brocard was too caught up in details ever to see the whole picture. So maniacally obsessed with order as to preclude the messiness of life itself. He was fated to go to his grave a stranger to his very self.

A blasting sound broke the silence as if a dead weight had fallen on a car horn. More high-pierced sirens followed. Rome was coming alive in that aggravating way that was all its own and still Antonio had not arrived. Getting back to his list, Bertie was a lost soul who was doomed to endless puberty. The order fed and clothed him but had long since ceased to truly nourish him. The same could be said of Dionysius, the failed academic and priest who didn't even have the nerve to move out and get on with his life, settling instead for a few droppings from the biblioteca—nothing escaped Manolo—and some veggies from the garden. The Irish priests were enigmatic but so ephemeral that, from Avertanus's perspective at least, they would pass through the life of San Redempto without notice. He thought for a moment to see whom he had missed, then remembered Brother Ephraim, who was better left forgotten. Never could separate the colors from the whites anyway. That sad list was the whole community in Rome. When Father Otger returned he might prove himself to be the only human life form at San Redempto with more than two cells. At least he saw life for the sick charade that it was and could manipulate people almost as well as the Basque brothers. He also had the considerable talent of procuring the most scintillating photos. Ultimately though, he too was useless. Flaying his weight about madly in some travesty of control. As if he and all his little schemes would amount to anything.

When Antonio finally did arrive his news was not good. Someone had taken the key to the treasury off the key board in his cell. He had no idea who had it or for how long. If someone was bold enough to do this, then they would stop at nothing. There was no telling how many secrets would come out, how much would be uncovered.

It took Manolo no time to decide what they must do. The luxury of time was no longer theirs. They had to take the next step.

"Today we organize, tomorrow we leave."

The plan was to tie up all the loose ends over the next thirty-six hours. They had full inventories of their holding, and everything was organized for a speedy departure. It was good that Father Otger was returning in a few hours because they had some unfinished business to handle. If anyone could tell them what to do about that roll of paintings stained with decay, he surely could. All the other articles of real value could fit into a truck, which Manolo would rent for the following night so they could load it and drive it up to Switzerland, where they kept their account. They had work to do.

As it turned out, they never were to find out that it was Dionysius who had borrowed the key that night, and someone else would inadvertently take the blame for him and nearly die for it. There was one certain truth, though. The indelible marks of hubris had been burnt into their flesh and anyone downwind from them knew that they reeked of sulfur. Fate, or perhaps the devil himself in whatever guise he was taking, had already determined their downfall.

30

$\mathcal{I}$s there a fixed point where pain becomes ecstasy? And if there is, can it ever be captured and marked so as to be replayed? Or is it fickle, contingent on who we are, when, and with whom we live. Emmanuele troubled himself with thoughts like this as he stared at Bernini's statue of Saint Teresa in ecstasy. As often as he had seen it, and it was something he habitually gravitated to in Rome, he could still find details to shock. The veins on the neck of the boy angel who torments her transfixed him today, as did the way in which her mouth opened longingly to the golden shower of heavenly rays.

Otger had always maintained that the Cornaro Chapel, in which the statue was placed, was the height of Roman Baroque perversity. The initial strangeness is due to Bernini's genius alone. This exceedingly large woman, reclining on even larger boulders and draped in yards and yards of fabric, floats untethered above us as if she had no weight at all. Defying all laws of physics or logic. The second oddity belongs to our time alone and shows the narrowing scope of our spirituality. She is an uncompromisingly sexual creature pursued by an androgynous youth of devastating beauty. The Baroque mind unified the body and spirit, God talk and man talk. Its spirituality didn't cancel out the body, or even the ecstasy of pain. But what he had often regarded as the most perverse aspect of all, and the mark of the unabashed theatricality of the period, were the two life-size opera boxes carved into either side of the chapel. Each held members of the family who had donated the chapel, the Cornaros, chatting and reading and above all peering out at the saint in ecstasy. They are the ones with the money and the power, have no doubt about it. The total sadistic voyeurs who are fully in control of pleasure, pain, and even sanctity.

The absolute appropriateness of bringing Emmanuele to the chapel did not fully hit Otger until he caught sight of him. He had to meet him outside San Redempto if his plan was to succeed. There were distractions there, but more important still, here, outside his domain, Emmanuele was much more vulnerable. Which is how Otger wanted it. The excuse he used was that he had wanted to see the Cornaro Chapel after its restoration, cleaned of years of Roman dirt. What he had not counted on was that Emmanuele, formal to a fault, would have worn his habit with full white cloak. Standing at the altar rail, he seemed at one with the starkly white figure of the tortured saint. The similarity was so riveting that he decided then and there how Emmanuele's final chapter was to read.

The suitability of Otger's professorial tweed jacket and knit tie were in stark contrast to Emmanuele's anachronistic costume. Once again, he had the upper hand. He went over and stood next to his old friend the prior, who almost imperceptibly shuddered. After some time in silence, Otger led him outside into the dank gray light of morning. Emmanuele vaguely remembered how the two of them used to laugh maniacally at the gypsy girls playing hunchback and the street hustlers rubbing their crotches. Today he had difficulty keeping his eyes from welling up with tears, his mind from going wild.

Otger's first objective was to unsettle him with silence and so for two long blocks he said nothing. Then, as they approached the Piazza della Republica on their way to the Via Nationale, he began to erode away the little confidence the poor man had left.

"I heard from that insignificant menial Brocard, and for your own sake I must tell you where his snooping has led. He has concluded that you and you alone must have masterminded the robbery or at least been accomplice to it. It seems he has done some research at the Farnesse and your young toy Thius had shown intense interest in our martyr paintings of late. This is just the tip of the iceberg. He has taken on the role of destroying angel and he will not be satisfied until all of the sordid details are out."

As they began to walk the colonnade of the Piazza della Republica, Otger's eye was too absorbed in flesh to continue talking. The silence tore Emmanuele apart even more powerfully than Otger's barbed words. Boys leaned against pillars, muscled men beckoned them into the cinemas, the vulnerable, ready for the picking, sat alone at cafe tables. What still excited Otger only enervated Emmanuele. He never felt so totally lost.

"You have no credibility left, my friend," Otger confided in him with mock gentility. "They are all on to you, it is as simple as that." Emmanuele could say nothing.

"I have one final gift for you. Tomorrow night, I will bring over some boys." When Emmanuele went to protest, he turned and covered his mouth. "No, I will hear no protest. They will do anything for you." Then pointedly, "Anything that you want, or need."

31

And then the Angel of Evil took him and set him on the pinnacle of the temple and showed him all the Kingdoms of the world. If forced to take a stand, would he choose betrayal? Would he even recognize it? And if he threw himself down, would his protecting angel swoop him up before his head cracked open on the slate of the cloister?

Or maybe, just maybe, Bertie thought as he stood with Cuthbert on the roof of San Redempto, they were just two old queens on a Roman holiday, ticking off the sights in their *Blue Guide*. Far less Christic a thought, but maybe more realistic.

"Bertie, look here." Cuthbert led him over to the edge, then, as he followed his finger, drew a line through the narrow alleys of the Borgo directly to the Generalate of the Jesuits. "This is a perspective most people never get of Rome. Fantastic, isn't it, like a Victorian Alhambra, a white veil, pure as any virgin's, concealing the black pope himself. Completely hidden from the street, as all things of real interest are in Rome. This is a city turned in on itself, fiercely protective of its secrets."

My, but the Irish sure can chuck it, Bertie thought. Still, he knew he had been invited to this tête-à-tête for a purpose which would come out soon enough. For now there was nothing to do but enjoy the prelims. Which was easy enough to do. Cuthbert spoke with such authority, with a voice so deep that it seemed to rise up magically from the ground beneath him. And he molded words with that shaman's touch with which even the soberest of Irishmen are often blessed. As if all this wouldn't be enough to amuse him on a bleak fall morning, there was the undeniable fact that Cuthbert Mullins was a man, rough around the edges and smelly as a sewer. To Bertie, he was charm writ large.

Cuthbert guided him over to the opposite side of the building and jumped up on the ledge. He had obviously not the slightest touch of vertigo, but Bertie certainly did and he pulled back when Cuthbert stretched out his hand to help him up. "You can hold on to me, don't worry, it is really very exciting. Please, you should see it from here."

Being constitutionally unable to deny a man anything, Bertie hopped up on the ledge, clinging to the Irishman like the little girl he was. The inner cloister garden with the statue of Our Lady lay four Roman stories below. "Oh yes, absolutely marvelous," he said, refusing to open his eyes fully. "Can we get down now, please?"

"Isn't it time for the line yet?" Bertie said when he got his breath back.

"Which is?" Cuthbert smiled, knowing the game that was being played.

"Which is, 'You must know why I have called you here,' or something like that. But I really don't, honestly, unless this is just a cheap trick to make a move on me."

"Don't you think I would have been more direct were that the case?"

Oh those Irish, Bertie thought. "Well just in case you were, I wanted you to know that I already have someone, and nothing or no one is going to separate us."

"I'm happy for you," Cuthbert said, and he seemed to mean it. "And for me as well, because that will make what I am going to ask you to do for me much easier."

"Quite direct now, aren't you?"

"Even more than you can imagine."

Then Cuthbert explained all that Bertie needed to know for the time being, skillfully giving the illusion that he was telling him all that there was to know. As he did, Bertie inspected him closely, still not certain that his agenda wasn't sexual after all. He had a tight little rugby body which sweated uncomfortably under his habit. Not that his body odor was any worse than Pino's—it was just that it was different, too many chips and bangers, he suspected. But the eyes were fine, warm and trusting. As was that smile, which seemed to invite him into a childlike conspiracy. If only he knew how serious it was to be.

He could not have known how conflicted Cuthbert was in having to speak in half truths and hold back any sense of righteousness. Or, for that matter, how saddened Cuthbert was to realize the lie that religious life, the vows and witness he had made, had become. At what point, he wondered, did Bertie abandon the challenge of serving God. But looking at him, mewing over his "boyfriend" like some pimpled teen, Cuthbert could not help but feel sorry for him. Not with pity but rather with a deep sorrow, the kind which comes from the knowledge that a system has gone so wrong that innocent bystanders caught up in it have been unwittingly damaged for life.

"So you want me to get you into the archives and treasury. May I know why you and your Irish confrere want to know what secret riches this pile of a building hides?"

Without skipping a heartbeat, and with blinding candor that so thoroughly impressed Bertie that he found himself giggling like a coed. "To take it all, of course, every last piece of it."

They fell silent, the two of them, like the conspirators they had become. Then, thinking of Pino, Bertie asked if he might take a few little pieces for himself.

"It only seems fair," Cuthbert said, putting his arm around his shoulder protectively. "Get the keys tonight. It is important we work quickly if we are to succeed." Tasting freedom, Bertie luxuriated in the smell of the man, and nodded yes.

32

⁘❧⁘

That Brother Ephraim had to die was not in question. How to do it was the only problem. There were more than enough loose ends to tie up without piling on another corpse. Still, when Manolo realized fully just how distraught Ephraim was and how likely it was that he might talk, he had no choice but to act. Nothing or no one could be allowed to get in their way at this late date. He had to act quickly and decisively.

This whole turn of events started with one of those reflex greetings that are meant to dead end: *Va bene?* How's it going? The civilized response is to grunt and leave it at that. Manolo had no reason to expect anything more than that as he passed through the laundry room midmorning on his way to more important things. But Brother Ephraim, who had not slept one wink in the two days since Father Pius's body came hurtling down the laundry shoot, saw it as an invitation to unburden his soul and share his deepest fears. A dangerous thing to do at the best of times.

Never the brightest light, Ephraim had been haunted by the delusion that Pius was calling out from the grave for vengeance. That his rotting corpse was writhing with a rage that seeped out into the very soil of San Redempto. Even were that the case, Manolo could see no reason for concern. After all, Pius was the most ineffectual monk in life. There was no reason to presume that he would gain powers in death which he had never known before. As if death in itself conferred authority, when the truth was that it merely fixed for all time the inadequacies we knew in life. Pius was never once, and could not now be, a threat to anyone. But Ephraim, in his utter

98

stupidity, was not able to see this.

So Manolo sat in his shuttered room, surrounded by the debris of a lifetime, amusing himself with the prospects of how he might do it.

One easy way, and one which would do poetic justice to poor Pius's ghost, would be to bring Ephraim down to the abandoned larder in the basement on the pretext of helping him look for something. Once there, it would be an easy thing to lead him into the room, pushing him in if need be because he was as light as he was dumb, and immure him forever. Very neat, that one. There wouldn't even be any messy cleanup.

A nudge off the roof would also do the trick. Everyone knew that he was the only one ever to go up there, occasionally using the clothesline on the roof to dry things that needed more breeze than the cloister garden provided. In fact, the winds howled so mercilessly around the monastery that should he be found splattered on the street below, who could presume anything more sinister than the *tramontana*, that most sinister of winds.

Despite the obvious appeal of both of these, he was leaning towards a kitchen accident. It was, after all, his major work area. And, as experience had shown, if you need a good accident, there is nothing more suited than a cluttered kitchen.

There were of course the myriad possibilities offered by knives. Slipping and falling on them so that they pierced a major artery was always good. Even a judicious slice to the wrist: "He was helping me chop the *melanzana*. I just don't know how he could have severed that hand." Sharp knives were essential for cooks, especially those like Manolo. So many ways, so little time. Realizing it was time to act, Manolo headed down to the laundry to confront Ephraim, knowing that inspiration would strike him when most needed. He was never at a loss for how to act; confusion came in the planning alone.

As unconsciously as he had done everything else in his life, Ephraim had made the decision for Manolo. He was not in the laundry room at all, but standing over Pius's grave softening the soil with his tears. The mud of the garden had begun to cover his feet and creep up his legs, inexorably claiming his body.

In one brilliant moment, Manolo noticed the wooden lid to the cistern and realized his course of action. It all went so smoothly that it seemed choreographed. Ephraim, gasping in grief, turned to him, and Manolo, his brow creased with pastoral concern, positioned himself on the ledge of the cistern and signaled Ephraim to sit beside him. The very instant the idiot sat down Manolo flipped him into the cistern and, with the dexterity which would have been impressive in someone half his age, sealed him in with the heavy wooden lid.

Avertanus, who was on his way to the laundry room to see if his weekly sheet was done—they got a clean one every week—thought he heard a muffled scream and thud.

33

❧ ❧ ❧

⨍ have been such a naughty girl." The words just hung there, sus-
pended in space, and for the life of him he didn't know what to say.
He was a Father, but certainly no one's daddy. There was something
engagingly sensual about the professoressa, or Zinka as she preferred
him to call her, but, as he had never been schooled in such things, he
was at a loss as to how to respond. "Should I tell you what I did? You
won't be mad at me?"

Zinka played him like a mandole (they had no fiddles in Slovenia).
She prided herself in getting men to do what she wanted. Years of
basic training as a man coupled with innate feminine intuition had
made her a virtual killing machine. She was unstoppable.

Having seen how disorienting her breasts were to him on their first
encounter, she deliberately chose a high-necked blouse for this meeting. But her discretion stopped there. She hadn't spent thousands of
lira on wax to hide her legs away. Those he would see.

Before Brocard had a chance to frame his thoughts—he never was
one for spontaneity—Zinka decided they needed a *gelato*. A pestilent
autumn morning, and Zinka could think of nothing but an ice cream
cone from Bianca Neve. It was only a few blocks from San Redempto
but on the other side of the Tiber from the Vatican. Her world, where
she could reign free, as opposed to the claustrophobic speak room
they were forced to meet in.

There was no objecting to Zinka when she had a craving, so she
swung her purse over her shoulder, took Brocard by the arm, and
whisked him away from the monastery. They made quite a couple,
the two of them. He in his brown work habit, cinctured at the waist

with rope; she with her pink skirt, silver pumps, and hair pulled back in a controlled chignon. She was a professoressa after all. Needless to say, they did not go unnoticed.

Even though they ordered cones—he had not realized he wanted anything until she insisted—Zinka was not one to prop herself up at a bar like Italians were wont to do. No, they needed a proper table and some mineral water (without gas) before she began.

"Father Dionysius, out of his deep need to know the truth, allowed me to see the paintings in the treasury." Brocard did not seem overly alarmed by anything she told him, but it became clear that he was personally unaware of San Redempto's vast holdings. "The historical and real monetary value of these paintings is enormous. It seems hard for me to believe that no one knows of the paintings, both as a scholar and as a woman who cannot keep a secret. Someone must know; someone must have told."

Zinka noticed that his *gelato* was dripping down the front of his habit, so she caught it with her napkin, then patted it clean with water. He was more comforted than embarrassed by this, like the good boy he was. Try as he might, he could not figure out what she wanted of him. That she wanted something was becoming increasingly clear.

"Let me be blunt. It is essential that we see if the painting of Saint Agatha is signed. Even if it isn't, a case can be made, stylistically, on secondary evidence, that the painting is indeed by Poussin. And I am reluctant at this stage, professionally, to send it off to Oberhauer or Tuilliers for their authentication. In a word, I want all the credit myself. I need all the credit, but enough of that." Patting her chignon with determination, she explained exactly what was entailed. "The cleaning solution I will use is a mild solvent used in all of the most advanced cleanings. It is perfectly harmless to the canvas but wildly carcinogenic. Life is such a risk, isn't it? But this will show us what we need to see without requiring a total restoration of the canvas." Then, with a determination that belied her sex, "I must have the painting, Father Brocard. I simply must." He considered for a moment how much these past few days had changed him. Such a question to a well-trained monk had only one answer, The authority is not mine to take, my obedience is to the prior alone. But was it really? Then as well as now. How often had he hidden behind obedience as a convenient way to avoid responsibility. A sure way of never making a mistake in God's eye as well as man's. He no longer had such an option.

"Let us go back to San Redempto," he told her. "You can take it right away."

Wise in worldly things, the professoressa hailed a taxi at the rank outside Bianca Neve and had him wait outside San Redempto while Father Brocard fetched the painting. Fortunately, Antonio was nowhere to be seen, so no explanations had to be made. They put the painting in the backseat; she sat up front with the driver. She always liked it better that way. "I nearly forgot," she called to Brocard as he was leaving, "Camille Blanchierdarie told me she has uncovered something of interest which she wants to share with us this afternoon. She is being distressingly coy about it. Shall we say at four?"

34

Their eyes locked unblinkingly and a bond was set in place which death alone could break. "O Bast, Egyptian guardian of marriage," Bertie solemnly intoned, "seal this love we have so that our very souls unite." Nothing pleases a feline more than being mistaken for an Egyptian goddess, absolutely nothing. As the young priest knelt before the laundry cart on which the cat had enthroned herself, he heard a purr of approval and watched as she leaned her head towards him as a sign of divine approbation, as much as for a good rub.

Not that she didn't need some serious petting—all deities do despite their protests to the contrary. As did the big tom nearby and dozens of others waiting their turn in the wings. It was safe to say that with the exception of Ephraim, who fed them, Bertie was the only one at San Redempto who had even looked kindly on the garden cats, and in return they showered him with affection. Until Pino, his had been a life devoid of any touch, stripped bare of the slightest hint of intimacy. These cats would never know how much it meant to him that they waited for him in the garden, brushed up against him when he sat down with them, or leaned their foreheads towards him and, eyes closed, purred when gently touched. Without them he might have been so totally driven into himself that coming out again might have been impossible. These cats were more than a lifeline, they had been his life.

He knew now that there was something more. Yes, Pino needed a good scrub and a bit of tarting up, as they say back in Blackpool, but it was going to work. Now that there was the possibility of getting some money, or taking a few expendable objects that could bring them a bit of cash, it seemed possible that there was a way out. Just a little house in the mountains was all they needed. Well, not too far out that you couldn't get to the flicks from time to time or have a little Chinese, but far enough.

When he realized the way these cats had saved him, the way they sustained him still in the midst of the madhouse that San Redempto had become, he knew that there was a God of goodness watching out for him. And when he thought of Pino with his jet black hair and chiseled features, he knew that this God was one of beauty as well. There were few times when Bertie felt a sense of inner peace. This surely was one.

As he was leaving the garden, Manolo was entering.

"Have you seen Brother Ephraim?"

"No," Bertie replied without looking up.

"Good," Manolo mumbled, "very good."

For some reason, he was not convinced. He had to see for himself. Moving slowly towards the cistern, he was confronted with two, then six, then a phalanx of cats, arching their backs and making a deafening hiss. Others circled around him, still more leaped out onto the garden wall until there was hardly space for any more. A lesser man than Manolo would have gone no farther. He gave no thought to turning back, only reached for a nearby hoe and flailed it madly before him, catching several cats off guard and tossing them to their deaths. When he looked down into the cistern he could see what they were protecting. The wooden lid had been tilted up and Ephraim's arm, in one final attempt to cheat death, was raised upright, clawing towards the sky. What infuriated Manolo more than this grand and futile gesture was the sentinel the cats were keeping for him. One had even jumped the three feet down into the cistern to rub against his outstretched arm.

Pushing the arm back down into the pit of water was harder than he had imagined. Presumably the corpse was bloated with water and fully buoyant. Still, with a bit of shoving and a lot of cursing he got it back under the lid and—to make sure he wouldn't pop up again— dropped a heavy stone on top. This did not have to be a permanent grave, after all. Once he and Antonio had crossed the border into Switzerland, it did not matter to him how many limbs flew out. But the cats, something did have to be done about them.

Legends aside, it is pretty easy to kill a cat. Their necks wring rather handily and they succumb quite quickly to gas. But hundreds of cats in a day's time, when there was so much else to do besides snuffing out life, posed a minor problem. It did not take long, though, for Manolo to remember the shards of glass which had cut up that boy Thius so nicely. In no time at all he had ground them so fine that, when he mixed it with the food that was left out that afternoon, not a single cat suspected they were eating their last meal.

Within twenty-four hours the garden would be littered with the corpses of the only life it had known and Bertie would know that all hope had gone. For rigor mortus had set in to San Redempto.

35

They stared at the dried-up papers in utter disbelief. What angel had led them to uncover them? What responsibility did it place on her to rewrite history itself?

"Oh, this is even better than sex!" Then, unable to control herself, she lunged for Camille and Brocard, folded them in her arms, and pressed their faces into her ample breasts, Camille content to stay forever, Brocard choking uncomfortably. Releasing him she said, "Do excuse me, Father, not very professional, I know, but this is all too exciting."

For once, Zinka had not overreacted. The information contained in the *liasse* Madam Blanchierdarie had skillfully uncovered was nothing short of earth-shattering. It had occurred to the directrice that it might prove interesting to reconstruct the trail of research left by Hoop Rhutten some ten years before. So she dug up all of his requisitions slips—being a research institute all materials earlier than the eighteenth century were controlled in this way—to see if he had requested anything out of the ordinary.

And he had. He had spent extensive time studying *Liasse 479*, one of the innumerable bundle of anonymous seventeenth-century papers stored in the mezzanine vault. It was not to the directrice's discredit that she was not aware of it. Vast quantities of such documents awaited the one researcher in any century who might stumble across them.

The papers were ascribed to "a disciple of the Master Nicolas Poussin." Interestingly, they were dated 1665, the year of Poussin's death as well as the year of the founding of the French academy in Rome, of which he was the first president. These papers were nothing more than a record of his wishes for the course of study at the new academy. But, were they to be believed, they would not only firmly contextualize the painting of Saint Agatha, but substantially alter the accepted view of French Classicism. There would surely be some Oxbridge dons and Ivy profs who would launch attacks on such findings, but the Professoressa Zinka Pavlic, Doctor of Storia d'Arte, was fully up to any challenge. In fact, she lusted after it like a bitch in heat.

The first pages of the documents were of historical interest only. They confirmed Poussin's abiding interest in "noble themes." Several examples from general mythology were given with one intriguing mention of bloody-mouthed Chronos devouring his children. There followed a major discursus on Ovid's *Metamorphoses*, his commonly recognized obsession. Then, quite unannounced, came the reference to San Stefano Rotundo.

"I exhort all those who would learn to live as well as to paint to use as their mirror the cycle of paintings in the Hungarian-German Novitiate, San Stefano Rotundo on the Celio." On reading this, Father Brocard wondered if these frescoes which had so regaled him just the day before had taught him anything about life. Before he was able to decide, for he moved ponderously slowly in such matters, Zinka had begun to dance around the room waving the precious page over her head. Camille, ever the concerned directrice, gave her stern look. Zinka darted back a shush which put her in her place. Then she took a deep breath, filled her substantial lungs, and declaimed the most exciting words:

" 'On my arrival in Rome, I myself spent many fruitful days copying those ravishing subjects, making in all seven paintings on canvas of fine proportion. Notable among these was the heroic Bartholomew flayed of his skin and the sublime Agatha denuded of her tender breasts.' " Then, pausing long enough to catch her breath, "He was a freak!"

"Oh Zinka, darling," then Camille caught herself, "Professoressa, I mean. Don't you think such a word is a bit extreme? After all, the great Poussin is the Father of Classicism." To which Zinka, who had spent far more time watching MTV on Sky than any art historian ever should, replied, "Oh chill out, Camille. Don't you get it?"

Seeing stupidity written all over their precious little faces, Zinka did her best to speak like a grade school teacher, presuming nothing.

Like sadism, French Classicism, of which Poussin was the *fons et origens*—she was not totally successful at talking down—was about control. Of the human body, above all else, but also the environment, of nature itself. The origin of French gardens with their tormentedly pruned allees, of history painting, with its brutal structure, of tortuous girdles and confining bustiers, can be found here in these seemingly harmless words. It means that the de Sade released from the Bastille was not a break with but rather a culmination of French Classicism!

Camille and Brocard, true friends both, were so happy for her.

36

For some among us it is said that nothing refreshes the soul like getting down on your knees in the garden. Alone. On occasion, Father Dionysius McGreel was one of those souls. That afternoon, weighed down by a premonition of doom, he felt the need to churn up the soil and uproot some weeds. Foolishly thinking that this could bring him peace. There was no need to garden, of course. It was October, after all, and the rains were coming in earnest. Nothing to plant, nothing to sow. The bleakest of times. Still there was always something to do in a garden if you chose to so torment the earth.

So hoe in hand he set off to nurture nature. But no sooner had he walked out into the cloister garden than reality hit him and, despite his best intentions, he became quite disheartened. Everywhere else in Rome gardens still showed signs of life. Not so at San Redempto. Here cyprus stood barren, unpicked fruit lay worm-ridden, and the weeds themselves seemed to have abandoned all hope. And as if that weren't enough, dozens of cats were vomiting blood and writhing on the ground. Still, he would not be deterred. One useful job that could always be done was removing unwanted vegetation. In that, this garden above all others offered ample opportunity. Considering his options he saw that nothing really needed to be touched in his personal vegetable patch near the back gate. But the area around the cistern was definitely in need of attention. It surprised him that the wooden cover had been placed over the water and, more unusual still, that a heavy stone had been dropped on it to weigh it down. Nothing to be done about that though. This was not to be a day of heavy labor, no putting out the back for him. No, there was a weedlike tree that had taken root on the far side of the cistern, neither big enough to strain him nor small enough to make him feel as if he had really not worked at all. That would do just fine.

He was not digging long when he hit something firm yet soft and a stench rose up as from the sewers of hell. Uncertain what to do, he froze in place. Only after considerable time, during which fear nearly overtook him, and the loathing he had harbored for the monastery and all it stood for rose from deep within him, only then did he decide to dig and not to run. So he picked up a rusted spade that was leaning against the cloister wall. But the initial jab of the hoe had caught the shroud and ripped it away from the head. What little the worms had left of Father Pius stared up at him. All he could think to do was to run. And run he did.

Why Dionysius chose to head back into San Redempto, he would never know. Force of habit perhaps. Or fate. All that can be said is that as he made the turn into the ambulatory, he ran head on into Father Avertanus, who, as was his custom during siesta prior to going to his study carrel, was shuffling back and forth reading his breviary. The impact sent both of them flying to the floor, with Father Avertanus, as luck would have it as he had the brittle bones, on top.

After the mandatory gasps and apologies, Avertanus rolled himself off Dionysius and, exhausted by this effort, lay back down next to him. When Dionysius made a move to get up, Avertanus stilled him with a gentle pat of his hand.

"No, no, this will do just fine for a while. It's really rather nice down here, you know. Vaulted ceilings, nice high arches. Pity the paintings are gone; I might have finally seen them. Strange, isn't it, how you can think you know a place and then the perspective changes and it all seems so different. Can happen with people as well, you know."

"Father Avertanus," Dionysius stumbled, "in the garden, Father Pius—"

Again Avertanus silenced him. "Quite dead, yes, I know." Then Avertanus propped his head up and took a good long look at his old disciple. What he saw did not surprise him. In his excitement—any would do—Dionysius had developed a most arresting erection. The old monk's face lit up with a smile so broad that it belied his years.

"You always were more blessed in that department than anyone I have ever known."

"That seems to be the only department in which I don't disappoint."

"Hardly true, I'm sure, but even if it were you get no sympathy from me." Then hardly pausing to think, Avertanus confided something to him which he had longed for the opportunity to say for some time. "Leave, Dionysius. This place is not good for you."

"But what would I do? How could I make a living?"

"If that is the problem, I can easily get you a position at the Vatican library. You know the system and the monsignori in the stacks would be absolutely beside themselves." Dionysius muttered something—he was too wrapped up in thought to really know how to respond. As he wandered away, Avertanus called out to him in the stagiest of whispers. "And do cover Father Pius back up, will you? It's time he got some peace."

37

Bertie adored shopping, especially when it was free. Years of fantasizing had taught him to be prepared, bring as large a sack as you can carry, because you never know what's on special. So it was that after compline, when the community had retired, Bertie met Cuthbert at the door of the archives with an extra-large duffel bag slung over his shoulder. His Irish friend, armed with pencil and pad alone, seemed sadly unprepared.

The first room was rather disappointing. Lots of musty old books. Cuthbert seemed interested though, making noises about the "rarity of the incunabula." Which was not exactly what Bertie had in mind. A little gold and some precious stones would be much better, thank you, even some silver and sparklies would do. Funny how much he had changed these past few months. "Camp" used to be something the Boy Scouts did. How much love had changed him. Was there any way out? He surely hoped not.

They then came to an even larger room, twice as high as the first. It was devoted expressly to archival matters. This was Brocard's domain. Circling his desk were two stories of boxes of loose papers, correspondence, official documents going back nearly eight hundred years. Bertie, with his desperate fear of heights, could not imagine what it would have been like to climb the ladder to the top. He was pleased when Cuthbert unlocked the door to the treasury, and puffed out his bag in anticipation.

Once inside, he went straight to the cabinets of liturgical objects on the right hand wall, while Cuthbert gravitated first to the stacks of paintings on the left. Neither was disappointed. Bertie could not believe his luck and muttered something about the treasures of the Sierra Madre as he piled a couple of chalices, assorted censors, and one, no two, monstrances into his sack. Pino would be so proud of him.

Cuthbert, whose taste was far more catholic than the professoressa's, and whose purpose was more all encompassing, made note of everything. The anonymous thirteenth-century paintings, the minor Lorenzettis, as well as the extensive collection of seventeenth-century works. Then the works on paper, drawings, etchings, cliché verre, everything. At one point he thought he heard someone moving in the other room. He stopped to listen but decided that it was just Bertie, fussing and dithering over whether he really needed a couple of jewel-encrusted pixes. Bertie decided that, yes actually, he did.

It had been a very exciting evening, and Bertie for one was sad to see it end. Cuthbert thanked him for helping him get in and told him that they would have to talk about what he had taken at the end of the week. There was time, he assured him, and don't worry, you will get something. Then, giving Bertie a gentle tap on the nose and the most engaging Irish smile, he vanished into the thick black corridors they called home.

Bertie, feeling a bit like Papa Christmas and every bit as festive, made his way undetected to his room where he quickly hid the booty in the back of his closet. The nerve of him, he thought as he registered what Cuthbert had said on leaving, thinking he could tell me what I could take and what I couldn't. The cheeky little thief.

He was far too excited to go to sleep, but it was too late to see Pino, who was forced to go with people to their rooms at night. As Bertie was in the custom of dreaming—it had got him this far in life why stop it now—he imagined what it would be like when the two of them didn't have to settle for people and places they didn't want only because they had no other option. He dreamed of the freedom the trinkets stuffed into the closet would bring and had no doubt that a God of love would be fully understanding.

He thought he might try to pray and so he sat down in his straight-back wooden chair, placed his palms on his thighs, closed his eyes, and tried his very best to center himself. But there was Pino again, smiling quixotically, shirt open to the waist, working his hand slowly over the surface of his hairy chest. Oh this would not do at all. Unless, he thought, it became his prayer. And so it did. Thank you, God, so much for letting me be around such beauty, for making me alive to myself and to the world. When I had almost lost hope of ever feeling anything. Anything at all. Thank you so much for Pino. For us.

Suddenly he remembered that he had yet to return the keys. No time like the present as Mum always said. So he quietly left his room and even more quietly made his way down to the porter's cell. Antonio almost always took a grappa with Manolo last thing in the evening. As hoped, his room was empty. Then, just at the moment when he was placing the keys back on the board, he turned to see the prior. But not Emmanuele really, rather some transformed harpy, Medusa herself threatening to devour him.

"I am on to you, Father Berthold, you despicable worm." He had looked into the eyes of evil and doubted if there were any escape.

38

It was rare these days to put anyone under obedience. But, with an authority which reduced him to less than nothing, that is exactly what Emmanuele did to Bertie. He ordered him to follow him, now. No explanation was given, none needed since authority had a logic unto itself. Trembling, because he knew quite well that he had been in the wrong, Bertie told the prior he had to pee, please. There was no response, not even eye contact was made. He realized that, being a bad boy, he would just have to hold it.

As they walked through the deserted hallway, Emmanuele first with Bertie trailing behind, he wondered why he had not run. Why he was following this crazed creature. Was it a sense of guilt for his silliness, or perhaps some unquenched thirst to be controlled that led him to put himself in such vulnerable positions? He was not a dumb boy, Bertie, by a long shot. Only a weak one. As they made their way back towards the working quarters, he thought of this vow he had so blithely embraced when he was still in his teens. To place himself under solemn obedience to those in authority, and their name was Legion. Priors and provincials, prior provincials and generals, bishops and then the whole panoply of Church officials. At times it seemed a bit top heavy to him. So many men with fancy hats and silk sashes telling little Bertie Langdon from Blackpool, England, when to bow and when to scrape. It was too much really. Almost comic. But not now.

Things turned from bad to worse when Emmanuele, who was thoroughly prepared for what he had to do, took a flashlight out from under his habit and led him down the grimy servants' stairs to the basement. Bertie had never known of this staircase, but, as he was to find out, there was much about Emmanuele and San Redempto that he never knew.

In Bertie's few brief years at the monastery, he had never had any opportunity to go down into the basement. Then again, he never went looking for one. The stories that were told of what had happened down there for centuries were blood-chilling enough. Anyway, he liked his gore nicely packaged, no real blood or real ghosties, thank you. Just darkly shadowed pictures and finely crafted words. He was, after all, quite a modern boy. Occasionally he had paused at the top of the stairs just inside the rear door to the monastery, the one that led into the garden, to consider the black pit over which the monastery stood. This was the only access he had ever heard of to the dungeon, as it was commonly called by the monks. Until that moment when Emmanuele led him down the servants stairs, the ones that would have been taken when serious punishment was given.

As they passed walls that sweat blood and rooms where, so the stories had gone, recalcitrant monks had been shackled and starved, Bertie knew that were he to continue to acquiesce to Emmanuele's depraved demands, he would have no means of escape. No one would ever hear his cries or see his tears. If, that is, he didn't bear this cross with some nobility. Which is what, in his foolishness, he decided to do. It was a decision he regretted.

They finally arrived at a large room with a stage built out from the far wall. Quite festive really, Bertie could not help thinking, with some swaths of red velvet and decent lighting. Festive was not what this place was to be, not even for the perversest mind.

When they got to the stage, Emmanuele told him to strip and lie down on the low table that had been placed there in the center. He bound Bertie's hands and legs to the legs of the table and slowly, because there was now no rush, placed votive candles around the lamb to ready him for the sacrifice. This is not, Bertie closed his eyes so that he could think, this cannot be happening to me. The last words he remembered saying were, "Please, Father Prior, can I pee?" This seemingly simple demand was the trigger that set off the gun. Emmanuele lunged for the *flagellum*, still freshly drenched in his own blood, and struck him hard against the stomach. Bertie let out a howl and pissed at the same time and this only inflamed the prior more.

The audacity, he shouted down at him, the audacity to tell our secrets to anyone. You shall not get away with this. Not this time.

Emmanuele tried valiantly to restore some shred of authority to a life that had been stripped of even basic respect. But he didn't realize this as he turned his rage on Bertie, the most vulnerable member of his rapidly diminishing community. All he knew was that he had to lash out at something or someone for the injustices that had befallen him. How could they all have turned so totally against him? They would suffer, he thought, as Bertie swooned into unconsciousness like a Victorian courtesan arousing her john.

Amazingly, as he caught sight of Bertie, really saw him, he was unable to continue. This wasn't an object anymore, this was a person with a face, a brother who had trusted him. The disgust which Emmanuele felt was turned inwards, his hatred internalized into a loathing which had not depths. How could he have so hurt this weak and trusting soul? How could he have so abandoned any sense of decency and goodness? Broken man that he was, he dropped the *flagellum* to the ground and walked from the stage.

Some time later Emmanuele untied the young monk's body, heard him moan, and saw that he was still breathing. Gratitude that his lunacy had been checked before another life was lost might have been his. But he was incapable of feeling anything at all.

39

Photo albums could rightfully be classified as lethal weapons. Harmless as a loaded pistol in the bureau drawer, they can fire off unexpectedly and shatter the complacency of years, ripping illusions to shreds and reducing them to memories devoid of life and joy. So it was for Brocard late that night, as Bertie was staggering out of the dungeon and Dionysius relentlessly plowed his woman, trying to forget the unforgiving stare of Father Pius. As he could not sleep, he took out the old family album his aunt had sent him on the death of his mother, unaware of where it would lead him.

He had taken the trouble to reorganize it so that nothing was out of place and no photo, no matter how extensive the group may be, was unmarked. Aunt So-and-so and cousin Who-gives-a-hoot were all set down in their rightful places, marked for all time. As he turned page after page he was struck by nothing. That was the first shock. No emotion was bubbling under the surface, not the slightest indication of life was present. His had been one of those lace-curtain Irish families that drank in private and no matter how heavily, only communicated their emotions with the most discreetly passive aggressivity.

Looking at these faces from the past with their lifeless smiles and dropped eyes, he could still hear them saying "Jimmy is going to be our little priest, aren't you, Jimmy?" And feel still the weight of responsibility come down on him, as if his self-offering would make the family right, at least in the eyes of the world. It was a responsibility he had never shirked, nor even consciously questioned until it was far too late to do anything about.

Then, somewhere near the middle of the album he stopped to look at a yellowing snapshot of his uncle Bref, his mother's unmarried brother. He was a deceptively benign-looking man, of far greater intelligence than anyone else in the family. Someone who always seemed to know what was happening before it in fact happened. He remembered a curious incident which happened when he was old enough to walk and young enough to wander the house at will. His mother was tidying up Uncle Bref's room, dusting his desk and then, out of curiosity, picked up some loose papers. As she read them her face changed as if, for the first time and very last time, truth itself had cast its shadow over it. "Of course, the little bugger knew all the time. He was behind it all."

At that moment the truth that Brocard had been searching for these past few days became clear as well, and he closed the album firmly. He had to find the documents which would verify his suspicion, so he made his way through the darkened halls to the source of all information at San Redempto, the archives. His domain which, like Rome itself, he had never made full use of, treading on it as lightly as he had on life itself. If the answer was to be found, it would be there.

Once inside, he knew immediately where to go: the request letters for access to the treasury from 1971 until the present. Innocuous enough yet able to blow a hole through every lie. Sliding the ladder on its tracks and climbing to the highest reaches like some fearless mountain goat, he removed fifteen large *liasses* from their shelves and began to meticulously work his way through the documents. It was early morning before he had gathered all the information he needed. He knew now who had given Hoop Rhutten access to research in the treasury years ago, and more important still, who had given him continued rights long after he left the order. The very same monk who had introduced the unfortunate boy Thius to the project.

Appearances, Brocard was finding late in life, are simply that. So armed with his findings, with the truth itself, he realized that there was nothing more for him to do but wait for the mastermind to return to the scene of the crime. It was all so Agatha Christie, so elegantly right that he had no doubt that truth would win out and justice would reign.

But the hours ticked away and he slept soundly cushioned by the musty papers, the confrontation never coming. Perhaps just as well, years in his religious community had not prepared him for facing things head on. Justice, as scripture had it, was God's alone.

40

*A*vertanus longed to believe that Good was to be found at the bottom of the unremitting evil that plagued San Redempto. Not some shard of nicety nor some lone redeemed feature but, like the gold that lay at the bottom of an alchemist's crucible after all the mixing and burning had been done, unalloyed Good. It was for this purpose that he set out early on the morning of the last day, intent on calling down those forces which needed to be with them, and setting others to rest.

One of Avertanus's pet theories which, in truth, had turned into something of an obsession, was that early Christianity leaned heavily on the rituals, indeed the spiritual energy, of the pagan cult of Mithra. The Roman religion, for his studies had convinced him that it was indeed a fully developed religion, was fiercely masculine, as Christianity had become in structure and ritual from the late third century. Both coalesced around a sacrifice which was meant to transform the initiates. What the comparative study showed was that a healthy, almost harmonious syncretism had developed between the two religions. There were far more similarities than differences to be found between the worship of Christ and Mithra by the fourth century, the time when both rituals were fixed. He was convinced that they had developed a spirituality of complementarity which could harness universal power.

Needless to say, his study was not warmly received at the Pontifical University. He was not encouraged to publish it, nor even to talk about it for that matter. Worse still, in his meeting with the rector, he had the distinct sense that his theory was less of a threat than an embarrassment. Loopy old Avertanus was at it again, eccentric as ever.

But it was a theory which he could not shake. One which he felt compelled to try out just this once. That is why, armed with two books—the *Christian Rites for Funerals* and a rare volume of *Rites for Mithric Rituals*—he quietly closed the door of his cell behind him and ventured out just as dawn was breaking

It took him back a bit to see Dionysius coming in the garden gate as he was going out. Not unexpected though. Among the graces of old age, at least as he embraced it, was the ability to judge less and accept more. Not everyone is suited for religious life, he recognized. Even fewer now than ever. And since their brief talk Avertanus had felt a bond with his young disciple which allowed him to understand him with greater compassion, to love him even more. They mumbled *salve* to each other like two brothers.

Everything went with such uncharacteristic smoothness that he knew some greater force had matters well in hand. The bus to take him up to Via San Giovanni was waiting for him, as was the seat he liked the best directly near the door. He did not even feel the weight of his years that morning and his skin glowed with youth—as often happens when we are inspired, regardless of what our age may be. Nor did he encounter any problem at the monastery entrance to San Clemente. He knew that his old friend the prior, an incurable insomniac, would be there to receive him at any hour. Once inside his request to use the chapel in the *scavi* was granted, although the strangeness of the hour and the place was duly noted. Taking the black fiddleback vestments from the sacristy and a torch to light his way, he made his way down the vertiginous steps to the temple of Mithra over which the ancient church of San Clemente had been built. As he vested, he wondered how many years it had been since any priest had worn this chasuble. In the face of death, black had been preempted decades ago in the Catholic Church by white, a sign of the Resurrection. But Avertanus knew that in this case, death must be seen as an absence of light, the existential void which allows no hope. Only then, only when the dead bury the dead, could those souls who were filled with goodness, those children of the light been seen once more. And truly live.

He placed the torch in the bracket on the wall, reverently approached the marble altar of Mithra and kissed the head of the raging bull on the bas relief which fronted it. Then he made a grand prostration before the altar, evoking the names of those who were to be released. Brocard in his kindly compulsiveness, Dionysius in his earthy openness, and Berthold in his hopeless naiveté. It was not humility which caused him to forget himself. He was old and in all likelihood would not make it through the violent storm which was bearing down on San Redempto. Then too he did not know if he truly deserved to be counted among the just or the stupid. Time had taught him that he was deficient in both.

First he read the prayers to Mithra, slayer of the bull and judge of the dead. They were powerfully masculine in their demands, unnuanced denunciation of all that was evil and all which had threatened to subvert Good itself. Avertanus did not know where evil had lodged itself at San Redempto, in which cell it lived, which choir stall it went to in its charade of sanctity. It could well have been the walls itself, the very foundation of the monastery which was drawing all within it to their doom. Mithra would know. He then removed a small kit from his belt, took out the cruets, paten, and chalice and opened the rite for Christian funerals for the mass of the dead. Then, placing a chip of plaster from the monastery on the altar, he anthropomorphized the building, dealing with it as he would a lifeless corpse. All went well until the consecration of the blood, when he shook uncontrollably and the blood of Christ spilled out onto the altar of Mithra, mixing inexorably with that of slaughtered bulls. Avertanus felt some peace as he completed his sacrifice, but wondered if all the blood which needed to be offered had already been spilled.

41

Unbeknownst to Avertanus, at the precise moment when the precious blood was spilled, the heavens opened and a rain poured down on Rome of almost apocalyptic intensity. The Spanish Steps became a waterfall and flash floods submerged whole stretches of the Via Salaria. Nowhere was the downpour heavier, nowhere more relentless than at the monastery of San Redempto. Until recently the old pile had retained a shred of dignity, a hint of its former glory. An old matron who could still ladle on the makeup and trot around in heals to face the world. Only today were the ravages of passing years to be honestly faced and the charade to be abandoned. The rains that began so early the morning of the last day made short work of years of deep denial.

The plumbing was the first to go, as it so often is. Water backed up from drain pipes in the garden and started to flood the basement. Pipes burst in the walls, exhausted by the abuse of time. Worse still, sewage backed up into the toilets and poured out onto the floors, which after some hours could no longer sustain the weight and gave way. Leaks became streams, streams rivers and rivers led into the ocean of mud surrounding the monastery. Drain pipes could no longer handle the water and acted instead as lips of a fountain, the largest in all of Rome. Water cascaded from the roof, washing away what remained of the outside surface as it crashed to the ground below.

Like a face bereft of muscle tone, the outside had long since been a disaster lying in wait. Centuries of sunbathing had dried the plaster, whole chunks of which dislodged in the torrent. Rome, which always prided itself on the weathered facades of its buildings, was mortified by the dilapidation which had so overtaken San Redempto. And quite unlike other palazzi whose exteriors hide the splendors of their interiors, this old matron was as ugly inside as without. Perhaps even more so.

Moisture had so totally taken hold of her that she never truly felt warm. A cold dampness clung to her walls, and even before the sewage had backed up an unpleasant smell clung to her, that persistent bad breath which cannot be disguised because it rose up from a rot which lay buried deep within. No amount of shawls could keep her warm; no colorful gargles could make her breath acceptable. She was old and worn out and nothing more could be done about it. Only death itself could offer any cure.

The pounding of the rain resounded throughout the halls and blended in with the howls which she alone could hear. The muted scream of Ephraim was the faintest of them all, being the most recent. The more distant the memory, the stronger the injustice rang out. A nameless student who died in his room of pneumonia because no one checked in on him. The endless stream of monks whose lives were circumscribed by her walls, dying enraged because life was leaving them before they ever tasted it. And who now wandered the vacant rooms and waited in abandoned choir stalls for final release. At times like this, when nature ravaged her, when the winds roared through her cavernous halls and thunder broke above her sagging roof, even those inured to spirits could not help but hear the howl. Nor could they fail to realize that one day God Himself would reign down justice.

If she closed her eyes and allowed the sight of the past to grip her, she could see the long rows of white-clad monks processing down the ambulatory towards chapel chanting that litany of unpronounceable saints the order had spawned on Christendom. Red martyrs many, white virgins all. Models of a way of life worth dying for, or in. In that clarified light of time, she could hear again the *salve* echoing through the ceiling vaults. See the procession of chasubles and dalmatics wending their way to the altar of sacrifice.

How could it all have passed so quickly? A mere four hundred years, over in a heartbeat. Would they think kindly of her, would they remember how well her refectory was proportioned, the fine detailing of her sanctuary, how finely shielded her garden was from prying eyes? She had surely served them well, thousands of them. Bore the tradition as no man ever could, kept faithful to the task she had set out to do.

But as sheets of rain washed over her and the blackness of the storm isolated her from all else around, hope itself abandoned her. It was foolishness to think that San Redempto would be remembered for anything but the pestilent sewer which it had become. Sheer lunacy to expect anything more than indifference on her demise and realistic to presume that many would indeed rejoice to dance on her grave. Sadness was all she felt. Surrounded by shining monuments to the ages, sturdy as the day they had been built, she knew herself to be a transitory pile of stone and mortar whose anonymity was to be forever secure. Realizing all this, she did not rail against the rain, but accepting its relentless assault, imploded in an inexpressible grief.

42

$\mathcal{N}$othing would deter them from their final plunder. Otger had as much time for the infantile wailing of the prior as did Manolo for the frantic concerns of Brocard. Nothing could keep them from organizing the booty which had to be moved out, as planned, that very night. So as the building groaned and the anxieties of the community mounted, they went on about their business with controlled calm. Intent on looking out for themselves.

There were distractions, though. The stench from the sewage spilling out into the hallways was impossible to avoid. Even Otger, who had a discreet interest in the texture and scent of excrement, his own generally, gagged for air. Unavoidable as well was the festering pool of water at the base of the waterfall which had once served as the main staircase. An entire ecosystem of water bugs and slugs had taken hold of it, proving once more the sheer indifference that nature has to human affairs.

Manolo had brought him to see the roll of paintings because he had realized that without Otger's help they would have no real value. Forms were needed, expertise must be expended on them before they could be sold for real money. And ever presentable as he was, Otger was the one who had made the contacts with antiquarians who would know how to correctly deal such objects. So, reluctantly, he and Antonio had decided to let him in on it. On the condition that they all share equally. As he unrolled the canvases they released the smell of Pius, which had nothing whatsoever in common with that sweet smell of sanctity talked about in the martyrology. Mercifully, they were in perfect condition. It was amusing for Otger to listen to Manolo blunder his way through some lame story about his complicity in the robbery. As if he had the brains or courage to execute anything of this magnitude. In a way it was good that Thius was out of the picture. He would have been a lot more difficult to get around than the bungling brothers Basque. Then too Otger could take advantage of the art appraisers in Rome, get all the documents needed and then have the canvases sent up to Holland. His dear friend Madam Blanchierdarie at the Farnesse had once mentioned knowing one of the world experts on Poussin. He had only to entrust the paintings to her.

So they rolled the paintings up again and wrapped them in sheets of dirty plastic so as to keep them dry. Manolo saw no problem in Otger bringing them over to his friend as soon as possible. The sooner they were authenticated the sooner they made their money.

Despite everything, the rain did get to them. Perhaps it was the way it hammered at the windows and shook the very floors they walked. Or maybe it was the overwhelming dampness which drenched their skin and soaked the clothes they wore. It was not that they were discouraged or even sad, two emotions which never figured in their personalities. Rather they were caught up in the death throes of a building and, indeed, a way of life, the force of which swept them into a frenzy and made them lunge in manic fury.

Otger had no concern for the taped boxes of scapulars and holy cards which Manolo had spent the morning packing. Useless trinkets for insignificant people. No, his concern was purely for the work stored in the treasury. And not all of it at that, only those pieces which, over many years of research, he knew had substantial value. This was the moment for which he had been waiting. No rainstorm, however biblical in proportion, would dampen his triumph.

Anxiety turned to panic when they entered the archives. The damage already done by the storm was substantial. One whole wall of records had tumbled down on Brocard's tidy little desk, thousands of waterlogged documents littered the floor, thousands more hung perilously over their heads as the remaining shelves buckled inwards. Manolo's hands were shaking so badly that he could hardly open the door to the treasury. Cursing his inadequacy, Otger pulled the keys from his door, unlocked the door, and flung it open.

All was safe. There was a bulging in the ceiling to the right over the case of liturgical vessels but everything else was in order. Losing no time Otger pulled out those paintings which Manolo and Antonio were to transport for him—there was no question at all whose they were in this case. He stacked them against the wall, inspecting them briefly as he did. A remarkable Dughet, the Lorenzettis, of course. Millions of florins' worth.

Then he began to set aside the *liasses* of drawings and other works on paper. He had no need for the bibelots which Emmanuele had used for his sport, nor did he need the rather gauche turn-of-the-century prints of the patriarch's, which he grandly gave Antonio. For all his fine work. Otger always did have a way with menials, especially dumb ones.

When they parted it was as it should be. Manolo scurrying around like the rodent he was, busy with a thousand details. Like the very rich whose ranks he was soon to join, Otger's affairs were being handled for him. Although the tempest roared all around him, he rested content in the knowledge that it could never touch him.

43

Brocard stared up at the medieval flood markers on the side of Santa Maria sopra Minerva, wondering whether the Tiber's embankment could ever burst. Would the great modern walls which held back the river be sufficient to this deluge? Or would it crumble as surely as the sad and broken umbrella which he held low over his head, spokes exposed and fabric blowing helplessly in the wind. Fortunately, just as the poor thing was becoming more of a liability than a help, the bolted doors to the great church opened and a fat little Dominican friar let him in. *"Bruto tempo,"* he mumbled. Ugly weather indeed.

Why the professoressa had wanted to meet here, and at such short notice, was a mystery. He was however becoming quite accustomed to her peculiarities and, if truth be known, would have been quite disappointed were she to have done anything predictable. The opportunity to get out of San Redempto was itself a relief. For the first time in all of his years in Rome, he had not been able to take his siesta and he seriously wondered if he would ever again be able to sleep in its walls, so pestilent had it become.

By contrast, the beauty of the Minerva overwhelmed him. Even devoid of light it shone in utter calm. It was as if the uncorrupted body of Saint Catherine, which lay under the main altar, was casting a loving glance over the interior of her church so that no tempest, no matter how great, could disrupt its solemn peace. Maybe the Beatific Fra Angelico as well, sealed into its walls, assured that no chaos, no confusion would break this reverential silence. Of course, neither of them had factored Zinka into things.

"Isn't it all too fabulous!" Brocard's heart skipped a beat. "Oh, so sorry my little monk," she continued, bending over him and rubbing his bald head with affection, "you were at prayer. Well enough of that now, we have things to discuss."

Rising to his feet, he was amazed to see so much of her. Not that she was naked, exactly, but the driving rain had done its best to reduce her simple sundress to a second skin, and there was not a crevice or a mound that was not fully visible. Exhibitionist that she was, she absolutely glowed with joy.

"It is so warm and full," she said running her hand through her matted hair and not dropping her eyes for a second, "nature gone wild and demanding us to be hers. It is so fabulous I never want it to end." Then forgetting all about the rain she took Brocard by the hand and, walking brazenly into the sanctuary, led him to the statue of *Christ Risen* by Michelangelo. "Come see here," she said as she signaled him around to the far side.

To his dismay, all Brocard could see were the massive marble buttocks of the Risen Lord. "That, my dear little Brocard, is the best ass you or any of us is likely ever to see." She knew she shocked him somewhat but rightly sensed that he was greatly amused.

"And this is the reason you wanted me to come out in the worst weather of the year?"

"You mean it isn't enough?" She smiled coyly. "No actually there is more. Much more." She paused for maximum effect and then, walking slightly out into the sanctuary so that she could move her arms more freely when she talked, began to preach her good news. Even Saint Catherine under the altar, supine behind her glass, was all ears.

"As you know, I have been a good little girl recently, applying my mild solutions and rubbing oh-so-gently on the bottom corner of our canvas. I've been as careful as those obsessive restorers who have removed the gunk and loincloths from the Last Judgment to reveal those bright fields of preciously tiny penises. They are so adorable."

Brocard said nothing but did look at her intently so as to get her back on track.

"Saint Agatha's breast is there, nubile and succulent as the day it was plucked. And," she paused because the excitement was really getting to be too much, even for her, "branded into it, with cruel assurance, the name of the master himself, Nicolas Poussin."

At this she sensed that even Brocard was excited and did not think twice when she pulled him to her breasts. "How wonderful," he mumbled into them, "how wonderful."

"As if this isn't enough," she said dislodging him, "Camille called with the most astounding news. Something which you will find very interesting indeed." Without pausing to breathe, "Dr. Otger Aarnack has dropped off the six stolen paintings at the Farnesse for the inimitable Dr. Zinka Pavlic to authenticate. All the little chickies have come home."

The news came too quickly for Brocard to assimilate, and looking far more womanly than his ravishing accomplice, he grasped the Lord's ass for support.

"Now, my other reason for coming is to pray. I do it too, you know, but only I worship the goddess upon whose shrine this church sits. The great Minerva herself, clad in armor and bursting from the head of Zeus." As she kneeled she cast a glance back at Brocard, and, glint in her eye, asked if she shocked him. The question was rhetorical.

44

Brocard experienced no relief whatsoever when he stepped back into San Redempto from the windswept streets of Rome, but he was relieved to catch sight of Bertie and Father Cuthbert sneaking down the hallway sometime later. There was a final mystery here that still needed sorting out.

"What is wrong with you, lad? Speak to me." But Bertie couldn't speak, hadn't been able to say a word since those horrible hours in the dungeon. He was brought up well enough however to respond to an urgent request like the one the Irish priest had slipped under his door earlier in the afternoon. Pain and shock still seized his body but he could almost hear his old mum saying, "Catatonia, Bertie dear, is no excuse for bad manners."

In the note he had promised to disclose his plan, one which would have a great impact on Bertie's future. For the goodness he had shown so that he might not suffer any additional pain, Father Cuthbert Mullins, his brother in Christ, wished to meet him.

Bertie was surprised to be led up to the roof of San Redempto one final time. Cuthbert's explanation was that they would have more privacy there. Which was true enough. With Brother Ephraim now gone, or like so many others permanently vanished, there would be no danger of seeing another soul. But there was space enough for privacy inside San Redempto as well. Even lakefront property went begging as the community continued its great shrink. No, in all likelihood, Bertie thought, he's just a wide-eyed romantic like all those Micks, returning to our little spot for one last time. Rather sweet really, were it not raining so bloody hard.

Brocard followed them at a discreet distance, reveling in his role of sleuth—then hid himself behind a small shed within earshot of where they stopped.

"Nice hard day," Cuthbert quipped with one of those very Irish lines. Hard, you see, not soft. Would have made more sense for Dionysius was all Bertie could think. He was not happy. As the wind tore through them and wave of clouds burst open upon them, he remembered how much he had positively loathed *Wuthering Heights*.

"You're afraid, aren't you?" Bertie was shaking violently and it wasn't just the weather. "What on earth did they do to you?" Cuthbert held him by the shoulders and tried to look him in the eyes, but Bertie would not look up. He actually couldn't. "I wanted to tell you that all of this will be over soon. It has been decided and nothing can save it."

Cuthbert whipped his hand over his face, clearing the water so that he could see. There was a clash of thunder so loud that Pius surely shuddered in his grave and a bolt of lightening so bright that the living were temporarily blinded. Then Cuthbert got an idea.

"Look!" he said, jumping up on the ledge. Bertie was horrified, it was so slippery, the wind could take him, he wanted to scream. That was his idea, of course, to shock Bertie so greatly that he would have to speak again. "Take my hand." Bertie would not go up on the ledge with him, he was not that submissive. "Take me hand!" Cuthbert said with an authority which, Bertie being Bertie, had to be respected. He did take Cuthbert's hand and was pulled up onto the ledge. "Squat if you want so you don't fall," Cuthbert continued, "then look straight down and with all the fear welling up within you scream to God Almighty!" In theory it was a good enough idea, unfortunately God Almighty had other plans.

Cuthbert was too near the edge to do anything when he saw the ledge crack and realized that it was he who should scream. That was not what he did. Sheer terror affects the loquacious differently, it seems. He never said another word, never did explain the grand plan to Bertie or to anyone for that matter. The ledge gave way so totally that he plummeted like a rock. As he was flailing in space he caught sight of the statue of Our Lady of Succor in the garden and, needing her help more now than ever tried to reached out to her one last time. Sad to tell he impaled himself, spread-eagle on her hands, folded heavenwards in prayer. It was a credit to Italian workmanship that the statue had been so firmly set into the stones of the cloister that it stood upright throughout the entire remarkable landing. A good thing too that Cuthbert had worn his habit, which masked the killing gesture of her prayer. It could not disguise the blood, though, which poured forth from between his legs like a woman in childbirth, mixed with the waters of heaven. Still Bertie said nothing. Could not even move. Did not know where to go or what to do. He had never felt so lost, had never known such desolation.

Then Brocard moved out from behind the wall where he had seen everything and, saying nothing, stood next to Bertie. With Bertie squatting on the ledge, they were at the same height. It made it easy for Brocard to reach out to him and gently put his arms around him, something which a week ago he could not have done but which now seemed the most natural of things. "There, there," he said to comfort him, "it is all over, he is with Mary."

"He's b-b-bloody impaled on her for C-C-hrist's s-sake!"

"That's good now, you're talking again," Brocard said feeling positively maternal. "Now how about we both get down from this nasty roof."

45

Stranger to tell, he really looked like quite a happy corpse. Needless to say, this being San Redempto, nothing had been done to beautify him, so cosmetics and stitching were in no way responsible for the strange little smile on his lips. In fact there was time for nothing. In the barely two hours since they removed him from the praying hands of Mary, little more could be done than scrub clean the visible areas, plop him in a box, wrap a white cloak around him, pull up the cowl, and gather the community around for the prayers of the dead. Were it not for the fact that the whole community saw him on their way into refectory, Emmanuele probably would have asked Manolo to dispose of him more efficiently. For a brief moment, he thought he might be able to get away with it even though they had all seen him. Avertanus, from his cloud of unknowing, actually thought Father Cuthbert was engaging in some quaint Irish rite, dancing with Mary, Celtic White Lady, or some other nonsense. Only when Dionysius threw up did he realize otherwise.

Brocard was too concerned about the secret which Cuthbert took with him to the grave to feel anything at his passing. Then again, he had become so accustomed to loss that even had all the questions been answered there was no presumption that grief would follow. So he walked through the ritual of death, with the full awareness that, as diminished as the community had become, more might well be on the way.

The chapel was the only one who wept. Tears ran down its walls and—it might have been the way the wind ran riot through the shattered windows—it seemed to howl. It had no electric light to shed on the dead Irishman, all power had gone out hours before, but it did make a valiant try to fight back the darkness with half-spent candles.

The prior began the prayers with uncharacteristic temerity. It was as if he were disembodied, the faintest shadow of a former presence which was once writ large. When his voice trailed off into nothingness, Father Otger took up his part, so as to get on with things. Rightfully this was Avertanus's place, as subprior, but no one objected. The truth was no one wanted to be there one minute more than was necessary.

At the end of the prayers, Manolo brought the aspergillum over to Emmanuele so that he could sprinkle the body with holy water. He was so absorbed in his own mourning that Avertanus had to direct his hand upwards so that some water touched the corpse. They then went through the community, each in their turn dousing a body which was so drenched with water that any drops which touched it were repelled instantly. Antonio was followed by Brocard, then Dionysius and Bertie. All passed the coffin as in a daze.

Finally, with a solemnity which stilled the others, Father Angelus Lennon, the forgotten Irishman, quiet to a fault, stepped forward. He sprinkled his confrere with the holy water, paused to pray briefly over the body, and turned to face the community. "I have something of grave importance to relate to you which cannot wait."

Then he took an official document out of the hidden upper pocket of his habit and in the most official of tones began to read:

"I, Luigi Cardinal Cicognetti, Prefect of the Holy Office of Religious, having made due study of the autonomous community of San Redempto of the venerable Order of Our Lady of Divine Succor, do hereby declare the community and the monastery in which it resides suppressed as of the moment of the formal promulgation of this document. The reasons for such suppression are numerous, ranging from depleted number to lack of due observance of religious life. All detailed accusations are on file at the Holy Office. There is no recourse to be made, no argument will be heard. The suppression is final."

Looking up over the body of Cuthbert, Angelus caught Avertanus's eyes, then Brocard's, and saw the downcast heads of the remnants of the community. Compassion, which he had in good measure, compelled him to explain the situation in a more personal way. Putting aside the text, he walked out into the center of the nave and told them how difficult it had been for both Cuthbert and him to have been living in their midst these past months under false pretenses.

"Nothing," he went on to say, "no system or group, however well intentioned, lasts forever. We have cycles of growth and decay. So too, in the Church. There are houses, groups, whole orders at times, which need to be cut off, like a gangrened limb, so that the body will survive. The general of the order, your general although most of you acted as if he did not exist, hearing stories of the lax and inappropriate behavior here at San Redempto, decided it was time to take action, should action be needed. Although this monastery had the privilege of being autonomous from the order in its day-to-day affairs, it remained connected to a larger system. Cardinal Cicognetti himself was called in when we were able to confirm to him the remarkable hidden wealth of San Redempto, which most of you in your own ways are aware of. These treasures are not, you realize, yours at all. You are, to a man, vowed to solemn poverty. This is and always has been the patrimony of the Church. Hers alone to preserve or dispense with as the need presents itself."

He walked over to Brocard, whose eyes were clouding over, and said, "The Church, to be a viable witness to the Lord, must rid itself of all that discredits it, all that causes scandal, all that does not build it up. Some of you must discern whether or not your vocations too still make sense. Others must renew that commitment, in light of a changing world." Dionysius's mind began to race. What did this mean for him, should he finally move on? Bertie shared the same anxiety.

Even before Angelus was finished the two brothers had left the chapel, more intent than ever on completing their plunder that very night. Emmanuele, on the other hand, could barely move. The world had indeed come to an end and all that was needed now was to make amends for the endless wrongs which he had done. But how?

As Angelus moved away from the body, the lights of the candles clustered around him and illuminated his face so that it seemed to shine from within. "Do not worry," he said with great compassion. "All of your needs will be met, no one will be put out on the street. You are, of course, free to go, all of you. As you always were."

It was at that moment of uncommon gentleness that Avertanus, struck by the aureole of light around him, recognized Angelus as the angel for whom he had so earnestly prayed. However, his hope that redemption had been won was somewhat premature.

46

*N*ever in their lives had they worked so feverishly, for never before was so much at stake. True to form Manolo had made a plan, the boxed goods from the second floor were to go in first, then blanket-wrapped items like the paintings and a few assorted pieces of furniture which would make life easier when they set up house across the border. Lastly, fragile objects on the top, all tied down by blankets and ropes so they would arrive intact. A good plan really, simple and doable under most circumstances, but as the deluge continued outside and the monastery disintegrated within, all hope of order was abandoned. A frenzy had taken hold of them and the two stolid Basque peasants were reduced to airhead socialites fussing over the coming prom. Oh Cindy, you forgot the sash! Do I need it anyway? He'll be here in five! Oh my God I broke a nail! Now calm down.

They couldn't still themselves, of course. Antonio did the major lugging of boxes, abandoning all order, while Manolo went to fetch what was to have been the truck. There was no time to complain when he saw it. Giuseppe from Santo Spirito had agreed to find a truck for them but because of laziness and lack of funds (he had not been given much to work with), when Manolo got there he found an old Italian Hearse, cavernous in size. Not at all the anonymous moving van they had in mind. Still it was roomy, had curtains to disguise the contents, and, as Giuseppe explained, the passenger seats were very comfy.

One part of the original plan did stand. Manolo backed the hearse into the unpaved area by the laundry room. A logical place as there were no stairs to negotiate and everything could be arranged in

Ephraim's abandoned work area before loading. As it would turn out, this was to be their fatal mistake. They gave no thought to the mud around them, the fact that as the rains drove down the soil was liquefying and the ground beneath them began seizing the hearse in a stranglehold.

But they were too concerned with gathering everything together to notice this. In his most officious manner Manolo ordered Antonio to put this here, no here you idiot, and place that over there. For once in his life Antonio would have none of it. He was not his brother's servant, speak kindly to him. There was no time for radical personality change though and, exhausted with trying, Antonio acquiesced to his brother's demands.

There was a writing table that Manolo cherished, a delicate little thing that had belonged to Father Joachim, a wizened monk who had been found dead on the toilet some years before. Manolo had taken it from his room before the body was cold and was not about to leave it behind. Although it was easy enough to lift, they were having difficulty maneuvering it into the hearse because it had been parked too close to the wall. So Manolo told Antonio to pull it up a few feet. That is when the disaster began.

As Antonio put the hearse in gear Manolo moved closer to the open rear door and twisted to get a hold on the writing desk. Then, as fate would have it, he pulled something in his back and in an attempt to aright himself slid under the spinning wheels of the hearse. He screamed, of course, so loudly that all the corpses were quickened with enthusiasm, but between the deafening sound of the rains, the revving of the engine, and the pounding of his own heart Antonio was unable to hear him. It was only when he realized that he was burying the hearse deeper into the mud that he looked up to see the body of Ephraim floating towards him. There was a simple enough explanation: the cistern had backed up and of course the bloated body was carried with the river of water which rushed towards him. But logic did not hold in the midst of that tempest when all the terrors which had been lodged deeply within Antonio's shriveled soul surfaced at once.

Terrified, he placed the hearse in neutral, or so he mistakenly thought, and turned to help Manolo, or simply to find out what he was to do next. As he jumped out he could feel something tugging at his feet. Looking down he saw the ground was littered with decaying cats who seemed, impossible as it might be, to be rising up in vengeance for the evils done them, their stiffened bodies spastic with rage in the lightning which crashed above.

When he made it back to the rear of the hearse he saw that Manolo had been pinned under the wheel, almost lifeless, with only enough energy to curse. Howling in the driving rain Antonio pulled him frantically but the more he tugged the deeper his brother sunk into the mud. Then somehow the hearse, which he had inadvertantly put in reverse, caught hold and pinned Antonio to the wall with the force of a runaway train, crushing his chest so flat that none of his vital organs survived. The car horn, jolted by the impact, set out a plaintive cry.

Avertanus was packing his bag at that moment and thought he heard something amiss—horns, screams. Silly old monk, he thought, what more could possibly go wrong.

47

Seven boys were led into the garden door later that night, the Seven Horsemen of the Apocalypse as Otger called them. They were the most beautiful he could find for his friend, dark creatures with softly muscular bodies and eyes so evil they caused the devil himself to tremble. In the darkness and the driving rain, they did not notice the dead bodies cluttering the far side of the garden. Their minds were fixed on other things.

Emmanuele was waiting downstairs, unconcerned that the water was rising to the level of the stage and that the ceiling looked as if it might collapse at any minute. So too were Otger and the boys he had procured. He, after all, would be on a train back to Holland within the hour. And they were not only being paid handsomely for their time but relished the opportunity for uncontrolled sadism, a luxury not often granted to the poor.

As Otger played acolyte they all silently undressed and then, as he had no will left of his own, stripped Emmanuele as well. When the ring of candles had been lit, they tied the prior to the table on which, only the night before, he had tortured Bertie. No costumes were needed this time, no sets required. Only brutal stark simplicity.

Otger loomed above Emmanuele's bound and stretched body not unlike the priest in the painting of Saint Agatha. He too pointed upwards as if to remind his friend of the great design of things. But there was no body part in his hands because nothing survived the lacerations of the youths, crazed by the sight of flesh ripped from the bones and driven to a frenzy by the gushing of his blood.

If he made any sound they did not hear him, so completely reified

142

had he become. An object of forbidden delight, laid out for their amusement. Occasionally they made noises of pleasure as their sweaty bodies rubbed together and they became increasingly aroused. But they did not let their excitement get in the way of the job they were being paid for and which brought them such longed-for revenge.

So as not to beat him into unconsciousness the young men concentrated on his chest and thighs. At times they miscalculated and hit his face. At others, when one of them saw that he was beginning to become aroused, they struck his groin. When they did Emmanuele threw back his head like Santa Teresa and let out an imperceptible groan.

Otger had been so engrossed by the whole affair that he had not realized how late it had become. Looking at his watch he realized that if he were to catch the night train to Holland, he had to leave immediately. He thanked the young men for their help and assured them that he would use their services again, but not for such hard labor next time. They laughed, winked, and, professionals that they were, continued to flay away. Otger threw a bag of money and objects on top of the pile of clothing, never looking back as he left.

He did wonder, as he made his way through the empty streets of Rome, whether anyone would ever confront him about the havoc he had wrought at San Redempto. Surely even Brocard, slow as he was, had figured out that he was behind Hoop's research these many years. As he was behind Thius's, even the last fateful trip to Rome. That there could be no doubt that Otger alone had masterminded everything.

Anyone with any sense would see that he was simply playing on the greed of Manolo and the lust of Emmanuele to achieve his goal—which was, and always had been, power, that most exhaulted of vices. Making his way to the Stazione Termini, one of Mussolini's more enduring legacies, he checked which track his train was on and could not help but smile.

Of course, no one would say anything. Evil, true evil, goes unpunished in this world. Perhaps, he smiled more broadly still, looking into the black hole of infinity, evil is simply absorbed into the cosmos like food for a brute animal. Nothing more.

As he boarded the train to Amsterdam, the passion of the seven young men working on Emmanuele diminished, and, as if on cue, they dropped their whips and fell upon each other, exhausted but satisfied. More would have transpired had one of them not noticed that the ceiling seemed ready to collapse and were they not to meet the same fate as the man they had just butchered, they had best go.

Upstairs the remnant of the community was prepared to leave. Father Angelus made his way through the darkened halls to collect them. Because of his seniority, he knocked on Avertanus's door first. The old man had a bag of books with him and little more. Next they went to Father Brocard, who took some time answering because he had to pack all his photographs, extra habits, and bits and pieces. Dionysius joined them next, and he had so little with him one would have thought he didn't live there any more. Finally they arrived at Bertie's room, where his door was open and his bags were packed. He sat on the edge of his bed in eager anticipation, a little boy going off on a great adventure.

Otger had told them he was taking the night train but Emmanuele was nowhere to be seen and Angelus was reluctant to leave without him. San Redempto was to be definitively sealed off that night. He must be found at all costs. They decided that given the state of the building it was safer to stay together. It was easy to check off areas where he would not be. The chapel where Cuthbert's body was being waked was one; the ambulatory now submerged in water another. But Bertie knew. He brought them to the servants' staircase, and then taking the flashlight from Angelus, led them down into the dungeon. It took what little courage he had left in him, but he knew that were he ever to quell the demons, he would have to face the dungeon one last time.

Emmanuele's corpse lay whiter than the virgin Agatha, his blood drained out in a river which swirled into the waters consuming San Redempto. As they struggled to set him free they slipped and strained and fell until his blood had drenched them all. As the final candles flickered, Avertanus offered a brief prayer to Mithra, realizing that the sacrifice had been made. Then the remnants of the community of San Redempto made their way to the front door, locking the monastery forever behind them.

48

Hustlers lose their luster after midnight. A certain harshness takes over, a desperation coupled with resignation which transforms the liveliest of faces into masks of death. Bertie wondered, as he sat at a cafe table in the Piazza della Republica still clutching his bag of belongings, if Pino would ever get this hardened look. He even feared, although he tried not to think about it, that he might already have it. There was nothing he could do now but wait. He had nowhere else to go, or rather, nowhere he wanted to go.

An hour went by, maybe more, the longest wait of his life. Finally he caught sight of Pino approaching with a fat old man with a wig, then shaking his hand good-bye. Bertie knew he had been paid in advance, he liked it that way. He was so good at business.

Trying his best to be cool, Bertie gave a discreet wave which, of course, Pino did not see. He tried again, still with no success. Finally, afraid he might lose the love of his life to a Japanese tour group, he stood up and waved in his direction. Yes, he saw him, and seemed to be pleased. Bertie lost confidence on the spot. He had never seriously considered the possibility that he might be making a fool of himself until then.

But Pino did come over and no he did not look jaded at all. The same beautiful man, a little bloodshot but not much worse for wear. When he saw him standing there before him with a look of such concern, Bertie could not help but cry. He cried for all the death he had seen and cried for all the suffering he had endured. He cried for a life that had gone—no matter how rotten it had been, it was his life—and for the years which could never be retrieved. He cried be-

145

cause Pino was so extraordinary and he so common and cried because, no matter how hard he tried, he would never be worthy of him.

Pino sat next to him and cradled his head in his arms. Fully aware that such sensitivity could ruin his reputation, he stroked Bertie's head and wiped the tears with his shirtsleeve. "There, there, Padre," he whispered lowly in his ear. "It's all right."

"Some padre," Bertie finally said, choking through his tears. "They closed my bloody monastery and butchered my prior."

"*Tutto va bene,*" Pino said. "Everything is all right."

"Do you think so, Pino? Do you really think so?"

His hustler didn't answer, couldn't really because he had never posed the question seriously before. Perhaps, he thought, it was time that he did.

"Where are you staying?" Pino asked.

To which Bertie replied, "With you."

The young monk looked up into Pino's eyes and realized that, hardened as he might be, they were welling up. He checked himself, stood up, and slowly walked away. Bertie's heart stopped beating and in the long pause that followed he thought that it would never start up again. Then stretching out one of his massively strong hands to Bertie, his man winked and signaled for him to come.

They went to a small pensione on a side street near the Statione Termini. Pino dropped some money on the counter and the old lady at the desk handed him a key. It was clear, Bertie thought with pride, that his man was well known. Once inside the room Bertie began to talk, haltingly at first, then with an eloquence which he had never known. He explained about the robbery and the murders, the agony of the building and the suppression of the community. And as Bertie talked Pino undressed him and then slowly took off his own boots, jeans, shirt, then finally underwear and socks. He couldn't help but see the makeshift bandages and bruises all over Bertie's body but, as he had seen far worse in his line of work, registered no shock on his face. But he could not hide his concern. Lying next to him Pino put his finger over Bertie's mouth to silence him. Do you realize, he told Bertie, that you haven't stuttered once in all this time. Really? Really, he assured him with a smile.

There was something Bertie had to show him that wouldn't wait. Reaching for the bag he pulled out the liturgical objects which he had chosen from the treasury. Pino handled them as the precious vessels they were, more thoroughly aware than Bertie of their true value. "Via Gulia," he said, "they'll pay good money for them there." Then he put them back in the bag; business could wait until tomorrow.

Bertie was afraid of looking up at him, content really just to be there, next to the warm, sweaty body of the man he loved. Pino knew that this was not enough, that the time had come for more. So he raised Bertie's face up towards his and, with a tenderness which shattered all reserve, kissed him firmly on the lips. They did not come up for air for quite some time and when they did it was Pino, not Bertie, who talked.

"*Ascoltami*, listen to me, Bertie." He had never said his name before. He would never call him Padre again. Then turning Bertie on his stomach and pressing the full weight of his body on him, he whispered in his ear, "It is time for both of us to grow up."

49

They left the monastery of the Minerva under a slate gray sky to watch the final destruction of San Redempto, their home for more decades than either of them cared to remember. For Avertanus it was a passing which had to be witnessed so that all of the many pieces of these past days could come to completion. There was no nostalgia at all in his desire to be present that day. For Brocard however the emotions were much more confused. Try as he might, the events of the past weeks and days made no sense to him at all. Nor was completion that easy. Kindly monks like Pius and Cuthbert lay dead in their graves. Simple souls like Ephraim and Antonio, whose bodies had been discovered in the demolition, and an unformed one like Thius, dead as well. Was there any reason God had to take them? Now Manolo, whom he never liked, that he could accept as part of God's wisdom. And Emmanuele. It was all so confusing.

The Dominicans with whom they were lodged had kindly offered to accept the two of them into community should they want to transfer their vows. In anticipation of a positive decision, they had lent them white tunics so that they wouldn't stand out by wearing the habits of a suppressed order. They both wore them that day, but felt somewhat strange, as if they were betraying the order and the house which, despite its faults, had been its mother. Still, Rome was a gossipy small town and this did make life easier.

There was a funereal stillness in the air which made it hard to breathe. The newspapers had called it a smog alert, but Avertanus knew it for what it was. No real air at all but rather the pestilence of Hades preparing to meet the ruins of San Redempto. Brocard only knew that he was having difficulty breathing but made no suggestion that they take a bus. A pilgrimage had to be made on foot and, in a perverse way, a pilgrimage this was.

From the Minerva, they took the road into the Pantheon where Avertanus had them pause. The temple to all the gods had been protected by all the gods and stood as structurally sound today as it had in the early second century when it was raised. As he bowed his head and silently prayed, Brocard offered a prayer that this whole excursion wasn't going to turn into a Cook's tour. He didn't need any more lectures. Or theories.

But theories were all that Avertanus had to give that day, and as they made their way through the Piazza Navone and along the Via Coronari he would not be stopped. Being used to the demands of community, the droning on of those one wished were not around, he said nothing. As Avertanus's tale unwound, he actually found that in a curious way, it had some merit.

"Recall if you will the number of paintings which were removed from the ambulatory wall, the canvases that put this whole series of events in motion." He was a good teacher, Avertanus, knowing how to frame his thoughts and ask questions that teased answers from a lively mind. "How many were there?" he asked Brocard.

"Why six. What does that signify?"

"Nothing in itself but I was suspicious enough that first day to absent myself from the community's investigation. Now tell me now how many dead bodies piled up immediately following this."

Brocard mumbled the litany under his breath. "Six."

"Precisely." Avertanus was clearly pleased with himself and would not be stopped. "Now how many days has it been from the robbery of the paintings of the martyrs to the suppression of the monastery."

This was harder for Brocard to figure out, as weeks had conflated into days for him and days into hours. Still, realizing the pattern that Avertanus was looking for he answered, "Six."

"That is it exactly, three sixes."

As they made their way across the Bridge of the Angels, Brocard confessed that he was not convinced. To him it was all some horrible coincidence. What happened to San Redempto and the dying little community which inhabited it was analogous to what happens to many terminally ill geriatrics. A system shuts down. When one thing goes, it all falls apart. Death comes not just to animals and plants but to groups and buildings, civilizations and great empires. What happened was a natural part of life.

Avertanus let him have his say. He was a respectful teacher, a patient one as well, but he was not going to step back from his theory. The excrement which covered the building, the inevisceration of the prime investigator Cuthbert, the satanic sacrifice of the prior, all this was proof of the presence of Beelzebub himself, the Prince of Darkness.

A crowd had gathered around the police cordon. Because of the threat of imminent collapse—San Redempto was that structurally unsound—this was the fastest the city of Rome had ever moved on taking down a building. An event in itself. As the first wrecking ball hit the outside wall, Avertanus prayed to God that the curse they lived through had been broken. But Brocard, having long since seen Otger's hand in all this, realized that as six members of the original community remained, and as Otger was evil incarnate, the cycle of evil could, and very well would, begin again.

50

$\mathcal{J}$s there anything more exciting than walking in stilettos? If there is," Zinka continued as they paraded through the Villa Borghese, "I simply can't imagine it."

The joy of being woman still overwhelmed her. Merely slipping on panties without having to wrap up some useless sausage was cause for celebration. So the uncommon pleasure of arching her feet, walking on toe and balancing her great yet dainty bulk on stilettos was nothing short of paradise. "Dante's Beatrice has nothing on me!" Then prancing out in front of Camille and hiking her dress up to indecent heights, she asked whether her lover thought that she was indeed the Beatific Vision. Beatific no, Camille longed to say but kept her thought to herself, a vision most definitely. Instead she smiled.

To say that the professoressa was in good spirits was an understatement. She was bursting with joy over all the good news. The painting of Saint Agatha itself would have been enough to secure her standing in the art world. To find that the remaining six Poussins had been brought to her lover was more than she could have hoped for. Now that she had found out that all of San Redempto's French School collection, recovered from a hearse, had been brought to the Vatican museum, she knew that her life's work was set out for her. She, Zinka Pavlic was destined to reconstruct the roots of French Classicism by studying the definitive collection of holdings. Art history was being rewritten, indeed the history of ideas. She was so happy she could pee in her panties.

Camille did wish that she could show a bit more restraint. This was, after all, the Villa Borghesse, not Pigalle. Still Zinka was a stunner and Camille was so inordinately fond of her breasts that she was willing to forgive her anything. Except, that is, a man. Zinka, free spirit that she was, had no knowledge of the deep water she was in until it was too late.

It had been nearly a week since they had come across Dionysius and his little family, accosted them might be more to the point. When they met this time it was like two middle-age suburban couples, passing the time of day. Until Zinka got started that is.

While the little boy went off to inspect dog turds—he was going to grow up strange make no doubt about it—Zinka pumped Dionysius for all the dirt. She had heard that San Redempto had succumbed to the wrecking ball. About time. She wanted to know what he was doing and was delighted to hear that he had taken a position at the Vatican library. She was sure she would see him in the stacks. She wanted to know about dear little Brocard, of course, and was glad to hear that he had found temporary housing with the Dominicans at the Minerva. She often went there to pray. Then she wanted information on all the corpses in the inner garden, the other one that hurtled off the roof, and the unidentified body revealed in the search of the vault at San Lorenzo. It was all so exciting. That was the word that did it, of course. A woman with her dress pulled up to her crotch using the word *exciting* was enough to engorge him for hours. So up he went. Zinka was so amused that she grabbed it on the spot—she never let a pair of trousers get in her way—and smiling at the others declared, "There's enough here for everyone, ladies, don't be greedy!" Well, silence descended upon them all. Were Dionysius half the man he was, he would have shrunk back to nothing. But that, being Dionysius, was not possible.

Camille could take no more. Rising with great dignity she went over to Dionysius's nameless woman and apologized. Turning to the affronting man she sneered, "And you." Then taking control of the situation, because if she didn't no one ever would, she said quite firmly, "Zinka darling, it is time for us to go." Releasing him, Zinka rose and followed.

They said nothing to each other as they walked. Zinka still could not get why her little Camille was so upset but as the sun set and they approached the Pincio Hill, she began to understand. This was one of their spots, the ledge overlooking the Piazza del Popolo with the dome of St. Peter's looming in the distance. One of the places they often went to at sunset, as did so many lovers, to watch the lights come on over Rome and thank all the gods above for having found each other. Zinka would never have wanted to hurt her and had to tell her so. Nothing as silly as a man would ever get between them. But nothing ever had to be said. As Camille leaned towards her and Zinka folded her into her breasts, they both knew that there was nothing that could get between them. Ever.

Dionysius and his woman didn't talk either, except to call for their boy, who picked something hard out of the grass, stuck it in his pocket, and scampered along behind them. Shortly after they got back to the apartment, she was slicing an eggplant when he came over to her to explain. The scent of her, her beautiful smooth skin so aroused him that there was nothing else to do but go to bed. Food could wait. When he felt the warmth of her tighten around him and heard her groan softly, he knew that he was home.

51

At midnight on the six-month anniversary of the suppression, Avertanus wrapped his cloak around him and with cowl pulled over his head made his way through the streets of Rome to the site where San Redempto had once stood. Except for the hangman's moon that hung low in the sky there was nothing of a sinister quality about the night. It was after all May, azaleas had been set out in large jardinieres, people were beginning to rid themselves of winter's pallor and all the fountains which he passed on his way sung of life itself. Still, he could not rid himself of certain fears which only this visit could set to rest.

Being a victim of habit he took his usual route, crossing the Tiber at the Bridge of the Angels. He was surprised to see swallows circling Hadrian's tomb by the thousands then swooping low over the ghost of the monastery in strict formation. Usually they only flew like this at dusk, devouring swarms of gnats along the way. But this nocturnal fly-by was far too vague. The sign that all was finally well would be impossible to miss.

The last he had heard, an effort was being made to save the chapel. But like every other part of the complex it proved to be so structurally unsound that it too had to be leveled. Nothing of the San Redempto he knew remained but much of the substructure which he expected surfaced and, in an irony of fate, it was that pre-Christian strata which was to guarantee the monastery some small place in history. To its credit, it had preserved intact Roman ruins which, had they been exposed, would have suffered the ravages of tourists and pollution. As archeologists began to work the area, they were amazed at the quality of the dig and the extent of material which had been preserved.

It seemed they had their own Mithric temple under San Redempto and it did not surprise Avertanus at all that it was situated under the old stage, or dungeon as the monks used to call it. Not far beneath the foundation of the monastery they located the staircase leading down to it, for Mithra was always worshiped underground where the blood of the bull could seep deep into the earth. One of the confusions which the archeologists could not yet resolve was that there seemed to be a Christian church in the same location at the same time. The two were in some way attached, which made no sense to anyone except Father Avertanus who saw in this clear proof of his own findings.

More remarkable still was what was being uncovered in the garden. After all the bodies were disinterred and the blood oranges uprooted, the serious work of digging began. It was not a blind dig, but one which was based on decades of serious research at the Sapientia. This was the reason why the city offered to help the Vatican in the radical suppression. All scholarly research indicated that this was indeed the site of the lost Circus of Nero, which had once stood outside the walls of the present Vatican.

The excitement of the archeological community and indeed all of Rome mounted with each small discovery. Nero's marble lintels, the father of perversity's fluted columns were reported in the press as if unique, substantially different from the imperial debris which threatened to bury modern Rome. As the millennium wound down it was Nero, fiddling away, whom Romans obsessed over. The site of his mindless, crowd-pleasing games and gratuitous torture became the empty heart of Rome. And threatened to become the latest tourist trap. None of this escaped Avertanus as he stood in silence waiting for his sign.

It was then that the young man appeared, moving in the night like a great cat waiting to pounce. He was the man who had unwittingly consecrated the rites in the Campo di Fiori that Avertanus had used to bring down the forces of change. Somehow he looked younger and more radiant, as if touched by God, and as he unzipped his trousers Avertanus moved towards him. As he started to piss he caught the magus's eye and did not drop it. The arc of yellow burst into the sky with the force of an explosion, the release of energy which would work its magic. Some tourists who were passing by shook their heads in disgust, but with the colors of pure light refracted in its arc, Avertanus knew otherwise. He pulled the cowl back from his face and he too looked younger than his years. As the moon bathed both of them in light he knew that he had his sign. For now at least, the evil was washed clean.

Then he scanned the empty site one last time and as he did, it seemed that San Redempto rose again. A glorified body filled with light and air, grace and goodness. He heard the sound of monks singing in choir, intent on prayer and pleased to be alive. He felt them walk by him with their great white capes billowing in the wind. He tasted the sweetness of their garden and the purity of their water. He saw that they indeed did love one another. Confirmed in his vocation, he knew with unswervable certainty that, even were it a dream, it was one worth dying for. *Consumatum est*, he said with faith renewed, It is finished.

Part Two

Mayhem

52

She closed her eyes and saw, more clearly than in any painting, the blissful figure of Agatha stretched out before her torturers as both condemnation and sacrifice. Collapsing back in her chair she took in every word of Avertanus's vivid description of the picture which had precipitated such chaos and the saint who had endured such suffering—sucking in every word with her mouth, allowing her body to drop limp before the image.

For his part, Avertanus gave thanks to a gracious God who delivered him out of captivity back to his homeland and, more wondrous still, into the presence of such a visionary as Sister Apollonia Van Barren. The move back to Holland, something he had resisted for so long, had proven to be painless and healing. So right and so easy, in fact, that it confirmed his suspicion that the correct path in life is the one which naturally opens out before us. The cosmic plan, God's will if you must, is clearer and easier to discern than most of us are willing to admit or able to grasp.

The frightening thought had not been abandoning Italian for Dutch or even abundant sun for endless rain, rather it was the very thought of returning to the monastery of Zenderan. He remembered it still as a vast and sinister pile of a building set down in the midst of fields which were far too gentle and a village which was far too small to accommodate it. Zenderan was the minor seminary of the order where his overwrought parents had deposited him when he was barely fifteen and from which he was dispatched to Brazil a mere year later. Coupled with this unhappy memory was the reality of what Zenderan had become: the final stop for terminally ill, burnt out, and ministerially superfluous monks. From what Avertanus had heard, it was a veritable roach motel—check in but have no hope of checking out.

Given all he had endured at San Redempto, Avertanus was not keen on the idea of continuing death and destruction. He decided that to the best of his ability he would, as Deuteronomy so wisely advises, choose life. So he settled into his freshly painted rooms, and doggedly determined to live. Being one of the few remaining scholars in the order-and a distinguished one at that-he had no problem getting the provincial procurator to purchase him a computer, complete with scanner, laser printer, and most wondrous of all, a speedy modem to go online. Zenderan might not be Rome, but cyberspace would free him up to connect to scholars globally. Not a bad trade-off.

To advance his desire to live in the present and not in the past, Avertanus relied heavily on some highly developed blocking techniques perfected in his years at San Redempto. He barely heard the sounds of his neighbor crying for more morphine and nimbly glided past Alzheimer patients drooling in their wheelchairs with the eager way of someone on a mission. Admittedly, the view from his window out onto the cemetery was disconcerting, until, that is, he began to focus on the manicured rows of tulips which linked the graves together. However, it was some time before the rains subsided enough for him to appreciate the hauntingly beautiful Convent of the Holy Sepulchre in the distance. When he did, it became his Klingsor's Castle, and the nuns he had yet to meet, its flower maidens and Sister Apollonia, about whom rumors swirled, his Holy Grail.

Although strictly cloistered, the nuns of the Holy Sepulchre readily invited a spiritual giant such as Father Avertanus Deblaer, Emeritus Professor of the Gregorian university in Rome, into their cloiser. However once there, even given his prodigious skills at blocking reality, he was forced to admit that flower maidens they were not. Clean and soft-spoken without doubt, but no way could so many wrinkles and widows' humps be seen as beguiling. Yet the mystery of the hermitage built within the cloister garden and the greater mystery still of the woman who had vowed herself to live in isolation within it, was more than enough to keep his interest alive.

The Van Barren girl had always been a bit strange. By rural Dutch standards, she was too beautiful and rich for her own good, too solitary and perverse, if truth be known, for any man in his right mind to deal with. Her father and brothers had long since despaired of what to do with her. It was therefore a blessing that she found religion, and a greater blessing still that she longed to lock herself away from the world as a bride of Christ. And the family was prepared to make any sacrifice to get her out of the way.

The first few years with the sisters of the Holy Sepulchre were blissfully unpleasant for her. After her novitiate, she took the name Apollonia, after the early Christian martyr who dry socketed into death after having all her teeth brutally extracted. How she longed to humiliate herself before the Lord and cleanse her willful self of all pretensions. Then one day, as fate would have it, she had enough. The wise old religious surrounding her became vicious crones; their communal praise cacophonous babble. A meeting was arranged between her anxious family and the disconcerted prioress, who, if truth be known, had seen the young Sister Apollonia as their financial salvation.

The plan they devised, although rather unconventional, addressed everyone's needs. As it was obvious Sister Apollonia was being called to distance herself from the community, a deeper solitude, a hermitage would be built for her at the edge of the garden, a cloister within the cloister. Although simple, it would be equipped with those basic comforts which an ascetic of her breeding would expect. A library, central heating, and a microwave, of course, for the good sister to heat up the meals which would be discreetly left at her door.

It was a small but momentous step from speaking with the nuns in the convent to becoming the private spiritual director of Sister Apollonia Van Barren. Being a great spiritual soul, the prioress readily conceded that Apollonia needed a similarly great and spiritual soul to guide the surging of her spirit. And so it was that Avertanus found himself describing in lurid detail the painting of Saint Agatha's breast to the delight and edification of the young ascetic sister of the Holy Sepulchre in her cozy little hermitage.

How fortunate he was to be able to see spirituality in action, to witness in his own life what he had only read about in dusty tomes. His pulse raced to know he was in the presence of someone who could show him truly what it was to find peace, contentment, and joy in suffering.

53

The next day Avertanus was looking forward to sending his first E-mail to Brocard in America when he happened to look out his window and see the one person whose very existence he had successfully blocked for nearly a year. Father Otger Aarnack, casually walking over the graves in the cemetery, was having an animated conversation with the prior, who from all appearances seemed to be taking great pride in the number of monks he had planted in his time in office. For someone who was purported to be evil incarnate, were Brocard to be believed, Avertanus could not help but note how fit Otger looked. The picture of health in fact. Nevertheless the very sight of him triggered waves of negative thoughts, painful memories which he was loathe to dredge up. Otger, it seemed, had no such qualms. Avertanus's heart sunk as he saw the prior pointing out his room to Otger. There was nothing to be done about it. A few minutes later Otger was standing at his door, nodding, grinning, and muttering *dag* in that convivial Dutch way.

"Such a long time," he said, oozing his way through the door into the room, "such a very long time, my brother."

"Moving from Rome has been all consuming." Avertanus grasped for a better reason. "To be honest, I wanted to distance myself from the San Redempto debacle."

"Yes," Otger replied in the most distant of voices, straining it seemed, to remember. "Nasty business that."

"Well, I am here to train the next generation. Did you hear the order has finally accepted a novice, and of all things, they plan to lodge him in this *casa della morte*?"

It had been so many years since anyone sane had applied to enter the order that the formation system had long since been abandoned. Who could this new recruit be? And, more to the point, what could have driven him to their door?

"He's a disaffected lawyer, a minor player on the world court tribunal from the Hague. Well educated, dreadfully idealistic, and loaded. Sounds like fresh blood to me."

Avertanus let the last line go. Despite his unremitting cynicism, he found it hard to believe that Otger had truly set in motion the evil which consumed San Redempto.

"Perhaps, this young man . . . what is his name?"

"Arne Wijmann—and he is far from young."

"Arne, then. Is it not possible he has a real vocation, a call from God?"

Otger fleetingly examined several of Avertanus's personal items, the photo of his long-dead parents, the *flagellum* he whipped himself with in novitiate intertwined with a blackened miraculous metal, and a framed blessing from some dead pontiff. Then he situated himself in the only comfortable chair in the room, leaving Avertanus awkwardly standing.

"My dear brother. The 'call,' as you so quaintly refer to it, can rarely be blamed on God. Even you can't believe such pious drivel."

"I choose to believe still that God has some part in it."

"A limited role at best." It was Otger's smile which was so off-putting. So inviting, welcoming even. Sweetening the most bitter of comments. "Who can honestly say what drew them to religious life? Domineering mothers, family expectations—Jan is going to be our little priest, aren't you, Jan? The grinding poverty the Irish faced? Sexual fears, the very fear of the world? Maybe even the fear of a wrathful God?"

Looking out the window down at the graves of hundreds of men who had given their lives to the order and the Church, Avertanus, normally placid if not disconnected, felt the faint rumble of anger. Where, he thought, did love and commitment come in?

"And the idea of service to others, or sacrifice to bring the message of love into the world? To live and to speak as Jesus did?"

"What a child you are. What a sadly disillusioned child you are, my brother."

Otger had the answer he wanted, which, after all was the only reason he wasted time on this visit. Even were Avertanus to be confronted by the truth, the hard facts of what Otger had done and was still capable of doing, he would not believe it. A warped sense of goodness had so lightened his soul that true blackness had no way of entering.

As Otger closed the door behind him, Avertanus wondered how two good men, schooled in Christian spirituality and husbanded in the ways of the religion, could have turned out so different. For the briefest of moments he entertained the thought that clear-thinking and rigorously logical Otger might have even lost his faith. But he dismissed it quickly—such diabolic wanderings bordered too much on that judgment of soul which was God's alone. He had another more concrete and infinitely more festive task at hand.

After years of burying himself in archives, of crawling through archeological digs and enduring countless scholarly symposia, Avertanus was convinced that the true *disciplina arcana* (the hidden knowledge which underpinned the human endeavor and tied all peoples together) was the World Wide Web. True, he still didn't know what on earth it was nor how to truly access it, but that too was part of its allure.

He did, however, know how to hook up to his local host,—the prior had seen to that—and how to call up the E-mail function. Ever so carefully, because he knew that computers broached no error, Avertanus Deblaer of the Pontifical Gregorian University typed in the address for his old friend, now transformed into bcurtis-@compuserve.com and, without skipping a heartbeat, leaped bravely onto the superhighway.

> *Dear Brocard,*
>
> *It seems so strange not to be able to nod at you in choir or pass you in the hall. It seems stranger still to think that there is no more choir or for that matter, any standing halls. Poor San Redempto! Still, I am making my best of the move back to my native soil, as I trust you are. My only real apprehension came just now when Father Otger paid me a mercifully brief visit. He is still as cynical as ever but I am afraid I cannot enter fully into your suspicion that he is evil incarnate. A victim of the laxity so sadly*

rife within the Church. Do write soon so I know these words got through.

Your brother in Christ.

With that the new, up-to-date, and modern Avertanus moved his cursor to Send, firmly clicked his mouse, and felt uncommonly empowered. Finally, he was connected.

54

So long as he stayed inside his tower, all was well, but the instant he ventured outside, even to the public rooms of the rectory or into the adjacent church, he felt as if he were under attack. Brocard knew quite well that things were objectively not as bad as he felt them to be. Many priests would kill for an assignment at Our Lady of Perpetual Help in Bryn Mawr, the most upscale parish on Philadelphia's Main Line. As money flowed so freely there, order reigned. The music at liturgies, for example, while a bit modern for his taste, was professionally handled, as were an endless array of parish programs, with mysterious anachronism from RCIC to CCD. And being rich, there were no sad-faced old ladies ringing the door of OLPH at all times of the day or night needing to talk. In Bryn Mawr, they all had either their own psychotherapists or personal trainers. Usually both.

It was just that Brocard was in delicate shape. Not only had the implosion of San Redempto taken its toll on him, but the lack of any real resolution had quite simply worn him down. Stories were, after all, meant to have happy endings; villains meant to suffer and good triumph. Neither of which, of course, had happened. Coupled with this was the culture shock of returning to America, a society and a church with which he felt sadly out of step. He conceded that his sister was right to insist that he return "home," nearer his only living relatives, rather than bounce around alien monasteries, never really belonging. Still, his ways had been so set over a lifetime abroad, all his edges so rubbed smooth, that he began to see himself as some quaint remnant of a world long since passed rather than the model of religion which for so long, in his delusion, he had thought himself to be. This was made painfully clear on his first excursion into Amazonia, as he had privately come to refer to this most woman-dominated and most unfeminine of towns. In retrospect, he knew he should not have worn his religious habit. However, for him it was the most natural thing to put on: a sign of his commitment to God, his vowed life, his marginalized position in society, as well as his lingering affection for San Redempto, despite all the suffering and grief it had caused him.

It was the first morning after he had arrived. He had risen early, out of habit really rather than any sense of excitement, and gone down to have breakfast with Monsignor Duhmbelle, the pastor. Besides being cursed with the most unfortunate of names—pronounced, he was told, with the accent on the last syllable—the good monsignor had a bulbous, mishapened skull which he unsuccessfully attempted to cover by torturing long strands of hair upwards from his earline and plastering them in place.

The contrast between the two of them could not have been more extreme. Duhmbelle, all done out in tartan green for a day of golf, was hurriedly placing his breakfast dishes in the sink for the housekeeper to deal with when Brocard, seeming to be composure itself in monastic brown, quietly made his way to the table.

"Oh, well, Father Brocard, the sexton will have everything set up for you for mass." He was not one to waste time on small talk, Monsignor Duhmbelle, all such social skills well beyond his ability. "Mrs. O'Connor will be in at nine. She only works half days Tuesdays but will make you a plate to microwave tonight if you want. Just let her know."

Brocard was so taken aback by the spectacle of a cleric parading out his spindly legs that he could not think quickly enough to ask even one of the many practical questions which he needed to have answered. Could he have a house key? Where was the nearest pharmacy or were there, perhaps, some aspirins in the rectory? Could he use the old desk in the spare room as a computer table or would he have to buy his own? It was clear to Brocard that the pastor had been forced to take him in by the bishop, that his presence was far from a welcome one. Still he was resolved to make the best of it.

"Is there coffee by any chance?"

Distressed at being so put out, Duhmbelle dropped his golf clubs, went over to the corner of the counter nearest the stove, and pushed it in to reveal a lazy Susan filled with jars of instant coffees and gaudy boxes of tea bags. Brocard, ever the naive, was quite amused at the ingenious design of the counters; Duhmbelle couldn't wait to get out.

Left alone in the kitchen, sipping his coffee and nibbling on Saltines—the only food he could find, being afraid of venturing too deeply into larders and pushing revolving counter fronts—Brocard found himself longing for the bowls of blood oranges he had become so accustomed to from his years in Rome and, strangely, even missing the company of community, dysfunctional as it surely had been.

As he sallied forth from the church after having said mass a couple of days later, all he knew about the physical plan of Bryn Mawr was that if he turned left he would end up on the main drag, as his sister had referred to it when she dropped him off. To his right stood a narrow bridge over railroad tracks to the terra incognita of Bryn Mawr College itself. A challenge which, silly man that he often was, he felt up to.

It was one of those brisk, clear days which the northeast of the United States does so well. The light a bit too brash, the air scrubbed too clean for someone used to inhaling the rich, thick soup of Rome. The wind too seemed different. In Rome, if it is found at all, it lumbers down from the mountains in great waves. Here it gusted capriciously, teasing him on his way, occasionally billowing his tunic and furling out his scapular into a banner.

Although it was a mere two weeks before, try as he might Brocard could not remember anything more about that walk. He must have had some response to the great Dickensian pile of Baldwin School, a place where rich children are deposited by their busy parents in much the same way poor children were warehoused by their indigent parents at monasteries in the past. The way cars actually stopped for pedestrians at crosswalks must have perplexed him, and the sheer preponderance of young women could not have escaped his notice. All he really remembered was what they said.

He was somewhere on the manicured campus of Bryn Mawr College, reading the small print on a plaque pinned to a massive ash tree, when he heard the first of several devastating comments.

"Jesus, look at that, will you? Someone is still wearing dresses after all."

He turned to see the backs of two young women, heard them laughing as they blended into a swarm of undergraduates determinedly making their way to class. Jeans, slacks, trousers everywhere. But not a dress to be seen.

"The new curate over at Perpetual Help," he heard one say.

"Mother Duhmbelle," her friend blurted out. And so he came to be known. Father Brocard Curtis, a man of gentle dignity, or so he had always thought, a man versed in the classics, steeped in Latin and Greek and fluent in Italian, turned into a clown for coeds.

And so it was that despite his love of nature and the beauty of the town, he retreated more and more to his room, a tower on the top floor of the rectory at OLPH. He said mass daily for invariably the same faithful group, occasionally saw the pastor on his way out the door for golf, meetings, or heaven knew what, and microwaved the plates which Mrs. O'Connor prepared for him each day.

His one hope was the new computer which the order had purchased for him, realizing that without it he might be cut off not only from most of his brothers in Europe but also from the Church in Rome, which, they rightly feared, was rapidly fading off the radar for the American Catholic Church. Together with instructions on how to set it up was a list of E-mail addresses (the same Avertanus had received) of members of the order, together with the official Lady of Succour Web page, the Vatican site, and other important destinations, like documents of the Catholic Church.

It took him some time to figure out how to hook it all up, but finding time in a rectory was no problem. After several days he was able to get on-line. After all of the initial anxieties, all of the misplaced wires and dialogue boxes, he was amazed at how easy it was. Opening the mailbox he was assigned, bcurtis@compuserve.com, he was delighted to see that he had two letters. If they were even called letters. One from his old confrere Avertanus and a second from the ever-amusing Zinka Pavlic. Neither of whom cared how he dressed. Filled with hope, he prepared to reconnect himself with friends.

55

Carissimo Brocardus,

Oh how that name rolls off my tongue: Brocardus, it is my night and day. Well, no Camille is still my night (she is irrepressive and how I love her for it), but you still do creep into my daily thoughts. You and your masterful sleuthing! Well let me get you up to speed (as they say in your Hollywood) on our little Saint Agatha because I know you are dying to hear everything about her. The cleaning and restoration have gone slowly—she was awfully mucked up you know—but very well. She is a stunner! I had to fire several assistants along the way whose talents, although great, had little to do with conserving art. Just used them and spit them out, to the delight of all! Amazing how many people adore being used, isn't it? But back to the painting. I am working on Saint Agatha alone, not only because she was the first of all our tortured lovelies but also because working with the whole batch of paintings would be a daunting task. Even for a prodigious talent like moi. My plan is to develop this one first, build reputation as they say, and sell it for a bundle of course, then the other works will fall into place. Now, professoressa that I am, let me explain what this entails because I know you are a cretin in such matters. But such a cute little cretin that I could never hold it against you. Simply put, it goes like this: scholars make their careers on knowing all there is to know about one particular artist. They supposedly know every work, every dropping of their chosen artist and are reluctant to accept a new work into the accepted canon (often the list that they themselves have compiled). Poussin scholars have been a particularly beleaguered lot until recent years, which means *that, like any persecuted minority, they are almost paranoiac. A key player in this is a distinguished and/or dubious (depending on who you talk to) scholar who is chair of art history at Bryn Mawr, the little college down the block from you. Personally I get all sticky just thinking about the grand communal menstruation which happens each month. Women pick up on each other's rhythms, you know. Just imagine the lacrosse locker room! But back to matters at hand. Dr. Charles Mitchum, an old lech of an Oxford don from all reports, is the reigning Poussin authority and without him in my court it will be awfully hard for me to firmly establish Saint Agatha's reputation. To insert her into the next edition of his Catalogue Raisonee, to have her name counted among the elect, he must accept my research—it is after all impeccable, and devious as he can be, I am supremely confident that in me he has met his match. But in order for success to be assured, I need a little favor from my precious Brocardus. Oh how that name rolls off my fingers. Go to him, any excuse will do. I have it: a courtesy call based on the extensive and tragic connection your venerable order has had with the arts. Find out if he has anything in the works with Poussin and do drop my name, highly recommended of course, so he is aware of my existence. My only fear is that he lodges objections to the research in my upcoming article on Saint Agatha in* Burlington *magazine, the indispensable link to establishing the painting's reputation in the art world. So, my bald little sleuth, the saga continues and I need your help as much as ever. I know you won't fail your Zinka. I for my part am yours forever (to the extent randy little Camille allows, of course). Don't get too American on us over there. Then again, some chaps and a lasso might be a hoot!*

Crazy Zinka had given purpose to his life, put a rudder on his rump, as she might say, and sailed him off into a glorious future. Or at least one in which he felt he was needed. Before hearing from Zinka, he had pretty much canceled out any thought of ever going onto the campus of Bryn Mawr again. Now, drawn back into her wonderful web of conspiracy, he could hardly wait. Of course he would leave off his monastic habit this time. Or would he? No, he thought determinedly, that was who he was and those women were just going to have to deal with it. Zinka, the ultimate outcast although she would never even remotely accept such typing, had worked her magic again. In your face, girls, he thought. And smiled broadly at his audacity.

After the excitement of Zinka's missive, poor old Avertanus's was dull indeed. Not to accept Otger as evil, despite the fact that Brocard had told him everything, was irksome at best. But what was Brocard to make of his observation about "the laxity so rife within the Church?" Was sweet, ditsy Avertanus turning Jansenist in his dotage? In his grief over the demise of San Redempto, could he honestly have forgotten the laxity which brought it down? Perhaps for the first time in his life, Brocard was beginning to look critically at things, to question the world around him, and in so doing to grow up.

And yet Brocard could summon up enough good memories and even a few warm feelings about the years he spent in Rome with Avertanus to be able to shoot off a brief response. If only to let his old friend know that the computer had indeed worked.

> *My dear Avertanus,*
> *Yes indeed your kind thoughts did get through. I too miss praying in choir and those many casual moments which bound us together as community and brothers. We were a sorry lot at San Redempto. But there were some good people. Do you remember the way Father Pius sneezed on cue with every Paternoster? My life here is very different, but more of that later. It's late in this part of the world and you know how I need my sleep. I will write soon.*
>
> > *Your brother in Christ, Brocard*

But try as he might Brocard was not able to sleep. There was simply too much on his mind: Zinka, new forms of communication, the harpies on campus. Impossible to sleep.

56

There was nothing to get a handle on. No specific thought worried him but rather an accumulation of doubts and anxieties. So he fluffed up his pillow, tried lying on his left side again, and then, when that didn't work, his right. In desperation he even lay flat on his back gazing heavenwards, the royal sleeping position which was far too commanding and assertive for little Brocard to seriously consider adopting. Even night itself did not seem to want to rest. A gibbous moon tenaciously refused to hide behind a cloud for even a moment and as it burned on, over and over he turned with increased fury, until the very thought of sleep was out of the question. Sometime after midnight, he jumped out of bed and walked over to the window to confront the night on its own relentless terms. Thinking he could stare down the moon, his mind raced with thoughts of the few friends he had, strange as they might be, and how deeply he missed them. Silly Zinka and intense little Camille, overly pious Avertanus, even profligate Dionysius with his throbbing privates—especially that, he blushed to think. And Rome. The outrageous transvestites—yes he could never keep his eyes off them—in the Borghese, the cars parked on the Janiculum, windows smoked with passion, ludicrously bouncing up and down, lurching from side to side.

It was at that moment that he realized he wasn't isolated, that there was a way out of the grave he seemed to have dug for himself. The Internet. The excitement of hearing from friends had been wonderful, but how more wonderous still would it be to be connected to someone new, someone who might open up different, new, exciting horizons. He couldn't move fast enough. As he turned on the computer, he reached for the package which the procurator had so thoughtfully sent on. Most helpful was the copy of *The Internet for Dummies*, which could guide him step by step into this brave new world. Less compelling were the sites suggested by the order, especially, given the exuberance of this moment, destinations like the official documents of the Catholic Church. No, he could not waste this moon, this surge of new life on a perusal of *Humanae Vitae* or even, *pace* the Blessed Virgin Mary, *Redemptoris Mater*. This night offered greater, more mysterious promise.

He was fascinated by how easy it was to change his screen name—he could chose five if he wanted so that his identity was disguised. A true Ballo in Maschera, masked ball as they would say Stateside, in which he could wander anonymously at will. Unfortunately his first choices, from Riccardo to Zorro were already snatched. He was, however, able to snatch up Scatface, for reasons that were beyond him. Escatology, the theology of the end time, was the improbable reference Brocard made for his tag. Scatface summed up, for him alone, that radiant smile of the elect at the Final Rapture. (As usual, his Roman training did not prepare him well for the real world, and over time Brocard's chatrooms and E-mail were to be filled with some of the most amazing and salacious requests.)

The next step was to select one of the several search engines offered. Not knowing one from another he simply clicked on the first one, Excite as he remembered, and when confronted with the blank box and pulsating cursor, looked over his shoulder like a bad little boy. Smiling blankly at the screen, he typed in the word: sex. After a moment of low-decibal rumblings, he was told that there were 9,472 sites available, the names of the first twenty given. Brocard scrolled down the list—he was getting the feel of this—and clicked on Cindy's Hot Lips. Within a minute there she was, not as well endowed as his friend Zinka, but every bit as bold. Cindy, it seemed had some videos for sale or rent. They could be downloaded—he checked out the term—for a "reasonable monthly fee."

Being a rather compulsive type Brocard was willing to work through all 9,472 sites. But as the time sped away and dawn approached, he realized that a more specific search might serve him better. In truth, he was getting rather inured to the charms of buxomy women with open orifices. Feeling free to say or do whatever he wanted, he typed in three search words together that summed up what he really, deeply wanted to experience: sex male Italian. Remarkably, this limited search turned up nearly eighty names. But after scrolling through the first two screens he noticed that one was actually in Italian. So it was that he logged on to ItalStud and opened up a relationship which was not to stop until fun had been had by all and evil brought to justice.

57

Things hadn't worked out exactly as he had planned, but when, after all, do they? As Bertie's mum back in Blackpool always put it, "Plan, plan, plan, luv—then expect sommit else." Still, against all odds, Pino and Bertie were making a go of it; had, in fact, made a pretty comfortable life for themselves in the Abruzzi mountains high above Rome. The village of Sant'Elmo Montanino was little more than a cluster of stone cottages tucked away in a rugged pass an hour or so outside of Ascoli. They had been able to buy a substantial aerie of three rooms with electricity and sporadically running water from the money they got from the booty pilfered from San Redempto. However, the key to their financial success was the fiber optics telephone line which they were able to get installed because of the house's proximity to the post office and the good graces of one of Pino's johns. Without that link to the outside world it is safe to say their relationship would have come and gone as quickly as a hundred lira hand job. Here is how it happened.

For the first couple of months after the collapse of San Redempto they were so preoccupied with the present reality of setting up a life together, from finding digs to discovering each other's habits, that they barely had time to consider the future. It was only when the fall rains came and the money began to run low that the larger issues of who they were and how they were to survive came into focus. As for the first question, it became patently clear that they were both endlessly fascinated by and deeply in love with Pino. Not that Bertie didn't think of himself a bit, it is just that he willingly became slave. That is the way it was and would always be. Nor is this to say that

Pino had no real feelings for Bertie. He loved him in a distant sort of way but his true love, his driving passion, was for himself. Everything, positively everything about himself interested him intensely. He was the sort of person who stared at his shit every morning to admire its color and form, who caressed his face lovingly and often, and who thought of his sweaty underwear and socks as precious, salable commodities. Which, indeed they were.

Although Pino needed and even enjoyed Bertie worshiping him, he began to be troubled by the clear fact that in giving himself exclusively to one person, so many other men and women, boys and girls were deprived of satisfaction. This thought burned in him as strongly as any call to ministry; as in any true vocation it would not let him rest until he answered it. Quite literally, it drove him back onto the streets.

But times had changed. Bertie had convinced him that he had to encourage more visual sex, perversely creative head trips, because of the exponential increase not only of AIDS but all those nasty venereal rots, from genital warts to unmentionable fungi. He also convinced him that it was time to hook bigger fish. God knew he was worth it. So, changing his wardrobe from leather jacket to shirt and tie, Pino moved his business out of the raunchy Piazza della Republica into the bar of the Hassler. That did the trick.

As long as he kept from smiling, something which was hard to do given some of the requests that were made him, Pino was devastatingly handsome. Were he to get into porno flicks—his fondest dream—he would have to have massive dental reconstruction. For the time being, a placid, immobile face did just fine. He stared down as a well-coifed matron handled his perfectly shaved balls like the child she never had looked on impassively as a CEO beat off with one of his feet in his mouth. And throughout it all he discovered the delightful truth that the richer and more powerful the client, the less demanding and passive they were likely to be. A thousand percent profit for far less work. Just the way he liked it. Because most men of a certain social echelon were impotent—that stress and those pills sure do take their toll—he never had to worry about them wanting to penetrate him. Well, actually, they always did but never could, which was a major part of their trip. Some women came prepared with dildos they liked to slide into him; but these were invariably antiseptic and so lathered down with oils that he had to keep from yawning while they worked them in him.

Usually he spent Wednesday to Friday in Rome, finding that for business types—most of whom had the family role to play on weekends—this was the time of greatest need. This suited Bertie fine. He was able to scrub their little house clean, go into Ascoli for the bulk of the groceries, do the laundry and other chores while Pino was away. That way, for four solid days he could worship him without any annoying distractions.

After only one month of this new, improved form of hustling, Pino struck gold in the person of Signor Vittorio Ambucelli. By day he was Ambucelli Communicatione Inc., one of the more advanced players in the European telecommunications market; by night he was an absolute pig who liked nothing better than to clean up after Pino. Details need not distract us here. Suffice it to say that Vito was fascinated by every substance which came forth from Pino's body, of which there was a surprisingly large amount.

Before long, every hour Pino spent in Rome was Vito's and he paid handsomely for it. Vito was able to spend many hours each day and at least one full night with Pino. He watched as Pino devoured tray after tray from room service and placed his ear to Pino's stomach to listen to the food making its delightful passage within him. However, not being one to be imprisoned in a suite at the Hassler for days on end, Pino was equipped with a portable telephone so that he could report on all his movements, from shopping to bowel. It seemed an equitable enough solution, and from Pino's perspective, a positively just and happy one. Nevertheless, Vito wanted more. More time, more ways of viewing and experiencing Pino, always more. From this primitive obsession, a truly modern plan was devised. One which was to alter both Pino's and Bertie's life forever.

Simply put, Vito wanted a way to be able to log onto Pino twenty-four hours a day, seven days a week. If Pino were sleeping Vito wanted to know if he was naked, restless, with or without an erection; if waking, was he sweating or spitting, taking food in or pushing waste out. It was all of interest, so what more logical thing to do than openly telecommunicate with his favorite object. Technically, it was easy enough to set up. Get Pino a decent computer with fast modem and good resolution camcorder; make sure his house was hooked up to the new telephone line which was being run through that area of the Abruzzi (easy for a man with his contacts); and log on. Even the existence of sniveling little Bertie worked out well for Vito. Years as a monk had trained him not only to be submissive to the demands of others but also terribly reliable. It was Bertie who could be counted on to keep the Pino Log, a list of what he ate, how often he urinated, how he wanted to be worshiped, or who he wanted to abuse. It was Bertie too who could service Pino, licking and cleaning him, on those days when Vito wasn't around to do it himself. What amazed Vito was that, after the briefest of time, he found himself looking forward to the digitized Pino every bit as much as the ostensibly real one. At first he missed the smells, one of Pino's stronger points, but that was soon resolved by daily deliveries of soiled clothes. No, the possibility to enter into another's mind, invade his life totally, violate his most private moments was deliciously exciting. In no time, businessman that he was, he saw opportunity not only to recoup all of the monies he had spent on Pino but also to use him for profit, another exciting prospect. It took only a few telephone calls and a few days for him to set up an interactive Web site for Pino, run directly from his cottage in the mountains. It was appropriately called ItalStud.com. And yes, it took Visa.

During those couple of days a week when Pino was away from the cottage the site would show still photos and accept requests for what the subscriber would like to see Pino doing or what they needed to know about him. Otherwise, he was on-line. As he needed to sleep alone and with a light on, the camera was placed in his bedroom broadly focused on his bed. If he got up in the middle of the night, he peed in a jar by the bed for all to see. Usually he would drink his own urine, not only because he was remarkably self-involved but also because an Abruzzi *strega*, purported to be ninety years old but sexy still, told him it was the secret of eternal life. During the day, which he spent naked, he dealt with requests and made plans for activities which people wanted to see during their respective prime times. For viewers in North America he scheduled his major activities to start around midnight (or around dawn his time, an easy thing to do for the son of a farmer). European viewers, of which there were many north of the Alps, tended to log on just after dinner. Perfect for Bertie, as there never seemed to be anything good on the telly.

So Bertie had his Pino, but so too did everyone on the World Wide Web. Thank God he wasn't a jealous person, because his lover was definitely being stretched thin. What concerned him somewhat were the numbers of requests from people to see Pino worshiped by a woman. Since Bertie's shoulders were always rather narrow, his skin smooth, and his hips a bit wide, a good wig and a pair of falsies worked well initially. Then Vito started sending up the occasional tart from Rome, even on one occasion a Brazilian hermaphrodite, so as to, as he put it, "maintain artistic integrity." For scenes involving pain, something Bertie really had no stomach for after the affair with Emmanuele, Pino could call on the help of one of the Seven Horsemen of the Apocalypse, the boys Otger had used on occasion for his scenes. Hustling was, after all, a small, close-knit community.

Not that there was anything overly sadistic about the ItalStud site. That, in fact, was its charm. A little spanking, a spritz of watersports—more titillating than anything else. But from its astounding popularity, it was all fully satsfying. For our friend Brocard, aka Scatface, it provided more intimacy and excitement than he could ever have hoped for. And, as more and more men and women subscribed to the site and the checks kept coming in from Vito, Bertie soon forgot any inconvenience this rather public twist had brought to their solitary life in the country. Before long, good wifey that he was, he was happy that his man had a paying job which allowed him to spend lots of time at home. And he couldn't wait to redecorate.

58

Camille rang her up as soon as she saw a response had come back. Despite the air of worldly modernity which she exuded, Zinka was a virgin to computers. The fact was the E-mail to Brocard had been her very first. She even had to use the computer at the Biblioteque Française because they could not afford to upgrade their old computer at home. Hopefully, the final sale of the paintings would change all that in time. For the time being, though, everything had to go through Camille's office, a slight inconvenience, with the benefit that the two of them could snatch a few moments together in the middle of the day.

However that was the last thing on Zinka's mind that day. She was so excited that contact had been made that, to Camille's dismay, she almost ran her over on the way to the computer. Not even a peck on the cheek, no less the usual squeeze and sigh.

"What do I press, click, oh, where do I click it, Camille!"

Gently placing her hand on top of Zinka's, Camille guided the mouse until the cursor came to rest on the name of the incoming mail. Then solemnly lowering her voice, she ordered her distracted lover to "double click, *bijou.*"

Zinka dislodged her hand from Camille's then squealed as Brocard's letter miraculously appeared, confident this new technology would help secure Saint Agatha's fate.

Dear Zinka,
    Your missive brought light into a very dark period in my life.
If anyone were to tell me that I would have experienced such

culture shock returning to my native country I never would have believed them. But there you have it, a native turned alien to his land. I have been made to feel strange and superfluous even at the church where I am in residence. It seems they need me to do sacraments, mainly the daily masses and a couple on weekends and the occasional funeral, otherwise the lay people seem to handle everything. The pastor contents himself with counting the money and playing golf. It is as if priests have become emasculated here, certainly there is no respect. I can't tell you the way I was abused when I walked onto the campus of Bryn Mawr College the first time. But, patienza as we say. Back to you. The challenge you set out for me is splendid and brings some direction back into a life which was sadly rudderless. How splendid to be a sleuth but how incompletely I did it. I now see the possibility of resolving what was so sadly left undone and have you, dear Zinka, to thank for the opportunity. (I just reread what I had written to see if it needed editing and realized what a pompous old priest I am. Everything I write sounds like a homily. So pat and so very rhetorical. Well, no chance of changing. I only hope you will know my sincerity even though the words might be inadequate and indeed misleading signs.) Back to our project. I telephoned Professor Mitchum at the art history department early this morning under the guise of being an aficionado of French Classicism. He was, of course, well aware of my order's disastrous six-hundred-year connection to the history of art. A sad but nevertheless compelling recommendation. Anyway, that very afternoon I donned my habit and girded my diminished strength to face the harpies of Bryn Mawr. Surprisingly I encountered none of the verbal hostility I had experienced on my first visit. It might have been because the undergraduates were all safely confined to class and I met only the occasional graduate student and faculty members on my rounds. Whatever the case, I was well received in the crammed rooms of the art history offices and library. You cannot imagine, dear Zinka, how low the ceilings are. Granted in Rome they are at times dauntingly high but what a sense of dignity one is afforded by volumes of useless space opening out above. My shock was intensified by the fact that the department is housed at the far end of a rather splendid building called the Thomas Library which fronts an equally splendid cloister. Although ersatz on every level,

182

it did so remind me of San Redempto, replete with a cistern in the middle like the one Brother Ephraim's body was stuffed into. Well, enough lingering on happier days.

Professor Mitchum's office is a sad little room overladen with books and cabinets and a desk filled with opened and presumably unanswered letters. From the look of the room one would have imagined him to be a distracted, unfocused soul but nothing could have been farther from the truth. He greeted me warmly, removed a pile of papers from a chair, invited me to sit and visit for a while. He seemed uncommonly warm and solicitous. He had heard about the demise of San Redempto and the rumors of some interesting art which had surfaced. I mentioned your name to him, waxing rhapsodically of your many talents. He regretted never having the pleasure of meeting you but carefully took down your name in the event your paths should cross, the art world being "incestuously small" as he put it. After some small talk about Rome I was able to secure some information which I believe might be of interest to you. First, Mitchum is indeed working on a new edition of the Poussin Catalogue Raisonee which is scheduled to come out at the same time as a major French Classicism exhibition at the Grand Palais in Paris in a couple of years. He is, as I presume you know, the principal organizer of the exhibition. What you may not know is that he is leaving for Paris in a few days to begin the initial work on the exhibition. Might you not meet him there? It seems he has an eye for women, an obsession, from what I could see by the way he drooled over the young women who were researching under his tutelage and servicing his academic needs. From my limited experience in these matters, it seems to me that he willingly places himself in a subservient role to them. Even though this may be an act, it might be one which someone of your un-doubtable strength and skill might well use to her advantage. If you know what I mean. So "Go to!" my dear Zinka, and keep me apprised of your activities.

Brocard

"Camille, my moist little melon, lock the door."

As exciting as this prospect sounded, Camille knew Zinka well enough to realize that a major favor was going to be asked. One which it would be impossible to deny.

"Don't you think," she said unraveling the ubiquitous silk scarf at her neck, "that we could steal away to Paris for a couple of weeks?"

"But, Zinka, I have responsibilities here, you know that. I can't just pick up and—"

Before she had a chance to finish Zinka pulled her to herself and buried her willing face in her breasts. Then, with her hands placed viselike around her lover's head she positioned it in front of her own and covered it in a series of very persuasive kisses.

"Well, yes, I guess I could." Suddenly, organizer that she was, she remembered her parent's offer of their small but well-situated apartment, were she ever to need a place to stay. "I will call Maman to see if they could stay in the country for a couple of weeks as they once volunteered. The apartment would be too small for all of us now that Papa is retired. But he loves nothing more than slaughtering rabbits . . . yes, it might work out."

"Perfect. It's done." Camille, thinking matters had been resolved rather than blown open into endless possibilities, simply wanted to cuddle. Realizing this, Zinka unbuttoned her blouse and allowed Camille to feed. In body, Zinka was all hers. As for the mind, that was another matter. It raced with thoughts of being back in Paris again, of the impending meeting with Mitchum, and, always, of advancing the claims of Saint Agatha.

There were two things in particular which she had to see to as soon as Camille unhooked herself. The first was to contact the general of the order of Our Lady of Divine Succor, whose interest in the paintings had never diminished, and see if he would underwrite the cost of developing the painting. In other words, paying for the trip to Paris and the various expenses that might come their way. The second thing she had to see to was hiring Dionysius to do some archival work for her at the Vatican library to fill in gaps in her research. Perhaps he might even be needed in Paris. Who knew, there might be a hole or two for him to fill. And God knew, he was the man to do it.

59

From all he had heard, communication breakthroughs were everywhere—except in his little corner of the Vatican. Granted, it was good
to be able to be put on hold by a real receptionist rather than an
automated message, but not to be making steps to have the library
put on-line or the catalogue computerized seemed less reactionary
than pig-headed. He remembered a conversation he had with one of
the head librarians after the American archbishop in charge of social
communications gave a workshop on the advantages, indeed the im-
perative, of using CD-ROMs. The librarian, Roman to the core, had
asked the energetic archbishop how long these CD-ROMs he was
proposing would last. Whatever the answer was, it was dwarfed by
the longevity of parchment. Goat skin round one; the digital revo-
lution nothing. Perhaps what galled Dionysius most of all was that he
himself could not jump on the superhighway. He didn't even have
his own E-mail—an embarrasment which cut deeply into his pride—
and although he had a responsible position at the Vatican library, he
was not even highly placed enough to be able to use their fax machine.
That was, quite simply, a perk which was well beyond his rank. However, his years in religious life in Rome schooled him well in how to
use restrictive systems. What he looked for was a menial with delu-
sions that grandeur might someday be his; a socially lame Vatican
supernumerary, a sycophant whose needs far exceeded Dionysius's
own but whose current position gave him access to necessary supplies
and services. The list was long but one name surfaced above others:
Padre Edmondo Ferugia, the quintessential Vatican rat. Maltese and
obsequious by nature, Padre Edmondo was a career bureaucrat who

had learned what to say and when to say it so as never, never to ruffle feathers. This was why Edmondo could always be counted on for getting the best and quickest papal blessings. More to the purpose, why he had his very own fax and, *mirabili dictu*, his very own E-mail. For the time being, he was making use of the fax; Dionysius was just waiting for the right moment, when he could supply the right favor or promise the right introduction, to step up to E-mail and the expansive world beyond.

Despite the restrictions he was under on all sides, Dionysius realized that he probably would not be able to function well or to be even remotely happy otherwise. His whole life had been one of negotiation and subterfuge and it was far too late for him to consider any serious change. The collapse of San Redempto had quite simply left a void in his life which only the labyrinth of the Vatican palace itself, all fourteen-hundred rooms, could begin to fill. There he could sulk and hide, suck up, or be bold as situations warranted. But coming in as an outsider to the system, there was much to learn and calculate before he could feel comfortably uneasy with it all. And live his duplicitous life.

The trade-off for use of Edmondo's fax was easy enough. A few times a week, Dionysius covered for Edmondo at the early morning mass for the Little Sisters of Loretto. Technically, of course, Dionysius was defrocked; but at five in the morning saying mass for a handful of old nuns who were cloistered behind a grill and simply delighted to hear a man's voice, who was to tell? It gave Edmondo the occasional day to go straight to the office and start early—he never considered the possibility of sleeping in, only functioning at his edgy best if sleep-deprived—and the good nuns a change of timbre. For Dionysius, who was after all a priest forever if that's what was needed, it was all one.

Just before going back to his woman the night before, Dionysius, at the main desk of the Vatican library, had received a handwritten note from Edmondo at his office in the requisitions for the Papal apartments, by means of the pneumatic tube which snaked its way through the palace. It read simply: "Have received a fax for you which can be picked up after you say mass for the sisters tomorrow morning." Favor for favor: the Vatican way.

That next morning Dionysius presented himself to the Swiss guard at Porta Santa Anna, the gate which gave direct access into Edmondo's sector and the servicing of the Papal apartments. No papers needed to be checked because Dionysius had made himself well known in the guards barracks on a few occasions. They were after all young, randy fellows who had to swear off sex during their limited service in Rome. Their needs had to be met from time to time, if only visually, and Dionysius had played that game flawlessly.

So in a flash he passed the guardpost and found himself in Edmondo's office. Although the room had no windows it was manically aglow with fluorescent light. By some bureaucratic legerdemain, Edmondo had secured more tubes than anyone else in a comparable space, a coup which filled him with childish glee at each turn of the switch.

"*Buon giorno.* Close the door, please." Edmondo was nothing if not discreet. Then, slowly opening a drawer, he removed an envelope and, as if it contained the final secret of Fatima, held Dionysius's eyes with his as he slid it along the top of the desk towards him.

Dionysius could not disguise his delight at hearing from Blessed Zinka of the Willing Ass, as he affectionately called her. Although he was annoyed that Edmondo could, and indeed did, read every fax that came through his machine, he felt confident that both the style and the content of her correspondence would be so alien to him as to be all but incomprehensible. To Dionysius, however, who was starved for exotic news from interesting people, every word was perfectly coherent and held out endless hope.

He found Zinka to be as lively in print as in person. Her excitement over that tormented picture of Saint Agatha was infectious and he could hardly wait to set to work on the task she set out for him. He knew he was up to it, knew how to access all the primary and secondary material, knew how to plod through footnotes and cross-reference texts. The prospect of being paid by his old order was perverse but gratifying. Part of him blamed the order for wasting the better part of his life; another part of him, the realistic one perhaps, thanked the older for graciously supporting him through his darkest years. Maybe they could both win in this situation. In any case, that was his hope.

Dionysius told Edmondo that he would prefer responding to the professoressa who had just faxed him by E-mail. More important he wanted his own, permanent address on Edmondo's computer. There was a pause during which Edmondo considered what he truly needed from Dionysius in return for such an extraordinary favor.

"Perhaps, if you get me a copy of the key to the Borghese chamber behind the library. It should be easy, you know where they keep it. I want to entertain some friends."

60

$\mathcal{T}$here was something about Paris which suited Zinka. Perhaps it was the slate gray skies which set off the imposing buildings so well, softening their well-trod exteriors and allowing their inner sparkle to be seen to best advantage. And there was no arrondissement in all of Paris more wonderful than the sixteenth, that bastion of wealth and privilege where Camille's father, an undistinguished but nevertheless pompous retired general, had chosen to purchase a pied-à-terre. It was little more than a closet with a view, as her mother the clothes-horse never tired of putting it. Still the building was a splendid old edifice set back from Avenue Foch not far from the Etoile. A perfect location for Zinka to promenade.

As Camille unpacked her few little items and tried in vain to find space for them in her mother's cluttered closets, Zinka decided to run a "lovely hot bath" for herself and assess the progress of her project. Needless to say, she thought best out loud.

"Isn't it just too wonderful how precious Brocardus has infiltrated himself into the enemy camp and won over that perfidious liar Mitchum? Can you just imagine if we didn't know he were coming to Paris? What an opportunity we would have lost!" She tried on a few dressing gowns before deciding on the apricot silk with cream tulle bunched at the wrists and neck. "Oh, *splendide,* don't you think, Camillle?" The question was rhetorical, as were all questions thrust her way when Zinka was being maniacally pensive.

"And that clever Dionysius knowing where to look for what. He is going to spare me any grief, hopefully even shore up my arguments." She tested the water with one toe then pulled it out quickly.

"So hot! Not Dionysius, my tight little kumquat, just the water. Don't want you having any tissy fits now, do we? Oh, I promise you our little excursion to Paris will cement everything together. Including us, you just wait and see."

Easing herself down into the bath like a supertanker going to berth, she groaned contentedly. "It is as if all my little chickies are lined up in a row." She then took loofah in hand and scrubbed rigorously. "Following their *poule* wherever she chooses to lead them. Allowing their Zinka to prod them along the road to success."

One of the first things she wanted to do now that they were in Paris was to pay a visit to the Galerie Malouf on Avenue Matignon. Somehow Monsieur Wilfredo Malouf, the owner and director, had gotten wind of their paintings and had contacted the general of the Order of Our Lady of Divine Succor to see if they might be for sale. How he had found out about the paintings would have been interesting in itself; that a major dealer on Matignon might be willing to put his weight behind the authenticity of the paintings could greatly advance the reputation of the pieces. So even before Camille had unpacked her final undies, Zinka rang up Malouf and, as he invited them straight over, whisked her out the door for their first business appointment, lurching ahead to the nearby taxi rank.

"It seems criminal to take a taxi on such a lovely day but we can leisurely stroll back. Perhaps we can stop for a *pastisse* if you're a good little girl." While the taxi tore up Foch and down the Champs Elysees, Zinka organized the papers in her attaché case. Everything was in place: authentication from a fellow scholar in Rome, infrareds of the underpainting, reports on the condition of the canvas and amount of original paint, ownership papers, and, of course, a full set of transparencies. "Now, Camille, don't be nervous. We must compose ourselves. Be as cold as the professionals which we are." With that she breathed deeply, caught sight of Camille nearly nodding off from something—who knew? exhaustion, lack of food, anxiety—and wondered if she was the only one in the world who took things seriously anymore.

In a word, the gallery was intimidating. Dark paneled walls, low lighting, high-priced masterworks framed in gold and set in wainscoting, a receptionist who sneered at you when you entered. Just the sort of place Saint Agatha would feel at home in, Zinka thought, her kind of torturers. After an awkward few minutes of waiting, Monsieur Malouf made his appearance. This being France, there was the obligatory ethnic probing.

"Zinka, what a charming name, Croatian, is it?"

"No, Serb actually. On both sides. Malouf, of the distinguished old Arab family perhaps? And Wilfredo, what an interesting juxtaposition."

"Lebanese on my father's side, Chilean on mother's. They met in Biarritz between the wars." Obviously not wishing to reveal any details of this extraordinary cultural clash, he turned to Camille, who only arched her eyebrow so as to silence any questions.

"Madam, I see, is French."

Once inside Malouf's office, he was all business. The documentation seemed quite interesting to him, particularly the copies of *Liasse 479* from the biblioteque in which Poussin "exhorted" students to pay particular attention to the San Stefano Rotundo cycle. He also felt that the transpa.encies read well, although several of the images were dull.

"Without doubt they need cleaning and some minimal restoration," Zinka rushed to inform him. "What cannot be denied is their quality and, from my position as a scholar in the field, their authenticity. They are without doubt early works by Poussin."

He watched with interest as perspiration gathered over the upper lip of Professoressa Zinka Pavlic, forming an unattractive but very revealing mustache. He had hooked her. All that had to be done now was to slow down, allow her to wriggle, and just reel her in. A daunting prospect, given her size, but a task for which many years in the art business had trained him well.

"My eye does not lead me to the same conclusion, Professoressa Pavlic." There was a long pause during which he placed each of the transparencies on a light box for a second examination. "Certainly nothing can be said definitively without examining the paintings in person. Still, compositionally they seem stiff, occasionally ill-formed. Incomplete, as you can see by this upper half of the Saint Agatha painting." He made an attempt to hand the transparency to Zinka for inspection but she would have none of it.

"I know it quite well, thank you. There is a minimal amount of damage to the cloud formation in that section of the canvas. This does not indicate compositional flaw."

At this Camille slid her chair closer to Zinka's and, in the most subtle of gestures, placed her hand on Zinka's forearm, which she was about to raise in anger, to still her.

"What exactly are you trying to say, Monsieur Malouf?"

"Precisely, Professoressa, that you have no solid case for your theory that these works are by Poussin himself, and from a market point of view, years, decades even, will have to be spent to have your theory accepted. Personally, I do not feel that it ever will be. I am however, prepared to make an offer to the order, which I understand is still the owner, with you as principal."

Zinka's head was throbbing in that uncontrollable way which only happened when she sensed she was being used. Camille tightened her grip. "Go ahead," she finally said.

"I would be willing to buy the lot of paintings for a fair market price as if they were School of Poussin. Consider well. This is a generous offer since all that can be said with certainty is that they are of the period."

At this Camille could not keep quiet. "But the signature, Monsieur, surely that counts for something."

"Not a great deal Madam Blanchierdarie. They are so easy to fake and, as the professoressa can tell you, often were added with first restoration, often as early as the later part of the seventeenth century."

Zinka wanted nothing more than to level the pompous crook but instead gathered up her material, closed her attaché case, and walked uneasily towards the door. "I am sorry we took up so much of your valuable time, Monsieur."

Camille scribbled their address and telephone number on a piece of paper and, feeling the inadequacy of not having a proper calling card—Paris not being their home—left it on the blotter of his desk. "Should you reconsider your position."

Humiliation and defeat do not make for lively conversation topics, so they said little to each other as they walked back to the apartment on Foch. Zinka even forgot to offer Camille a *pastisse*, her very favorite drink. As they waited for the lift, Camille reached for Zinka's hand. Closing the door behind them, she led her over to the sofa near the window and gently eased Zinka's head down onto her lap. It was a heavy load to bear but something which friendship and love required.

Back at the gallery, Malouf placed a call to Professor Mitchum, who had just checked into the Georges V, to tell him that the art historian they had spoken of had come to see him. Furthermore, the paintings were extraordinary and most probably authentic.

61

*T*he room was ablaze with light, and were it not for the absence of mulled wine and fancy dress, it would have been easy to imagine that this were a happier time, one in which clericalism was respected not scorned and being a man still carried a certain cache. In reality, he found himself seated on a panel held in the great hall of Thomas Library at Bryn Mawr College, surrounded by an alert and eager group, all of the female persuasion.

As fate had it, the day he was asked by Monsignor Duhmbelle to represent the parish in a discussion at the "girl's college down the road" was the very day Brocard had so successfully spoken to Professor Mitchum of the art history department. Puffed up with confidence, he felt up to the challenge. Foolishly, he had not asked how public the forum was to have been nor for that matter, about the exact nature of the discussion. After all, he remembered thinking, even though he did not have a pontifical doctorate and had not really kept current with academic matters, he had earned a licentiate and was a priest. Surely that would tip the scales to his advantage when pitted against mere undergraduates.

But as he was escorted through the couple of hundred women who were crowding into the great hall to the formal table at the far end of the massive room, he sensed he had made a mistake of tragic proportion. The audience of youthful and open faces he looked out on seemed far from hostile, nevertheless he felt all eyes on him as he took his seat. Unconsciously he ran a finger around the inside of his Roman collar in a vain attempt to loosen it and reached for the pitcher of ice water nearest his place. Nothing to be done about it. He was there and God be with him. Smiling wanly at the frighteningly academic woman seated next to him, he braced himself for the worst, and hoped against odds for the best.

The moderator announced that the format for the evening's discussion on the place of women in Western religion was to be informal and participatory. The panelists who had graciously accepted the college's invitation had no prepared statements but were rather resource persons who could respond to the opening comments to be made by Dr. Ronny Freedburg of Barnard College or from observations and questions from the floor. At that Dr. Freedburg took command of the podium and as Father Brocard turned in his place to look at her a firm and relentless catatonia overtook him. Not that anyone would have noticed. With his head inclined towards her, his eyes fully opened, and his facial muscles uncontorted, no one would have suspected that he was in no way present to what was happening. Words came in but he could make no sense of them; her questions tore through his brain whole and undigested so that there was no way for him to lay hold of them so as to begin to organize any response. In word, attitude, and form, he found himself in an alien world. One which he suspected to be of superior intelligence.

"Father Brocard, Father Brocard." He came back into consciousness at the sound of his name, although when the question was addressed to him he sorely wished he hadn't.

"Could you tell us how and if the official Church accepts the mounting evidence showing that women did in fact have a major role to play not only in the formation but in the day-to-day working of the early Christian community until they were suppressed by the misogynism which swept over all of Western Europe in the fourth century?"

"I am unaware of this systematic misogynism you speak of but only know that Jesus and his disciples who formed the early Church had great respect for women."

"Respect sounds rather condescending, don't you think?"

A low chortle rumbled throughout the women assembled while he tried to recoup.

"We do know that there were deaconesses in the early Church, yes, but the ranks of priest and bishop were always reserved for men."

"On the witness of written traditional texts, Father Brocard is quite right," Dr. Freedburg interjected and for one brief moment he did not feel alone. "However," she said measuring her words as the seasoned academic she was, "some intriguing research is being done in the emerging field of funerary monuments which seems to indicate that there may well have been female presbyters and even one woman bishop." Another rumble, this one of satisfaction bordering on vindication, rose up from the assembly. "Even were this not the case, it seems we cannot dismiss out of hand the possibility that, as early Christians often met for prayer in houses of widows, with whom they often stayed and always broke bread, that these same widows would not occasionally, or perhaps even regularly, preside at services. Break bread for those praying in their house churches."

Roman trained, Brocard was compelled to speak the truth as he knew it.

"The Catholic belief, as fully as I can speak for it, is that as Jesus Christ was a man, only men have and can take his role at the sacrament."

The same young woman who had asked the original question was quick to respond. "But isn't this reducing the Eucharist to theater? Shouldn't it be an inclusive representation of salvation, far deeper in significance than role playing or even gender?"

What struck Brocard most about these women, indeed the whole tenor of the evening was the seriousness with which they treated the issues. If there were hostility in the room, he did not sense it. Confusion reigned on his part, however. A deep, almost exciting uncertainty about what he stood for and what he even believed in reared its head. Although he did not know it at the time, this panel, this moment, was his coming of age.

To be sure there were some topics raised that evening which struck him as so extreme as to be easily dismissed. That any thinking person could take seriously the notion of worshiping goddesses, as many of these fervent young women professed, was simply beyond his ability to comprehend. Yet in their strange, searching, and passionate way, he had to admit a certain respect even for these women.

When the evening drew to an end he did not feel too bruised or too terribly alienated. He even stayed for a mochaccino and a little chat with Dr. Freedberg, or Ronny as she insisted on being called, before heading back to the rectory and, he hoped, a good night's sleep.

* * *

Once again, sleep did not come and so he found himself logging on and dropping in on ItalStud. He was entertaining a young woman that evening who seemed interested in little more than licking his feet. Not the most riveting of encounters.

Later that same evening he decided to E-mail his old friend Avertanus to tell him of his virgin experience with feminists and, throwing caution to the wind, life as Scatface.

62

My dear Brocard,

It pained me to read your E-mail of yesterday. You were too
flip, my good brother, a quality so unlike you as to make me
consider carefully from whom this letter came. You were too open
all together with me and I trust, as much as I have confidence in
the strength of our friendship, that you will not be so ever again.
Your letter has born out my worst fears about your returning to
America after so long away. It is too strong for you, too twisted
in its ways, too immersed in self-indulgence for someone who has
been isolated for so long from the world. For someone, as well,
who has been through such a difficult period as you—we both—
have had these last months. The loss of a monastery is bad enough
in itself, but the erosion of your faith and loss of your very soul
would be unbearably tragic.

I must confess that these issues have been much on my mind
recently. The Church in Holland, indeed the very morality which
gave greatness to this tiny country of mine, is in an utter state of
collapse. The Kingdom of Darkness has clearly won. Euthanasia
has gone well beyond mercy killing into the right to die, when and
if someone chooses. As if God the Creator had no say in the
matter. Now I have heard there is a movement to lower the age
of consent to fourteen. As if a child of that age can decide matters
of sexuality. The very difference between the genders has been
rubbed smooth, as I suspect it is in your country. The unique
beauty of what it is to be a man or a woman blurred beyond
distinction.

It is good that your young women at Bryn Mawr College are

wrestling with issues of faith, but this does not override the primacy of tradition. If the weight of time has taught us anything, my dear brother, it is that the witness of centuries cannot be so easily dismissed. As compelling as new research may be, it must be tested against the sensus fidelii, that belief the community has learnt from the Spirit over the course of time. Excuse my sounding so professorial but your tone and ill-digested arguments require I speak in this way.

As for your fascination with the interactive Web site of Ital-Stud (excuse me, the very word sticks on my fingers), I can only warn you to beware. Both of us have been schooled in solitude and isolation from relationship and my fear is that this solution is too easy, too perverse, and ultimately too controlling. This young man has already drawn you into his life, seized your attention, and I dare say your affection. I am not concerned for your sexual proclivity, my dear brother, years in the monastery have innured me to such feelings. What concerns me deeply is your vulnerability, the possibility that you will lose your head over this affair.

Please never speak of this again to me. Above all never disclose your new screen name as I fear that, were it to get in the wrong hand, it might be used against you. Think carefully of this, dear brother, and heed my warning.

I pray to God that someone as pure and good as Sister Apollonia comes into your life. Her dedication to prayer, penitential lifestyle, and commitment to spiritual growth has been a beacon of light for me, without which I might have been lost. My research into other religions, especially the pre-Christian mystery cults, which so marked my final years in Rome was so all consuming that I was in danger of losing sight of the uniquely Christian message of sacrifice and suffering. With God's help, Sister Apollonia has restored my sight. She is nothing short of an angel and her ministry nothing short of salvation itself.

I do not doubt that you may feel that I am overreacting to your news and perhaps from your newfound perspective I am. But consider well all I have said. Take it as fraternal correction if you will, but understand it always as a sign of my deep and abiding affection which neither time nor distance can diminish.

Your brother in Our Lady of Divine Succor,
Avertanus

199

After Avertanus sent his E-mail, he knew that he had indeed gone too far, reacted too strongly to what Brocard had told him. What a prig he had become! He knew that he had really written a letter to himself, that his intransigence was grounded in his fears rather than in some immutable truth. If he could have snatched the E-mail back, he surely would have, but it was already coursing from carrier to carrier along the pathways of the Web to unsuspecting Brocard.

For his part, Brocard did not know quite what to make of the pious diatribe. He sensed real concern on Avertanus's part but it was so couched in the party line, one he himself had down pat, that it was hard to extricate the personal from the pontifical.

What was clear was that Avertanus was going through a very stressful period. Transitions are never easy for old religious who are more set in their ways than any spinster. Still, there was more going on here than Brocard could even begin to get a handle on. Was it a culture shock, a crisis of faith, or, on a far more mundane level, could it have something to do with this bizarre and bewitching hermit, Apollonia Van Barren?

Father Brocard Curtis, Philadelphia-born and Roman-trained, was quite content with his strange and challenging day. The women at Bryn Mawr had given him much to think about and ItalStud had amused him in a perverse yet strangely intimate way. Shutting down the computer, he yawned deeply and fell soundly asleep.

63

$\mathcal{I}$t always happened. Just when you got unzipped, prone, and ready to go, the phone rang. For one brief moment, Zinka considered not answering. After all, there was little Camille, lips pursed and thighs parted, waiting for the big embrace.

"This better be good." She dislodged herself from her anxious lover and ran to pick it up. Luckily for her she did. It was that snake Wilfredo Malouf with a proposition.

"Professoressa." His tone seemed slightly arch to her so she offered little more than a dainty grunt in reply. "Professoressa, I have just gotten off the telephone with Dr. Mitchum, Dr. Charles Mitchum, surely you know him."

"Of him, yes, a fine scholar." Zinka did not let down her professional guard.

"He has recently arrived in Paris to begin work on a major exhibition."

"Yes, at the Grand Palais. I am familiar with it." She had to let him know that she was not completely outside the art loop. "French Classicism, I believe."

"Exactly. Well, anyway I mentioned your series of School of Poussin paintings—"

"Poussin, Monsieur Malouf, Poussin."

"Whatever, and he expressed interest in seeing the material you have."

"I would be pleased, colleague to colleague, to meet with him. But of course I can let no material leave my hand, as a professional like you can well appreciate." What she had wanted to say was "sleaze bag" or "maggot" but Camille's good influence had gotten to her. "Should Dr. Mitchum want to meet with me in person, I would be most happy to show him the infrareds and whatever else he might care to see."

"Excellent, Professoressa. Shall we say about four this afternoon for tea? Dr. Mitchum is staying at the Georges V, which I believe is not far from the address your friend Madam Blanchierdarie left with me. Which is, I believe, where you stay as well?"

"The Georges V is very near, yes." She refused to dignify his intrusion into her personal life with a fuller answer. What she wanted dearly was to kick him in the groin.

As they walked over to their meeting a few hours later, Zinka was so preoccupied that she was unable to appreciate the funereal grandeur of a perfectly bleak autumn day in Paris. The experience did not escape Camille though-she simply adored wearing her Hermes scarves to full advantage. In Rome, she recalled, it was like owning a thoroughbred and not allowing it to run. The dampness of the day freshened her cheeks but was unable to penetrate through the layers of radiant silk wound around her neck and trailing out behind her. "*Ah, quel temps,*" she muttered inaudibly to herself. "*Comme c'est splendide!*"

They walked in silence down the Champs Elysees to Fouquet's, the ever-elegant café on the corner of rue Georges V. Camille, conscious that Zinka was incapable of talking or being talked to at that moment, pressed tightly against her arm so as to let Zinka know that they had to turn. She did so want to tell her that Fouquet's was pronounced with a hard *t* because it was the way the proper name was pronounced. Without this knowledge, Zinka would surely sound like some *habitante*, or bumbling peasant, and Camille would never forgive herself for allowing her love to be so disgraced. Still, there would be time for such little lessons. Now, she had to stand with Zinka during this next trial and, as much as possible, control a passion which could too easily go wild.

"Oh Camille!" Zinka pulled Camille close to her as they entered the lobby. "*E paradiso!*" So operatic was the splendor that spread out before her, so opulent the scene, that Italian alone would do. "You didn't tell me the fall shows were on!"

★ ★ ★

Haute couture, that endangered species in a world of ready to wear, was everywhere to be seen at the Georges V. Lagerfeld here, Ferre there, and everywhere a Valentino. And women, women, women— no matter what gender they purported to be. It was all too glittering and too wonderful for Zinka to take in. Thank God she had plundered the closets and found the trendy little Armani suit she was wearing. Initially she had been concerned that the jacket could not be buttoned up. But seeing cleavage everywhere, and even an occasional exposed breast, she knew that her major assets had finally arrived. She felt powerfully affirmed and knew that she had truly invested wisely.

Her desire to meet Professor Mitchum was increasing exponentially. What reputable art historian, except her of course, would possibly consider staying at the showy Georges V, even were the fashion houses which surrounded it not mounting their shows? Could he too see the academic world as no more than fashion? And dreary fashion at that, lacking in all panache. Could the two of them share a common interest in the ephemeral and glamorous? Could they, she blushed at the blatant pun, be cut of the same cloth?

Both Camille and Zinka barely acknowledged Malouf's presence in the lobby; for his part, the distraction of several old flames and possible new conquests far outweighed their allure. A sadness came over the three of them as the elevator closed its doors on the festive scene below and quietly glided up to Professor's Mitchum's suite. And reality.

"My dear Malouf. And this must be the professoressa and her good friend." His convivial American way didn't fool her for a minute. It did however flatter her to know that he had been interested enough in her to be armed with a physical description. Otherwise how would he have known who was who? "Please, do come in."

The suite was large enough to impress and delightfully ornate. "I've ordered up some tea, I hope that will be alright with you?" Malouf went over to the trolley to organize things while Mitchum focused his attention on Zinka. He perhaps too gallantly escorted her over to the chaise lounge he had been sitting in when they arrived and motioned for her to join him there. Poor Camille, left standing by the door, fussed with her scarf compulsively in the vain hope that someone would notice her. That failing, she sidled over to a straight-back chair near the tea and quite convincingly disappeared.

It was clear that Professor Mitchum had a detailed game plan. After an hour's examination of all the documentation, restoration notes, infrareds, and photographs of Saint Agatha, he was prepared to make limited concessions about its authenticity pending examination of the painting in person. Before he kissed Zinka good-bye that afternoon, he had gotten her to agree to cut him into the painting and for Malouf to have exclusive rights to exhibit it. Thinking he had played her well—having no idea of who he was dealing with—he squeezed her with uncommon familiarity as she left.

64

❧

Some might think it strange, but for Sister Apollonia she was merely following the dictates of her conscience and her spiritual director, Father Avertanus. When she had promised her superior to live like a hermit—or more technically an anchorite since she was attached to a larger community—she had always insisted that her mind, that most glorious gift of the creator, be allowed to grow and flourish. She was to have her spiritual reading, her little library, even her periodicals. All within reason, of course, nothing too worldly or bothersome, nothing that would disrupt the placid nature of her contemplative life. Initially the problem was space. As she was a voracious reader, her little chalet, as she liked to refer to it, was getting overrun by books and papers. Something had to be done.

Father Avertanus had been the first to mention her getting a computer, although, in truth, the thought had crossed her mind much earlier. He was very enthusiastic about its capabilities. Consider, he mentioned to her, having a full concordance to the Bible, the full *Encyclopedia of Mythology*, as well as access to every major document of the Church. Imagine being able to set down religious experiences, then cross-reference them with those of orthodox mystics so as to see in a heartbeat if they are of God or the devil. A telephone line would have to be run into the chalet, but that would be easy enough. Furthermore, a technician would have to be allowed access to the cloister to set it up, because, despite his newfound enthusiasm and seeming proficiency, Avertanus was still very much a novice in such things.

Sister Apollonia needed little persuasion. This new tool seemed to her part of God's unbounded grace. The prioress and the community, all ancient in mind and body, did however need some talking to. The deciding argument came when Avertanus assured the convent that the Van Barren family would not only purchase Sister Apollonia's PC but also wire the entire convent. At this, the prioress herself finally conceded that God's hand was guiding them, as surely as it did Miranda in the *Tempest,* into this strange, new world. Just how strange and how new, she could never have known.

So as not to do violence to her solitude, Sister Apollonia spent several hours in chapel while a female technician installed the computer in the hermitage. Later that same day, Father Avertanus arrived for her weekly spiritual direction armed with a manual and a folder of Web site and E-mail addresses. With almost apocalyptic zeal, he impressed on her that there was no time to waste, the future was now. The kingdom—which exactly was never stipulated—was at hand. In his enthusiasm, however, he had made one fatal mistake.

After he left, Sister Apollonia paused to take stock of the momentous change which the computer had already brought to her simple life. Not only did she have ready access to spiritual books and resources but she also had unlimited access to untold worldly data which, if she didn't discipline herself well, could flood her mind and overburden her soul with issues and concerns which were, she had to remind herself, of no concern to her. The Bible, yes, but not even the numerous classical music sites. "Narrow is the gate, Apollonia." A little while later, she discovered the list of sites which Avertanus had signed on to and said, because she talked to herself incessantly, "Well just a few."

In his haste, Avertanus had gathered together all of the slips of paper on which he had written down Web sites these past few weeks since first logging on. He was far too disorganized to make copies of them for her, rather he simply threw them all in an envelope for her to peruse, confident that Apollonia, who was precision itself, would misplace nothing. Unfortunately, he had neglected to take out the slip marked ItalStud. So together with the Netherlands bishops conference and the documents of the Roman Catholic Church, Sister Apollonia found herself logging on to ItalStud. Her surprise at where it took her could not have been more pronounced.

What she saw in Pino was a vulnerability and a passivity which far outstripped anything she had ever imagined. He was, quite simply, giving himself totally to others; allowing himself to be reified so that those who were unable to understand true intimacy might know some form of life. So it was that GloriaDeo, for that is what her screen name was, began to correspond regularly with ItalStud—and couple in cyberspace.

65

$\mathcal{E}$verything about her fascinated him, absolutely everything. The way she posed questions, her complete disinterest in seeing him as an object, the totally nonjudgmental way she dealt with his life. Everything. Yet, remarkably he would probably never know what she looked like no less ever physically share the same space with her. Theirs was a totally disembodied sharing which in some strange way was more tangible than anything he had ever known; more profound a relationship than he had thought possible.

Thoughts like this showed just how emotionally bankrupt poor Pino had become. Nevertheless these were his thoughts as the correspondence with Sister Apollonia intensified, and although both of them were surely blowing this whole thing out of proportion, given their life circumstances, there was intimacy here. And some truth.

Bertie, for his part, did not quite know what to make of it. He went about his daily shopping, cleaning, and cooking as if nothing were amiss. Yet GloriaDeo—Apollonia had not yet revealed her real name—had changed Pino. Softened him somewhat, made him vaguely pensive and showed a heterosexual side to him, a fascination with things female, that mere sexual performance had never convincingly revealed. Pino had always said he was bisexual, but until this cyberaffair with the nun, Bertie had never considered how this might impact their relationship. Pino was, in Bertie's mind, a universally attractive object; for GloriaDeo, he was a man who was sacrificing himself so that others might understand their true human weakness. This Christic, human self-giving seemed to be particularly attractive to women, as if it triggered all of their nurturing instincts, all their need to protect and shield with undying love. As Bertie went about his daily chores of cleaning up after Pino, he only hoped that just because he had a bit of extra flesh between his legs, Pino wouldn't forget that he, Bertie, shared many of these feminine longings. Still, Sister Apollonia aka GloriaDeo seemed to have brought these innate traits to a new and feverish pitch. In the intense silence and solitude of her life, she imbued Pino with a purpose which far outstripped the purely human. Deifying him in his humanity unlike anyone had before.

At first, Apollonia simply asked Pino how he felt to have his privacy stripped away, to be at the whim and call of everyone. Amid all of the hundreds of questions which had come his way, no one had ever asked that before. Surprisingly, her concern seemed far more piercingly intrusive than any request ever made of him. It took him back and made him look inwards where there were no props to rely on, no stock poses to strike.

Some of her language was strange to him. Occasionally, he would open his E-mail to find that he was an "occasion of grace" or, more perplexing still, that "last night was a *kairos* moment bringing me into the presence of the Transcendent." At times like this, he leaned heavily on Bertie who hadn't spent a lifetime in a monastery for nothing. This was a metaspeak he was well versed in and he willingly helped the infatuated Pino through this maze of language so that he at least knew what Apollonia was getting at. Of course Bertie thought the nun was laying it on a bit thick but could never make his true feelings known.

There was a strange double standard at work in Sister Apollonia which would have been more typical of a Latin woman. Chastity, for her, was a natural virtue for women and a physical impossibility for men. Added to this was the fact that she had been brought up in house filled with men. She was unfazed by the male body and its incessant need to be seen and admired. From an early age she learned that men were by far more vain than women and more truly self-involved than anyone of her sex could ever be. To Apollonia, this was fact not vice or flaw but simply the way things were. Virtue built on this reality.

Every evening after compline, the night prayer that all religious faithfully say, Sister Apollonia logged on to ItalStud to see how this beautiful god-man was meeting the needs of others, and, when the spirit so moved her, she shared her deepest thoughts with him, her most probing questions about life. Pino never answered her right away. On the practical level, he usually had to ask Bertie to translate what she was saying, first from English to Italian and then from her language to his. But even when he began to learn her words and enter more deeply into her mind, he took his time responding because of how important this relationship was becoming, for how it was revealing Pino to himself.

66

45 Ave. Foch,
Paris 16
20 October

My dear Father Angelus,
   It was an extreme joy to have met you at the Curia recently.
Happily, I am able to report that finally some progress is being
made with the development of Saint Agatha. In our conversation
before I left for Paris you will remember that I told you of a
Professor Mitchum of Bryn Mawr in the United States. Without
Mitchum on our side, I was afraid that all of my efforts might
come to naught. He is a very influential scholar in the field and
it was essential that I win him over to our painting. Victory seems
to be within our grasp. He needs to examine the painting himself,
which does not concern me as I know well what he will find and
am confident this will confirm him in its authenticity. There is,
however, one delicate issue which must be addressed before he will
move forward. I assured him I would clear it with the owners, the
Order of Our Lady of Divine Succor, for which I believe you, my
dear Father, are still agent.
   Before entering into this difficult area it would be remiss of me
not to ask after your well-being. You suffered a severe loss, I
believe, in the impaling of your dear friend Father Cuthbert. The
only consolation is that he landed firmly and decisively, from what
I have heard, in Our Lady's hands. A riveting image. Now,
where was I? Oh, business.
   Art historians, as you may know, are a pretty disreputable lot.
Myself excluded, Father, but then you know that, don't you?

They are fortifying their little fiefdoms and advancing their pet theories. They are also, like so many others in this Valley of Tears as you monks might put it, on the take. For money, favors, just about anything really. Professor Mitchum seems to be, to my great relief, one of the money types. He is willing to upset his little canon of Poussin paintings, to embrace our Saint Agatha and company, if he is given some silent ownership of the painting. His thought was fifteen percent of the eventual sale, a considerable sum if it sells for ten million pounds as it certainly might. For this he would give us a handwritten appraisal (any other might be forged, so these are the only ones that truly count) and stand fully behind the painting. As I said earlier he still must see the painting in person. He is also adamant that some confirming evidence be given from documents of the period. This too I am quite confident will surface as I have a researcher scouring all the documents at the archives and parchments at the library of the Vatican, while I myself am working furiously at the Biblioteque Nationale here in Paris.

If you will excuse my being graphic, my dear Father, he has us by the balls. Professor Mitchum has within his power the ability to diminish and even damage my efforts. Without him, the painting would be worth a mere fraction of its true value. With the professor on our side, Saint Agatha might well garnish record prices at auction.

Please do talk this offer over with your superiors, good Father Angelus, and have a signed and notarized document stipulating Professor Mitchum's interest in the group of paintings ready for him when he comes down to Rome in a week's time. He will be staying at the American Academy on the Janiculum and will call you on arrival.

Thank you, dear Father Angelus, for seeing to this and rest assured that I will continue my efforts to establish your order's paintings to their rightful place in art history. I remain, warmly,

Your friend,
Professoressa Zinka Pavlic

Although there was undoubtedly some good news in the letter which Zinka expressed to him from Paris, there was more that was unsettling. Not that Angelus was one of those monks who had no mechanisms for dealing with the real world. On the contrary, his feet were firmly on the ground and had they not been, the debacle of San Redempto would most definitely have placed them there. No, it was just that he hated the fact that his order, indeed his whole way of life, was prey to hosts of charlatans. Zinka was right, of course: they had no choice. They were not in the financial position simply to hold onto the paintings. And even if they did, how would they establish their authenticity and value without entering into yet another corrupt system? He had once heard that some American theologian had stated that the only empirically verifiable Catholic doctrine was original sin. Just look at the world and our experiences in it and you know, empirically, that it is riddled with sin, that systems of corruption abound. Now art history. Was nothing sacred?

So later that day, he took the 64 bus up to the Statione Termine and walked several blocks up Via Marguta to the generalate. There he waited for the briefest of time before the Most Reverend Fernando Otero, the general of the order, was able to see him. Together they went through the professoressa's letter. To Father Angelus's surprise, Otero, true Spaniard, saw nothing amiss in Mitchum's request. "My good brother," he said as he paddled around the room in worn-down flip-flops, "you are so very Jansenist at times. You Irish," he added with a knowing smile, "are all the same." He regretted immediately what he had said, recalling the sacrifice Father Cuthbert had made routing out evil from San Redempto.

"Please do inform Father Brocard about this new evil surrounding Saint Agatha."

67

It seemed to Brocard that progress was being made at the expense of the order. The undeniable truth was that they were as ill-prepared to deal with the world as the world was to deal with them. From what Father Angelus told him, ownership of the paintings was beginning to be taken away from them. What, if anything, they would get when all the so-called experts and various middlemen took their cut might be small indeed. Brocard took it as a point of honor, especially as justice had yet to be done, to see that his order maintained some control over the paintings' fate. So he was very glad to hear the general thought it important that he position himself so as to oversee the order's interests.

Once again, the computer came to the rescue. Realizing that it would be necessary for Brocard to be in rapid and regular correspondence with the professoressa, Angelus had Zinka's librarian friend Madam Blanchierdarie contacted at the Biblioteque Nationale through the Biblioteque Française in Rome. Once E-mail contact had been made with Camille, being in touch with Zinka was only a wink away. Armed with this new E-mail address and strengthened by a confidence which only affirmation can give, Brocard dashed off a message.

> *Carissima Zinka,*
>
> *Life here continues to perplex. Without doubt this pastor is indolent and possibly far worse yet after all that happened at San Redempto—I hate to say it—I have almost become inured to indiscretions. No matter how egregious they may be. You were*

blessed it seems to have been born to freedom. I come to it quite slowly. Father Angelus tells me that you are making some progress with our Saint Agatha. Congratulations, I believe, are in order in having won over Professor Mitchum. It seems to me that the price he is asking is rather high, but then again I know nothing of your world. I can only trust that you do. As I understand it more research still has to be done to "establish," as you put it, the painting. Might you not consider trying to find out what research the elusive Hoop had done on the painting? Father Otger thought him important enough to hide from us back in the San Redempto days. I think he might have something to tell us. If you think this might be helpful, E-mail Father Avertanus in Nijmegen (AveMagus@NederInstitut/Zenderan.com). I have no doubt he can help. Be good and keep in touch.

He was in such a haste to move forward with his plans that he forgot to type in his name—an old fashioned habit he could not shake. Then again, he smiled to himself, how on earth could Zinka and Brocard ever be mistaken.

68

$\mathcal{T}$his wasn't meant to happen, but Zinka being Zinka, it was hardly unexpected. There they were, two art historians coupled like two love bugs, flying aimlessly throughout Mitchum's suite at the Georges V. For her part, it was important to seal this new working relationship with Mitchum; for his, it was the rare good fortune of finding a big-breasted woman who liked anal sex. They both were experienced enough in such things to know that the reasons for engaging in sex are rarely, if ever, shared equally by the participants.

"We must, absolutely must have a proper *vernisage*, with champagne, the press, and even dreary art historians gathered around our dear Saint Agatha!"

All Mitchum could really manage was a grunt, as he was trying to maneuver her over to the divan without slipping out. Sadly, he wasn't able to sustain an erection for a long time anymore but his desire to show athletic prowess was as keen as ever. Realizing he was going limp within her, Zinka guided him gently and tightened her sphincter so that magically, he started to come back to life. She knew she had him now, so no demand would be considered too extreme, no request would go ungranted.

"It is so important that the entry for our painting in your updated Catalogue Raisonee be printed up and handed out for all the non-believers." Zinka was wet with excitement as she thought of the way in which this discovery would set the art world on its ear; Mitchum, working himself up to a furious pitch, pushed down on the small of her back and, imagining he was some young stud, tensed his legs for the final thrust.

"A reproduction!" Zinka could not control her excitement at the very thought. "A full-page color reproduction is what we need!"

"Yes! Yes!" The battle-weary scholar felt transformed as a few globs channeled their way from him to her. "Yes!"

For Zinka and Mitchum, it was business as usual. For Saint Agatha, however, eternally writhing in transforming pain, this was a moment of monumental importance.

69

If it hadn't been for the information he had received from Zinka, there was no way that he would have discovered the precious document they needed. Dionysius had no doubt how the professoressa had sucked the information out of the American Poussin scholar and, not having a jealous bone in his horny body, only wished they had both enjoyed themselves immensely. He only knew that without the tip, he would be wandering the stacks still, buried in moldy parchments and the occasional, well-worn monsignor.

At first glance, the Vatican archives are every bit as organized as the Vatican library. As intent on appearance as any Italian, miles of shelves are organized with bound *fondi* (individual documents) and *buste* (boxes with loose documents), organized by size with the smallest volumes or cartons on the top shelf and increasingly larger on the lower shelves. But looks, if greater proof were ever needed, are deception itself. The fact was that documents had piled up this past millennium quicker than anyone was ever able to read them. Even knowing exactly where certain papers might be was confounded by several often-conflicting filing systems. Most problematic of all was the great organizational scheme initiated during the relatively short Napoleonic occupation. Dionysius had rightly suspected that papers relating to French artists in Rome working for the Church might have been included in this aborted reorganization scheme. Where exactly was a mystery.

The American professor had spent endless hours in the archives, only coming across a potential treasure trove during his last bout of research. All he was willing to confide in Zinka—never suspecting she might have a willing and able subject on site who could begin working as quickly as fax transmitted—was that there was a small room in the Tower of the Winds which contained *buste* upon *buste* of unresearched papers, largely, it seemed, relating to Church art commissions from the early seventeenth century. More specific than that, he would not get, but for Dionysius, who had come to know the labyrinthine stacks as well as seasoned sailors learned the remotest of red light districts, no further information was needed.

So this was how Dionysius found himself in the square and airless room on the mezzanine just off the Meridian Stanze, an airless storage place where not even the most adventurous of researchers would normally think of going. Except Monsignor Prienzi, one Friday last May. But that is a red herring not worth telling. What was important was the remarkable document which flew out of an overstuffed *buste* longing to be read.

> *Signor Nicolas Poussin, a French artist of good talent, has proposed a series of paintings based on sanguine drawings he had made shortly after arriving in Rome of the cycle of frescoes at San Stefano Rotundo.*

What followed was a description of the easel paintings which Poussin was commissioned to paint by the Order of Our Lady of Divine Succor which conformed in every detail to the San Redempto works.

His excitement was so great that he made a nearly fatal mistake.

Even though Dionysius was well out of the order, he had a deep allegiance to it. Without thinking he made his way to Edmondo's computer and E-mailed the news of his find to Father Avertanus in Holland, knowing that he would long to know it. It was only after sending the E-mail to Avertanus that he began the second note. Unfortunately, although Dionysius completed writing it, that all-important E-mail to Zinka never did get sent.

Edmondo, saying he had important things to do on the computer, insisted Dionysius save the note. He assured him that it could be sent later in the day. In reality, he was tired of Dionysius using his services without returning the favors which he had promised. Not of the physical type, which bored the asexual Edmondo even to think about, but practical ones. As Dionysius got up from the computer, Edmondo reminded him that he had embarrassed him by not being able to get copies of the keys to the unused Borghese offices which he had requested. For Dionysius, this was of no consequence; for Edmondo it was enough to assure the E-mail never would be sent.

70

$\mathcal{A}$ rivulet of blood, slow-moving and thick, made its way down from the nipple and arched around his breast before the sweat pooling in his armpit. "O delightful wound!" A favored mystical poem came to mind as she strained to focus on the image taking shape on her monitor. "If it be Your Will, Tear through the veil of this sweet encounter!" The needle that had been inserted into his chest twisted and raised up his already inflamed nipple.

Apollonia Van Barren in her hermitage in Zenderan was not alone in watching Pino have his tit pierced—in fact more people had logged on to this part of his life than any other. However, it is safe to say that Sister Apollonia was the only one who imbued this act with deep, spiritual significance. She alone connected Pino's exhibitionist escapade to the extraordinary acts of self-giving of the early Christian martyrs: Saint Lawrence, Saint Barbara, and, above all, the gentle virgin Agatha. How open this beautiful man was to the pain which the whims of others had inflicted on him. And, cowlike moaning aside, how nobly he dealt with his pain, confident of a higher reward.

At times it was his torturer who commanded her attention. So cold and evil. The Prince of Darkness himself, precise in all actions, a minister of doom playing to perfection the role which fate had dictated. " 'O gentle hand,' " she murmured still quoting John of the Cross, " 'that tastes of eternal life and pays every debt!' "

Bertie himself was rather shaken up by the whole affair as he did not like to see his man in pain. Still, it was something Pino had talked about doing for some time and when requests came in for him to be pierced, he realized the time had come. It was no problem finding someone to do it—all seven of Otger's Horsemen of the Apocalypse had made it a point to stay in touch with Pino. He had, in his own small way, become a bit of a celebrity on the meat racks of Italy.

But it was only when Pino started to exchange E-mails with the intense Apollonia that he saw beyond the gold imbedded in his chest to the larger significance of his act. Even were it an illusion, it filled him with purpose to think that was part of a cosmic plan.

71

Not only the Horsemen of the Apocalypse but Father Otger himself, the Prince of Lies, realized it was time to resurface. Money was no longer a driving concern and he had more than enough booty from San Redempto to support the grandest of retirements. No, he simply needed to stir up mischief in order to feel complete. To deprive others of peace and joy in order to find true satisfaction in himself. On top of it all, he felt that he had been unfairly duped out of the paintings of Saint Agatha and companions and could not rest until that injustice, as he saw it, had been arighted. As he rightfully saw it, dotty, trusting old Father Avertanus alone could advance his machinations. With this in mind, he arranged to move to Zenderan for a couple of months. Being adept at using the system for his progress, Otger proposed he spend time with the novice in Zenderan to work him through some formation issues. Once there, he devised a way to break into Avertanus's mind and life—a project which proved to be easier than even he could have imagined.

There were two problems with Father Avertanus, both of which could be put to great use by Otger. The first was that he was incapable of lying. He would drop his eyes and his ears would turn red whenever he merely avoided talking about something. That is how Otger quickly realized that Avertanus was in touch with Brocard, Zinka, and the general in Rome. The second was that he was a pack rat who saved everything. Which meant that the information Otger needed could be found somewhere in his room.

Years of religious training assured that Avertanus kept to a rigid schedule and, being of that old, more trusting generation, never locked his door. So one morning when the old man was off tending to the spiritual needs of Sister Apollonia, Otger let himself in and riffled everything from file cabinets to underwear drawer. In no time at all, he opened the computer and to his delight found that Avertanus had saved all sent and received mail. He intercepted Dionysius's shocking news about Poussin and erased it from the computer and then he took down all the information from Brocard, Zinka, and the titillating news about good Sister Apollonia and ItalStud he found in their emails. All of which could surely be used to his advantage.

72

A renewed sense of purpose energized Otger as he sped down the motorway towards Maastrich past faceless cyclists and clumps of besotted cows. Surprise was his best tactic with Hoop, get him off-guard. Not that Hoop was ever difficult to manipulate.

What a relentlessly dreary place the Maastrich Institut de Spiritualitit was. Housed in a few anonymous rooms in the rear of an equally anonymous building, desperately underfunded and unrealistically bloated with self-importance, it was all that Otger hated about academia. What never ceased to amuse Otger was how many desperate young scholars fluttered around Hoop's pathetic institute, as if the dim light of his ideas about art and spirituality could give temporary shape and form to their hopelessly fragile little lives.

Otger had planned his arrival for the most awkward time: the mandatory eleven o'clock coffee break. Hoop, religious trained, insisted that his brood abandon their terminals and gather in his office to pass around the cookie tin and hang on his every word. Standing outside the office for a moment so as to regain complete composure, Otger opened the door without knocking and stood before the motley group.

"Professor Aarnack. What a surprise."

"My dear Professor Hoop Rhutten, do forgive the intrusion. I found myself with some time to spare and was anxious to know how your research was coming." Otger's elegance and assurance was a perfect foil to Hoop's awkward apprehension. "Please, don't let me interrupt."

Every one of the six people crowded into the small office—even

Ineke who had been clinically depressed for years and who barely existed to herself—rose to their feet and offered Otger their chairs. He gratefully took Hoop's, forcing him to squat on the library stool in the corner despite the protests of his disciples. No one knew how to respond to a visit of such import. Of course Professor Otger Aarnack positively loved being a large fish in a small pond, and as the cookie tin was passed to him, he splashed around contentedly.

"Blood interests me enormously." The professor was adept at controlling conversations from the middle out, starting them as if they had been there already and bringing them to a predetermined end. "I trust your research has been flowing freely?"

In a hushed and impersonal tone, Hoop mentioned that "Doctorante" Ineke was hoping to be able to show them her work on Gregory the Great and blood shortly. Realizing what torture it would cause her to be the center of attention, even to have to speak, Otger feigned interest in her tiresome research and insisted she "tell us all now."

A small and frightened voice devoid of affect rose from one of the lower circles of hell. Covered in sweat, eyes focused on her worn Birkenstock sandals and woolen socks, Ineke told them of her work with the *brandeum* or shroud which had purportedly been in the possession of Saint John the Evangelist. "Yes, yes," Otger said in his most dismissive tones, "we are all aware of how the empress rejected this relic and how when Saint Gregory pierced it with a knife to prove its authenticity blood flowed out of it." Ineke retreated deeper into herself, seeing how trivial her research had surely been. There is nothing more devastating for any scholar than realizing that the unique territory they claim as their own is nothing more than common ground. "What intrigues me," Otger continued, "is how this blood incident connects to other bloody garments. Say, just as an example, the bloodstained tunic given to the Patriarch Jacob as false proof that Joseph had been slain. Is there truth or subterfuge in the blood of the shroud? Did Jesus Christ ever die, we might ask ourselves. Or was this too, as was Joseph's feigned murder, a plot to deceive?" Ineke could only think how well the devil quoted scripture and wished she had the presence of mind to quote scripture back to him. Instead she felt like throwing herself off the parapet.

"Blood, the root of faith and delusion. We thirst for it still, like the chicks clambering for the blood of the pelican, who like Christ, fed her young with her very blood. Such a perversely rich symbol." Then, arriving at the purpose for his visit, "Especially when it poured out from the early virgin martyrs, like the glorious Agatha."

Finally understanding the reason for this unexpected visit, Hoop dismissed his brood. Once left alone, Hoop became painfully aware of his own shortcomings. He could only return Otger's vapid toothy, brilliant smile with an embarrassing display of gums and protruding teeth, and Otger's full head of silvered hair seemed even more robust when compared to the few straggly strands which he torturously arranged in some vain hope of hiding his baldness. His shoulders drooped profoundly to see how well Otger held himself.

"I need you to produce a document for me, dear Hoop." There was no reason for Otger to ask for a favor, they were in this together, and even were they not, commanding came far more naturally to him than asking. "The characters who have taken the San Redempto paintings away from us are trying to have them authenticated as Poussin's work. Our only way of derailing this is to come up with a document saying that they are merely School of Poussin, period pieces with no enormous value."

"What purpose would that serve?" Poor Hoop was not fast on the uptake. He had no mind for scheming, little facility at all for deception.

"For one very obvious reason: to dash their expectations of profit."

"But if they are, as I have always suspected, real Poussins?"

"My dear Hoop"—Otger could not have been more condescending as he slowed his voice and measured his words—"if they are real, we can then devise to purchase them for little money and make the profit ourselves. Or, if these cretins insist on trying to fight us, we can blackmail them very nicely into allowing us to be principals in the paintings."

"But coming from you . . ."

"That is why you must prepare the document, making it look like something you found in the bowels of the Vatican, microfiche it, and photocopy it so it cannot be traced. I will handle everything else, you need not concern yourself about that. For your pains, I will see that some money is transferred to your indigent institute."

Crumbs. Hoop could barely contain his rage at the way Otger always used him.

73

My cher Monsieur, this long-distance connection is unclear. Please be so kind as to speak up." Not only did Malouf feel terribly inconvenienced by having his lunch interrupted by a business call but, adding insult to injury, he was being forced to speak English to the Dutchman on the other end of the line. When, and good God why, did the Dutch abandon French so completely, he wondered. "Please, Monsieur, slowly again."

The problem was compounded by the fact that Malouf had asked for a banquette in the deepest recess of the trendiest new restaurant in the Marais. It was as if the gossip and stress of *tout Paris* was coming down around him. And the little he could hear distressed him greatly. Somehow the caller, a dealer from the Hague whose name Malouf vaguely recognized, knew about the painting of Saint Agatha. More distressing still, he seemed to be privy to some information which, if not suppressed, could upset everything.

Normally Malouf never minded inconveniencing the dining of others by holding telephone conversations in public. However this was so critical that he realized that the restaurant would not do. So, keeping the caller on line, he walked out into the arcade of the Place de Vosges, an ordered and grand location. Perfect for focusing on such matters.

"What documentation exactly do you have to prove this assertion, Monsieur?"

As the caller answered, a woman with particularly large breasts brushed by Malouf. Nowhere near as well endowed as the professoressa, he thought, but really not bad at all. "Oui, oui," he mumbled back at the caller, "blah, blah, blah." Finally, realizing his *steak frites* had probably been dropped on the table and was getting cold, he cut to the chase.

"Let us say this document is real, not that I doubt you but let us just put it this way, Monsieur. And let us say that I have the experts on my side who can and will authenticate this painting as a true Poussin. What do you propose we do about this, dealer to dealer, *franchement* as we French say, so that everyone is happy?"

Life is so very full of choices. Blackmail or limited profits. A tasty lunch or the company of a luscious woman. What ever was an art dealer to do?

74

It is the smell of this place which attracts me so deeply." Breathing
deeply, eyes closed, peace or its semblance registered on his face. "The
mustiness of it all! Despite trying to scrub it clean as any operating
room, blood has seeped into its stones over the centuries. The tears
and despair these airless chambers have known—it is all too deli-
cious!" His companion could not help but laugh—foolishly thinking
he was joking.

"A strange place for a rendezvous, Professor Aarnack, but you always surprise me."

"I have always had a fond place in my heart for this museum of
torture. There are others, you know. The one in Milano readily comes
to mind. So near the decaying body of San Ambrosio. A lovely location and a fine collection. But nothing really compares to our museum here in the Hague. What I find most intriguing about it is the
fact that these once-working torture chambers stand not far from the
pompous world court, that self-important arbiter of morals and a travesty of colonialism. We must never forget that we Dutch plundered
and raped better than most Europeans. That we invented and used
some of the most devious instruments of torture ever devised. Denying this is to deny our past."

Businessman that he was, the dealer tried to pull Otger back on
target. "You have asked me here to find out about my conversation
with Malouf, I presume?"

"Look at this. Have you ever seen such a beauty?" He ran his hand
lovingly over the glistening breasts of the iron maiden, then as slowly
and reverently as if he were opening a tabernacle, he opened the

hinged front of the life-size female case to reveal the razor sharp spikes within. "Such a cruel and certain death." Then, flashing the most radiant of smiles, he asked what Malouf had to say about their proposal.

"He will give us thirty percent of the selling price if we destroy the document."

"Forty percent or a guaranteed three million dollars, whichever is more."

"I don't know if he will agree to this."

"He has no option." Otger continued to look dreamily at the iron maiden's blades, wondering how many they had impaled. "He will agree to our demand."

75

Dear Dionysius,

How pleasant to hear from you, my old friend. It is so good you have not forgotten me. It is good as well that you have not forgotten the debt you—we all—owe to the order. There were certainly some problems at San Redempto but as your communication rightly points out we must never turn our back on the order and must always remember the good it has done for us. It does my heart good to know that even though you have returned to the world, you have not forgotten your brothers nor the debt you owe Our Lady of Succor.

Now, to the point at hand. Like you I am excited about the document which you have found. This is surely a great find for the order and, for the order's sake, I am gratified that you have not made this public yet. My fear is that others less scrupulous than you will use this information to exploit the paintings for their own profit. Please, my dear brother, if you have not communicated this information to anyone yet, don't. I will talk this over with the father general to get his advice on how we might best proceed. Then and only then, when the order's interests are protected, can the vultures be set on the poor, embattled body of Saint Agatha.

I will try to contact the general before leaving on my ten-day retreat, but as he travels so much these days, I do not know whether I will be able to give you any news for a couple of weeks. Be assured that I will work as quickly on this as possible and that, even if it is a couple of weeks before you can reveal your great find, given the fact that the document has gone unread for three hundred and fifty years, this is not such a long time to wait.

My sincere thanks again for allowing me to be the first to share in this joyous news and my assurance that I will deal with it as cautiously and expeditiously as the gospel itself, I remain,

Your brother in Our Lady of Divine Succor
Father Avertanus Deblaer

Otger was proud of his deception. Avertanus himself had never sounded more like Avertanus. So pompous and so very convoluted. Confident the E-mail would work he sent it on to Dionysius in Rome. He then sent a brief E-mail to Hoop thanking him for his excellent work but telling him that, unfortunately, the present owners had no intention of selling the paintings at this time. Still, in consideration of his having put himself out, Otget would see if he could throw a few guilders his way.

When Dionysius received what he believed to be Avertanus's E-mail, he felt badly that he had written about his find to Zinka. Never for a moment did he suspect that priggish Edmondo had aborted the correspondence.

76

What was it that was so comforting about mushrooms? The way in which they hid unobtrusively waiting to be discovered? The nourishment they gave, the healing they could work, the deadly poison they could inflict on the uninitiated? Mushrooms were a challenge of nature, hundreds of types each carrying a different benefit or warning for those who cared to learn their ways. A taste which once acquired developed into a love. At least this was the way it was with Bertie who loved nothing more—Pino aside that is—than to wander through the deciduous forest which backed their mountain home in search of chanterelles and, if the gods were truly smiling, the rare King Boletus Fungi Porcini.

But this day Bertie had a graver reason to seek out the dark spaces of the forest. He had finally heard from the mysterious man who had been logging on to Pino for the past couple of months, the one who wrote so sensitively and caringly. Not like that Dutch nun who had her wimple on too tight. No, this one seemed to be normal. Well, not completely normal perhaps because who, after all, would follow the toilet activities of anyone if they were that normal. Comparatively speaking, that is. The E-mail which he had received, because it was written to him, Berthold Langdon, was so unsettling and ultimately so joyful that he had to make a hard copy of it and read it over and over again so as to convince himself that yes, it was indeed real.

So Bertie hid himself in a secluded corner of the forest, surrounded by a flush of chanterelles too yellow to pick but perfect to look at and, removing the printout from his pocket, unfolded it and began to read the words yet again, shrouded still in disbelief.

My dearest Berthold,

I don't know when it was that I first recognized you on the ItalStud website. For some time you were wearing that interesting red wig, trying unconvincingly to pass as a woman. Perhaps it was the time you sported the Tyrolean cap and lederhosen. Those shapely legs of yours are a dead giveaway. Maybe I always knew. What so impressed me as you took care and serviced that beautiful young man so selflessly was the humility and honesty you brought to your task. I knew this when we were together for those many years at San Redempto but in the foolishness of that time was never fully able to appreciate it. Yours is a beautiful nature. You are attractive because you are so giving and I stand in respect of your ability to be for others in a way which, try as I might, is beyond my ability.

I am writing you this with no ulterior motive, I am too old and silly for that I assure you. I only want you to know how much I miss your cheerful presence and how much I pray that you will be rewarded for the good you do and the thankless service and pleasure you give.

Your brother and friend always,
Brocard

Funny, kind Father Brocard. For the life of him, Bertie could only remember his bald head, wrinkle-free brow and rather stern look. He remembered him as tightly built, perhaps even muscular, surely not fat. It was so hard to tell what anything was like under that habit which Brocard never, ever took off. Did he even have buns? Bertie felt just like the silly girl he always told Pino he was. Particularly silly because it was pretty clear to him that this was not a love letter at all but just a letter of appreciation. A little moment of grace placed in a bottle and cast out into cyberspace, happily landing at his shore.

God knew he needed a little affirmation. Things had not been going well with Pino ever since he started to take Sister Apollonia's bloated gumph as gospel. Thanks to the wacko, his man was actually getting a Christ complex. Even his frigging tit-piercing had been turned into a Way of the Cross. Where it was going to end was hard to say but that it was spiraling out of control was patently obvious.

As Bertie was getting up to leave the woods, he was shocked to discover a whole flush of King Boleti. Remarkably, the caps of every one of them were at least six inches in diameter. Drawing close he noticed that the network of veins in their caps had already turned a deep, greenish hue. This was beyond anything he could have hoped for and, more clearly than a comet in the night sky or the ranting of any soothsayer, this was a clear sign that his luck was changing for the better. The truth was undeniable: his future, like these grand, luxuriant mushrooms, was ripe for the picking and ready to be enjoyed.

77

erde, do you hear me? *Merde, merde, merde,* and *merde* again."
This was quite simply the most ludicrous thing she had ever heard,
an assault on her integrity. Not to mention being an insupportable
insult to Saint Agatha herself. "I will not, I cannot accept this."

The telephone rang, once again it was Professor Mitchum, trying
his best to be conciliatory. "Carissima Professoressa, please do not
hang up on me again."

"There is nothing I have to say to you so long as you insist on
talking rubbish."

"Zinka, carissima mia, the research is not mine, I have not even
seen it. I only tell you what Malouf has passed on to me and how
seriously he takes this matter."

"Saint Agatha is by Poussin, not," she struggled to catch her breath,
"by some anonymous, clumsy *school* painter, some nameless follower.
The brushwork alone proves that, the infrareds of the underpainting.
Surely you can't believe this foolishness?"

"Whether or not I believe it is beside the point. Such a document undermines everything you have been working for and effec-
tively dashes our hopes for placing the painting correctly. Unless,
that is—"

"No deals, Mitchum! No deals!" The phone went dead again.

The professor was well aware of the arrangement Malouf had been
forced to make with the art dealer from the Hague and knew that in
time Zinka would be forced to go along with it as well. For now he
needed to calm her down, prepare her for the inevitable.

Frantic to get some news from Rome, anything that might counter

237

this spurious document which had no doubt surfaced from hell itself, she dashed off an E-mail to Dionysius, begging him to work harder, to uncover something, anything which might put this matter to rest. But when Edmondo received the E-mail he deleted it immediately. Whatever inconvenience this might cause Dionysius or the over-wrought woman who was seeking his help was nothing in comparison to the embarrassment, the *bruta figura,* which Dionysius had made him suffer. Edmondo thought himself the most wronged of men.

78

Carissimo Brocardus,

I am so distraught I barely feel myself! Where to begin? Our project for beauteous Saint Agatha which was going so very well has run amok. There were more vipers in the pit than I had suspected. Professor Mitchum, whom I never fully trusted, has just told me that a document has surfaced—supposedly from the Vatican library—which proves conclusively that our painting, that the whole series of paintings, is not by Poussin himself but merely a period piece. A School of Poussin, if you can imagine anything more insulting and ridiculous. He promises to have a fax of the incriminating document in my hands soon. He is already trying to buy me off for a fee. It is all too horrible. I have given so much of myself to this and now he wants to buy me off like some tradesman. Well, it cannot be. I am certain that the hand of that slimy Malouf is in this as well and doubtless some even more corrupt, greedy figures lurk in the shadows. What they are surely trying to do is to get the painting away from your order for the smallest sum possible and I fear that unless something is done quickly all will be lost. My hope, our hope, my dearest Brocardus, lies in Dionysius uncovering something in the archives in Rome. For reasons which I cannot understand he does not respond to my E-mail and, as you know, he never did have a telephone at the house of that woman he lives with. Poor Dionysius, still living in fear of being discovered even when there is no one looking over his shoulder anymore. For myself, I pray to God, my very dear Brocardus, that I act in a ladylike fashion always, however I must confess to you, my precious little Father, that the Milorad in me *(figuratively speaking, of course) wants to take out the semi and gun down the lot of them.*

For Brocard, sitting at his terminal late at night, the news was more distressing than he could have imagined. How capricious the art world was. Then as he was gathering his thoughts to respond to Zinka—he did nothing spontaneously after all—another E-mail arrived.

> *Carissimo Brocardus,*
>   *I miss you terribly and long to spend time with you. A rendezvous in Paris, a weekend together would cheer me up so very much. It may seem rash of me to presume you can drop everything to be with me but such is my desperation. Rush your answer to me at the new address I am sending this from as I do not want jealous Camille to know of our plans. Tanti baci.*
>
> *Zinka*

This second letter, so soon after the first was very unsettling indeed. Otger, who sent it, wanted to confront and embarass Brocard with what he knew and what he had done and Brocard, the monk with no guile, conflicted more than ever about intimacy and relationship, wondered if he might not have positive, even lustful feelings for Zinka.

79

Why is it that the smaller the handbag, the harder it is to find anything? A bit of concentration might have helped Camille somewhat, but Zinka would allow none of that. She had begun ranting the evening before and with barely a pause for a dream cycle, had continued throughout the night. First it was Mitchum, the duplicitous scumbag; then Malouf, pathetic little pecker that he was; and finally all of her anxieties, all of her rage was taken out on Dionysius. How could he disdain from answering her? Even if he had no news for her, courtesy required that he be in touch. And how could he have come up dry? What about the lead which Mitchum had given her, the cache of papers hidden in the Tower of the Winds. Could Dionysius be so self-involved as to put her project aside? Probably, knowing the perennial erection he flaunted, he had set up shop at the Statione Termini and was busy servicing incoming trains of sex-starved Polish pilgrims.

Finally, despairing that they were getting nowhere, Camille picked up the phone and made a reservation for Zinka on the next flight out of de Gaulle to Rome. Her hope was that the packing (Zinka did not travel light) and the trip to the airport in the morning rush hour would dissipate some of her girlfriend's frenzy. No such luck. In the midst of tearing around the apartment for pantyhose and spare pumps and offering directions and instructions to the taxi driver, she still had more than enough time and, as it turned out, ever increasing energy, to bitch and rant and scream to God about the injustice of it all.

As they made their way to the gate, Camille searched madly through her handbag for her parent's telephone number in the country. Well before this last episode, she had decided that she needed a

241

break from all this madness, and a retreat into her mother's anal compulsiveness looked comforting indeed. Finally finding the crumpled paper, she pressed it in her lover's hand, kissed her, and whispered lovingly in her ear that things would be all right, just have a bit more patience. To which Zinka, livid her lover was so controlled, so very French at a moment like this, could only say: "Oh shove it, Camille!"

80

Silence was what she did best: it radiated from her very being with
an aereola of sanctity. When Avertanus sat with her in prayer, he felt
a deep inner peace which could only have come from her because,
in himself, there was little peace to be found. Ever since he was exiled
to Zenderan he was incapable of stilling himself. Except, that is, in
the presence of Sister Apollonia who, if truth be known, had become
more his spiritual guide than he hers. Especially since Father Otger
had taken up residence in the room next door to his. Now in their
weekly sessions, it was Avertanus who did more of the talking.

Nevertheless his monk's intuition—every bit as keen as any
woman's—told him that there was something which she was keeping
from him. Some secret wordly attachment which she had not broken.
It went beyond her intellectual attachment, her love of books and
ideas. This she had reconciled well by modifying her vows, like the
Brigetine Sisters, so that book budgets could never offend poverty.
No, he was convinced it had something to do with the heart, some
affective link which strangely seemed to give her life. A vibrancy
which was uncommon among cloistered sisters and even more so
among hermits.

"Where is your heart, Sister?"

Never one to rush into a response, Apollonia breathed deeply, eyes
closed and hands folded loosely in her lap. "With Jesus, my Spouse."

"How do you image him, good Sister?" Here the pause was even
longer than normal and her breathing became shorter, more agitated.

"He is the Suffering Servant of Isaiah. His luscious skin drenched
in sweat, his sinuous body writhing in pain, blood gushing from his

distended nipple." With this her eyes opened wide and saw that Father Avertanus's jaw had dropped open. "I mean, he, Jesus that is, he was . . ." At this, tears welled up in her eyes and she dropped to her knees at Avertanus's feet, asking for his forgiveness. Not knowing how to handle such unexpected and, quite honestly, unwelcome compunction, Avertanus simply put on a pastoral look.

"Father, forgive me but I do not know if it is a sin or a grace I must confess."

"If it is grace, we will praise God together for it; if a sin, my good Sister, the compassion of Jesus will forgive and cleanse you of it."

"Father, it is the computer."

"The computer is not sin, nor can it lead us to sin unless we choose to be led."

"The choice has been mine, Father. But the Web site was yours. Do you remember the initial list of addresses and sites you gave me?" Avertanus nodded, never suspecting anything more controversial was on it than the documents of the Church homepage. "There was one site for ItalStud, which, foolishly I thought had something to do with Italian Studies." Avertanus's eyes widened—this surely was the site silly Brocard had mentioned to him, but how could he have been so foolish as to pass this on to a solitary? "Father, it is so captivating, he is such a precious, fine human being. I have never known a man to be so self-giving, so concerned to please others. It brings me such joy, Father, to communicate with him. Only recently have I begun to understand how this might be a violation to my cloister. Does my vow of solitude extend to cyberspace, Father?"

Avertanus was having difficulty keeping up with her. At first it had seemed that she was confessing to a carnal attachment to this ItalStud, but then the sin, if sin there were, seemed to be more about violating cloister, the hermetical isolation she had vowed herself to. Or maybe sin permeated the whole affair. Then again, since moral theology had not yet dealt with issues of cyberspace, right and wrong was a mute issue.

Seeing his confusion, Apollonia went over to the computer and downloaded a few images from last night's session so that he might decide for himself. Having a particularly fast modem, her images came up in no time. Pulling up a chair next to her, Avertanus examined several colorful images before coming to one with two men. Or rather one man and a foot stuck in his face. "Good God, it's Bertie," he exclaimed.

This time it was Apollonia's turn to be shocked.

81

Dear Father Berthold,

I realize that you most probably do not go under this title in your new line of work, but you are a priest forever according to the Order of Melchizedek, lest you forget. I am writing because I have just seen a disturbing computer photo of your worshiping a man's foot. Really, Father Berthold, morality aside, isn't this unseemly behavior for someone who should know better? Consider the fungi, Father. Did the order teach you nothing these past twenty years?

My concern lies less in you—I must say I despaired of you, my brother, many years ago—but the damage which you and your cohort might be doing to a Sister Apollonia, whose spiritual well-being has been entrusted to me. If you cannot think of your own soul, then do please try to consider the damage you might be doing to this poor, trusting soul who, innocent and unsuspecting, might be lost by your callous foreplay. Or whatever foot sucking is called these days.

> Your brother in Our Lady of Divine Succor,
> Father Avertanus

Dear Avertanus,

My, oh my, everyone is coming out of the woodwork! What a delight to hear from you, although you are sounding a wee bit sour to me, if you don't mind my saying. Now first of all, Pino scrubs his toes very well before any sucking. So there. Now, as to that poor wilting virgin of yours, listen here, Avertanus, she is the one who is hooking Pino into all sorts of weird things, puffing his head up with thoughts of sainthood and worse. No, I won't have you blaming me for that. Truth is, they seem to need each other, hard as it is for me to say, and the sooner we get this over with the better. Can't you bring the little tootsie here for a few days, let her see what Pino is like in person, let him go gah-gah over her wimple? Odds are they would both get over it soon enough. Now, as for me, I have just received the most appreciative E-mail from Father Brocard. It is a shame none of his goodness rubbed off on you. In fact it was he who indirectly encouraged me to throw off my wig and bury the heals and simply be Bertie on the Web. Which is probably how you recognized me so easily. Good thing too. It's time to come clean, don't you think?

Cheers,
(Father) Bertie

Dear Bertie,

I am duly castigated. Perhaps sucking a few toes is not too evil, cosmically speaking. Especially if they have been well scrubbed. As for arranging a meeting between your friend Pino and Sister Apollonia, I am afraid that travel is out of the question. She is a hermit, you know, and as you might remember, they do not travel well. However if you and your friend ever find yourselves in Zenderan I could arrange a meeting in the speak room of the convent. Do pack some clerical outfits if you do decide to take me up on this offer. I am afraid that the chains and chaps which both of you were sporting in those photos will simply not do. You see, Father Bertie, I may not have the savoir faire of Father Brocard or the intensity of Sister Apollonia, but I am trying.

Yours,
Avertanus

82

Dear Father Brocard,

Greetings from Rome. I trust that America is treating you well and that despite the many lively distractions it surely offers you still think often of those of us who labor in the tired Old World.

My reason for contacting you is that Professoressa Zinka Pavlic has just paid us a visit at the generalate. She was, to put it mildly, quite overwrought. She had urgent need of contacting Father Dionysius, who as you know is on leave. It seems that her E-mail, have not gotten through to him or, fearing the worst, that he lost all interest in assisting her and us in the Saint Agatha project. As he has never given anyone his home address or telephone number I have taken the step of sending a message to him at the Vatican library by means of the old pneumatic tubes. It is times like this that I thank God we never abandoned the reliable old technologies in favor of these yet-to-be-perfected electronic ones. If all goes well, a meeting can be arranged here at the generalate between the professoressa and her erstwhile researcher. Hopefully, this matter can be readily put to rest. What all of this does is trigger concerns which go far deeper than the authenticity of a painting or the validity of research. What I see happening is an erosion of truth and a rubbing smooth of distinctions between good and evil. When we buried poor Father Cuthbert in the crumbling shell of San Redempto I had foolishly hoped that, in some small way, the goodness of his sacrifice might be redemptive. I hoped against hope that the hemorrhaging—for that is what it surely is—of goodness from our witness of life had stopped and that even though our numbers were greatly diminished, we might still have something to say, some light to give to this selfish and despairing world around us. I feel now that I had deluded myself, that I had been dancing a little gig while Rome burned. The general sends his kind regards to you, Father Brocard. He and I both ask you to vigorously pursue the Saint Agatha project, not only for the money which the order so desperately needs, but above all so that sin and corruption do not completely envelop this project, as it seems to be doing in so many areas of religious life. Do forgive my Irish bleakness. Keep me in your prayers and pray too that our poor struggling order may yet survive.

Your brother in Our Lady of Divine Succor,
Father Angelus

Brocard emotions were conflicted as he read Father Angelus's note. He could not help but feel saddened by the way in which his order, a whole way of Christian life was devolving. However, overriding this apprehension for the order's future was a renewed sense of personal purpose. A deep and abiding joy that Saint Agatha herself was reaching out to him in her need.

83

Like some peripatetic Greek philosopher of old, Brocard always thought best while walking. So early the next morning he donned his walking shoes, pulled on his relaxed Gap jeans—yes, he had not been immune to the siren song of American advertising—brought along a bomber jacket because there was still a chill in the air, and strode confidently out into the mainline splendor of Bryn Mawr.

Order is what he sought that overcast spring morning. Not any parochial, limited community but a shape, a form to the events which seemed to be tumbling down around the beleaguered figure of Saint Agatha. As he made his way past the Baldwin School and onto the main campus, he had difficulty believing that all of the mayhem of the past months was random. Not that he was yet won over to Avertanus's detailed, numerological reading of events. However, Brocard too was trained in Scholasticism and so he longed for some over-arching design which would draw all these disparate pieces into one. He was even more convinced of this as he walked past the Thomas Library down the great bowl of earth into the playing fields at the far end of the campus. A game, he thought, surely this is all a game. Enormous banks of forsythia and carpets of wildflowers gave testimony to a God, mastermind of it all, who could not long endure chaos. Which he knew to be the work of the devil. The devil: that very word conjured up the image of Otger.

It was just a suspicion, but he wondered if in some devious way Otger's hand wasn't somehow behind this latest development. Avertanus had after all mentioned the curious fact that Otger had moved into the room next door to his in Zenderan. Perhaps it would be good to gather together all of the information needed to snare Satan himself.

As he settled in to watch a team of tartan-clad undergrads play an early match of lacrosse, the course of action he had to follow presented itself to him. First he would send two E-mails. One to Bertie to ask him to see if Pino had any contact still with the young boys Otger had used to dispose of poor Father Emmanuele; and second, to ask Father Angelus to secure all documents stored in Rome concerning the access Otger granted to the treasury at San Redempto.

It was a good day, he thought, to watch a game unfold.

84

When the Blessed Virgin Mary appeared to Thomas à Kempis in the last decade of the fourteenth century, she was fuming mad. Her exact words—and this we have on his own witness—were "You ingrate!" Thus began one of the most passionate obsessions in the history of Christendom.

Intriguingly, when the Professoressa Zinka Pavlic stood before Dionysius McGreel, she too was ablaze with righteous anger. Even to the extent of using the same exact words: "You ingrate!" Although the intensity Dionysius felt for Zinka after they sorted out their misunderstanding was nowhere near as long-lasting as Kempis's feelings for Mary, it was similarly extreme. History does have a way of repeating itself.

Zinka being Zinka, it had not been easy for Dionysius to explain himself. What exactly happened to the E-mails both she and he had sent was a mystery which only that quintessential Vatican rat Father Edmondo could answer with certainty but which took little intelligence to figure out. As for the miraculous document Dionysius had uncovered at the Vatican archives, she made him read it over and over to her like a child hearing her favorite bedtime story. Loving it more with each hearing, finding security in its words.

" 'Signor Nicolas Poussin, a French artist of good talent, has proposed a series—' "

"Yes, yes, slowly, slowly."

" '—series of paintings based on sanguine drawings . . .' " Dionysius found it hard to resist Zinka as she was bearing down on him with each phrase. Fortunately, they were meeting under the grape arbor on the roof of the generalate, well out of sight and sound of everyone. Reveling in the power of words he prepared to reel her in. " ' . . . drawings he had made . . .' " Closer, closer. " ' . . . the cycle of frescoes at San Stefano Rotundo.' " Contact.

However, no sooner had lust taken over than Zinka extricated herself from his grasp and, eyes ablaze with inspiration, proclaimed in the tones of the minor prophet that she had become: "Pack your bags, my chunky cucumber. We're off to Paris!"

85

Who would have guessed that Dionysius, whose groin never knew a still moment, would have had motion sickness? This was why he refused to fly to Paris and why, foolishly, he thought that taking the overnight train might be a better idea. It wasn't.

The journey started off well enough. They both arrived at the Statione Termine early and were able to settle into their cabin well before the train departed. In fact Dionysius was buried deep inside Zinka's rear, furiously squeezing her breasts and making all the appropriate noises well before the train pulled out. From Rome to Milan there was little problem, except for Dionysius noticing a few anatomical incongruities in Zinka which he readily blamed on the bumpiness of the rails. No, the problem started around Lugano when the train lurched wildly to the left to enter a tunnel through a mountain pass. To put it simply, Dionysius threw up all over Zinka. The smell was horrendous. Never before had any cabin seemed so small. There was no escaping it.

This was just the start of a truly unpleasant night, one that could take the zest out of any affair. He longed to pull the emergency cord, stop the bloody train, and walk back to his woman in Rome but Zinka, a woman driven by a mission, would have none of it. Her solution, which fortunately she did not share with him, was to take the documents from him and chuck him out of the moving train so that not a minute's time was wasted.

They did try playing around one more time when they arrived at Camille's parents apartment in the morning. But even though they had both scrubbed themselves well and washed all of their clothes twice, the smell of vomit hung over them making it virtually, but not totally impossible, for them to enter into the so-called joy of sex.

There was nothing to be done but to farm out Dionysius. Camille was bound to return soon and, the passion being gone, there was no reason to pursue this relentless phallus. She decided to throw Dionysius, as a bone to a dog, to Malouf, who could use him to lure women to his den. That was all she decided to give Malouf for the time being.

86

*S*pecial permission was needed of course, but given who he was, Father Avertanus had little problem in having it granted. Two young priests of his acquaintance from Rome—one British, the other Italian—impressed by the austerity of life and reputation of the holiness of Sister Apollonia, requested to meet with her. So arrangements were made with the prioress for the hermit sister to meet them in the convent's speak room, that neutral space which had one door in from the cloister and one out to the world where such extraordinary encounters might take place. Once the time was set, anticipation mounted.

Nerves ran high as Avertanus introduced his two friends to the prioress. Father Berthold, looking every bit the priest he was, maintained a quiet dignity. Pino, looking particularly fetching in clerical black—at least from Bertie's perspective—did the quiet part well as he loathed the way he spoke English and could not even conceive of Dutch. As for dignity, as soon as he started scratching his crotch any thought of that was over. Still, they were Father Avertanus's friends and everyone knew that the quality of vocations to the priesthood was not as high as it was years back. So she willingly turned an eye.

They seemed to be waiting an eternity before Apollonia was escorted into the curtained enclosure at the far end of the room. On hearing her enter, Father Avertanus signaled for Bertie and Pino to stand and move nearer to the railing behind which she would be seated. Then, when she was seated in place and the sister who had accompanied her slowly drew the curtain and, obsequious to a fault, closed the door behind her, Sister Apollonia slowly raised her eyes.

Studying her visitors as the aliens they were, she smiled broadly. "How lovely of you to come and visit me. How very gracious."

It was clear from the outset that Apollonia and Pino had things to say to each other and that both Avertanus and Bertie were unwelcome chaperons. Sensing this, they decided to leave the unlikely couple alone, language problems notwithstanding. Bertie thought it a risk but a calculated one. After all she was a hermit. How far could it go?

87

*D*oing her nails was the one part of feminine hygiene which came naturally for Zinka. Even while still trapped in Milorad's body, she had always been attentive to pushing back her cuticles, filing the tips, and applying a shiny finish. Now, thanks to the wonders of surgery, she was able to fully engage her sense of color, which in a word was loud.

Nevertheless it was distressing that Malouf called just as she was finishing off the last few nails. She knew that she had to take the call yet was damned if he were going to louse up her polish. Camille was due back soon and she wanted to look devastating.

"You heard me right, Monsieur Malouf, I insist on seeing the original documents that worm of a dealer in the Hague purports to have." She put down the telephone for a few seconds while Malouf ranted on so as to attend to the index finger of her left hand. It was good to hear someone else losing it for a change. Then picking up the receiver again, "and I want a restructuring of our arrangement reflecting my original position of principal ownership to be in place in the event that their papers prove to be false. Which I have no doubt they are." This really got Malouf going. How could she be so unprofessional as to recant on an arrangement all parties have already agreed on? Then the telephone went dead but she sensed that, remarkable as it might be, it was because he was thinking.

"Professoressa Pavlic, Zinka my *cherie*, what is it you discovered in Rome? What are you hiding from me?"

"Nothing that you need know about now, I assure you. Just inform Professor Mitchum as well that I insist on a return to our initial agreement should the Hague papers prove false. And one more thing, Monsieur Malouf." She had him where she wanted him, helpless and confused. "Not a word of this to that scumbag in the Hague or you and Mitchum will end up with nothing. Nothing, do you hear me!"

Her nails were done, blood-red and shiny as could be. They looked truly fabulous.

88

*A*vertanus pressed the scented letter to his face and tried to imagine that it was a billet-doux from someone who pined for him alone. How wonderful it would be, he thought, as the rickety old train wended its way from village to village, if God in his wisdom had set someone aside for him alone. Instead he was rather thoughtlessly added to Zinka's lineup. Well, at least she hadn't made untoward advances as she had recently made to poor old Brocard. No she had simply sent a handwritten letter, saying that he was all she trusted anymore, asking him to make a trip down to Maastrich to talk with Dr. Hoop Rhutten in person. As Bertie and Pino had already pushed on to Amsterdam "for research," as they put it, it was an opportunity to get away from Zenderan and the oppressive presence of Otger.

The institute was only a short distance from the train station. Given the fact that the community in Rome had acted as if Hoop were hidden, unreachable, and "dead to us," Avertanus found that, to his pleasant surprise, nothing was farther from the truth. To the contrary, everyone he encountered exuded an almost cultish benevolence, good will, and desire to help him in his search which was most unsettling for someone who had spent the better part of his life in Rome. He had to ask directions a couple of times to find his way to Hoop's office. In each case he was handed over, like some precious parcel from researcher to researcher. They even tapped the door for him.

"Dr. Rhutten, I doubt if you remember me . . ."

"Father Avertanus Deblaer, how could I not. You honor us by your visit." Hoop rose, offered him a chair, and sent one of his assistants off for coffee and the cookie tin.

"I must confess I am here on a matter of great importance and secrecy." Then after the briefest amount of small talk about their time together in Rome many years ago, Avertanus explained that magnitude of the problem that the Hague document, as it was now being called, caused to Dr. Pavlic's research, not to mention the millions of dollars that were at stake. As a friend and scholar, speaking with a sincerity of heart which Hoop had rarely experienced in his years in academe, he asked Hoop if he could shed any light on the matter.

It was at that moment that nothing short of a miracle happened. Because that, in fact is what conversion is. Hoop was so overwhelmed by an accumulation of guilt and feelings of betrayal—he had so lost sense of the very meaning in his life—that he dropped to his knees in front of Avertanus.

"I know I am doing this all wrong, I don't even know how it is done any more everything has changed so much, but, Father, I want to—I need to—confess."

Something in his gesture, his remorse, struck Avertanus deeply. This, he knew, was the reason he had been ordained—to be there for someone in his need. All of the arcana, all of the intellectual meanderings were like straw. This alone mattered.

He leaned forward and placed his hands on Hoop's shoulders so as to signal him to stand up. But Hoop would not budge, shaking his head as if to say, It is here, on the floor at your feet that I belong.

"That document you ask about, it is a forgery. Otger Aarnack put me up to it, as he has put me up to far worse for more years than I can remember."

"Do you take no responsibility yourself?" Avertanus' asked this softly but its purpose was loud and clear. Without taking responsibility, without an understanding of sin on some level, absolution cannot be given. "What is it you really want to confess?"

"I confess and I accuse myself of stupidity and weakness, of avarice, and even of someone's death." As he placed his hands in Avertanus's lap, he dropped his shoulders as if the greatest of weights was placed upon him. Hoop then began to tell the story of the theft of the paintings at San Redempto. How Thius, whom Hoop had sent there at Otger's behest, had managed to get the monastery keys from Emmanuele, the unsuspecting prior, for the promise of favors which he, presumably, found easy to offer. The whole elaborate plan was Otger's, from the timing to the accomplice who was to help Thius—one of the many street boys Otger knew so well—to the hiding of the paintings in the very back of a hidden storage room where even the brothers would not find them, and where Otger could retrieve them on his next trip to Rome. But it all went so terribly wrong. Some old monk—probably Pius from the description he got when Thius called him in Holland that evening—caught sight of them as they were nearly finished removing the paintings from their frames and then, in their rush to dispose of the paintings, they threw them into the dark room rather than hide them where Otger had said. How could they have known this dark, forbidding closet was ever used? And then, the final tragedy, Thius was found slashed to death in another closet. How or why he did not know, but he always felt responsible for having sent Thius down to Rome on this ill-fated mission.

In his silence, Avertanus knew. Brocard had told him but, like so many things he had blocked for so many years, he had not wanted to hear. Confessor that he was, Avertanus did not offer shock but only a compassionate ear, as Hoop told of a life filled with lies, of an academic career advanced by subterfuge and deception.

Before giving absolution, Avertanus asked if he might be able to speak of those matters brought up in confession which pertained to the paintings, the forged documents, and the robbery so as to begin to bring the light of truth into this whole, convoluted matter. Yes, Hoop mumbled, yes please. Whatever you can use to help, please do.

Then, after Hoop declared that he would try to amend his ways with God's grace, Avertanus placed his hand on the penitent in blessing. Saying first that light comes into the world only through the death and resurrection of God's only Son Jesus Christ, saying next that forgiveness is given by the ministry of the Church and the power of the Holy Spirit, he absolved him of his sins, in the name of the Father and of the Son and of the Holy Spirit.

Suddenly the burden was lifted from Dr. Hoop Rhutten and it was as if, strange as it may seem, he had been brought back to life.

89

Later that night, exhausted by the journey yet energized by the news he had received, Avertanus decided that, regardless of the expense, he must telephone Brocard in America. This was another instance where the bond of the brotherhood took precedence over professional duty. After all it was Zinka Pavlic who had encouraged him to pursue Hoop and who arguably had the greater vested interest, but she barely came to mind.

"Avertanus, is that really you? How wonderful to hear your voice."

"More wonderful than you can imagine, my brother, when I tell you what I have just found out."

Then Avertanus carefully revealed all of the information Hoop Rhutten had given to him about the decades of deception and theft Otger had masterminded, the most recent being faked documents which were being used by the dealer in the Hague to discredit Saint Agatha's attribution.

"I promised Hoop, a weak yet good person, that the order would not prosecute him at all but would turn its attention completely on Father Otger."

Avertanus smiled to hear Brocard castigating him like an old wife. "Yes, I know I should have believed you months ago. It is just that I can't conceive of such evil lurking within our community. Much as it pleases me to know the truth, it hurts me to know that a brother could have so badly used the order." As he spoke a gibbous moon broke through the clouds that had been obscuring it, drenching his room in the most sinister of light.

"Theft, my good friend is only one of the crimes which will come crashing down on him. The seals are about to be broken. The horsemen are thundering towards him."

Rather than pursue these arcane references, Avertanus told Brocard about Pino's visit to Sister Apollonia and noticed that who Brocard really wanted to know more about was Bertie, whom he too had recognized on the Web. They spoke of the irrepressible Zinka too. And even before Avertanus had the opportunity to suggest that he come to Europe, Brocard told him that being in Paris in the spring was not a wish but a necessity.

90

*T*ears welled up in her eyes and a wave of nausea came over her as she stooped to pick up the spent condom from the bathroom floor. Camille was so overcome with happiness at seeing Zinka again that she thought it best to go to the toilet rather than risk peeing in her panties. Little did she imagine she would find such an unwelcome reminder of Zinka's continued infidelity. Nor did she know how she was going to deal with it.

"Now don't play hard to get, my moist little melon, I have something to share with you and you alone." As she delicately lifted the dripping condom off the bathroom floor with tweezers and flushed it down the toilet, Camille found it inconceivable that there was any part of Zinka which was not part of the public domain. She soon realized that her disgust was because of Zinka's contact with a man rather than infidelity in itself, and then, being pragmatically French, she was confident that a faceless cock was no credible rival for a woman of beauty and character. Drying her eyes, patting her short cropped hair in place, and fluffing up her ubiquitous scarf, she decided that this small indiscretion did not even warrant notice. After all, Zinka still did have the biggest heart and largest tits in *tout Paris*, and from all that she still heard and felt, Camille had priority of claim to both.

"Well, finally! Come over here, dearest, sit down and close your eyes for the grand surprise." Always one to follow directions, Camille did exactly as she was told, confident that she was going to end up with a face full of Zinka. "Open!"

All she saw was a piece of paper, attractive enough but hardly worth such theatrics. "It is only a mock-up as they say in the trade, my tight little kumquat, the color will be far more vibrant, the text will shoot out in luminous gold." Focusing in on it, Camille saw that it was an invitation to a private *vernissage* of the "newly discovered" Poussin *Saint Agatha in Agony* at the Galerie Malouf on Avenue Matignon.

"There is so much to tell you, Camille." Smothering her fragile lover in kisses, Zinka could not have looked more radiant. "Oh, what a party this is going to be!"

91

One dark night,
Fired with love's urgent longings
Ah the sheer grace!
I went out unseen,
My house being all stilled.

Inspired by the mystical text of John of the Cross, Sister Apollonia Van Barren decided that the dictates of love transcended any human vow. So aided by the help of her spritual director, the faithful Father Avertanus, she realized her dream of fleeing into the arms of the one who spoke to her more clearly of the incarnate Love of the eternal Spouse than any person, concept, or theory ever had before. This is how they planned it.

Sister Apollonia was obliged to make an annual ten-day retreat, a time in which she was to have no contact with anyone. No sisters would drop food at her door; the whole convent was firmly directed to close the shutters on all windows that overlooked her hermitage so that she would never be drawn from introspection by outside distractions. These ten days were the grace she needed in order to leave and possibly even return.

It must be conceded that Avertanus himself was not completely convinced about the wisdom of her plan. He was not even sure that it was the best path Sister Apollonia's spirit should travel to be united with God. What he finally realized, however, was that even were this longing of the devil, unless it were allowed to be brought to completion, it would never go away. She would find no inner peace. So, in the middle of the first night of her scheduled retreat, after the sisters had finished compline and the surrounding convent was as dark and still as a tomb, she slid out the back door of her hermitage. She was dressed in a simple black tunic which Avertanus had bought for her some days before and she had spent a better part of the day combing the knots out of her waist-length auburn hair, which hung loose under a maroon hooded cape. All she carried with her was a small bag with a few toiletries. But her heart and mind were crammed with feelings and expectations as she made her way to the ladder which Avertanus had waiting at the rear of the garden wall.

> In darkness and secure,
> the secret ladder, disguised
> Ah the sheer grace!
> In secret, for no one saw me,
> Nor did I look at anything,
> With no other light or guide
> Than the one that burned in my heart.

Like the greatest of mystics, she moved as if guided by a force far greater than human will. Not once did she look down to see if her feet were firmly placed on the rungs, not for an instant did she pause as she flung her satchel over the wall and pulled the ladder up behind her. Even though Avertanus walked beside her, she might as well have been alone—silent, determined, and filled with that burning expectation which only lovers know.

It was not only Pino who drew her away from her hermitage, but beautiful Saint Agatha. When Father Avertanus told her of the *vernissage* in Paris in which the art world was finally to know her true importance, Apollonia thought of her own coming-out party. She felt that prayers were not enough to sustain delicate little Agatha at such a moment; the presence of all who had supported her in her journey to be recognized properly in the world demanded that she, Apollonia—who truly understood joyous suffering—must make every human effort possible to be there in person. But Pino himself was no small lure.

As they boarded the train to Antwerp which was to connect to the Paris express, Avertanus looked back to make sure no one was following them. Years of religion had taught him to be on guard. Sister Apollonia on the other hand had her gaze set on the one she would soon be united to. The beloved stag, as John of the Cross had elsewhere referred accurately to him, with whom she might finally find rest.

> *He wounded my neck with his gentle hand,*
> *Suspending all my senses.*

92

❦

*T*rue anonymity, as any New Yorker knows, can only be found in crowds. Aware of this, they had arranged to meet in that great open space in front of the Centre Pompidou, or the Beaubourg as Parisians referred to it, that garish heart of the new Paris which is invariably teaming with tourists, hucksters, and art wannabees. To assure a maximum crowd, the time had been set for four o'clock on a splendid Saturday afternoon. Seasoned religious that they were, both arrived early so as not to put the other out.

"*Salve*, brother." Brocard smiled broadly and gave Avertanus one of those chaste hugs which could never be mistaken for a sign of intimacy. Yet close they were in their own way, having lived together for the better part of their adult lives and having endured not only the demise of San Redempto but also, in all probability, religious life as they had known it. "Come, let's take the escalators to the roof, the view should be splendid today."

So Brocard followed Avertanus, who was far more at home in Paris than he. They merged into the crowds funneling into the clear plastic tubes that whisked them up the façade of the building to one of the finest views of Paris imaginable. It should have been a truly *herlichkeit* experience, as Avertanus's Swiss theologian friend Van Balthasar had been fond of saying. A moment of such beauty that it was transformative. As it was they found themselves crushed against the inside wall by hordes of children, several of whom were yelling that they had to "go pee-pee" but most screaming for seemingly no reason at all. Neither of them were used to talking above such noise and were so distracted that they only caught snippets of what the other was saying to them. Not an ideal way to catch up on each other's life or to make their plans for how to proceed, but the best they could do.

"... a necessary risk but she had to come. Yes, Bertie ... Paris too, yes."

"... women ... real power." Brocard's face lit up as if he had discovered some deep truth. It frustrated Avertanus slightly that he had no clue what this might be. Still, seeing Brocard excited about anything was infectious. America seemed to be agreeing with him.

As neither of them could really hear the other they looked carefully in each other's eyes and gave far greater value to body language than they might have otherwise done. What was clear to both was that they were alive—more alive than either of them had ever seen the other before, or even imagined they could be. To be sure, they were both lacking in that lobotomized veneer of peace which many associate with being enlightened. But their eyes sparkled and their skin had that flushed glow about it that showed that there was life within and an urgent desire to share it with each other, despite the noise and confusion which swirled around them. Laughing out loud at the idiocy of even trying to talk, Brocard grabbed Avertanus's arm and indicated that it was time to find a better place. As it turned out, this was inside the museum—where most of the throngs would never conceive of going. Breathing a sigh of relief they found a quiet, open space along the railing overlooking an ominously empty stage set up on the floor below.

"With our luck a troop of Australians playing garbage can lids will descend on us. Or worse still, ebullient Irish tap dancers with poles up their backs." Avertanus found his friend's facetiousness as refreshing as it was surprising. "My God, they are coming!"

Sure enough, a bevy of fresh young people dressed in black began to position themselves like wilted flowers along the periphery of the stage. Then someone who looked to be as old as Merce Cunningham himself froze in an awkward position center stage. At the first squeal of formless music he began cavorting about in blissful defiance of age.

"There is hope for us, Brother." Avertanus was obviously amused by the spectacle of so many wrinkles being squeezed into tights. "But the outfit will never do."

"Maybe later in life, my friend. For now there is too much work to be done." Then Brocard explained to him what had to be done before the *vernissage* later that week. How meetings had to be arranged and plans set with the authorities. When Avertanus asked him to be more explicit, he would only coyly say "both civil and aesthetic authorities." He was playing his cards close to his chest, Brocard, but he had to if he finally wanted to win.

93

It was highly unusual for Dr. Emil Rothenburg, the director emeritus of painting at the Louvre, to schedule an appointment on such short notice. In fact, it was virtually unheard of for him to have any appointment anymore at his office because, as everyone in Paris knew, Rothenberg was a gourmand who had long since decided that the only place in which things of substance could be discussed was over a vintage bottle of Givrey-Cambertin in a four-star restaurant. Fortunately for him, he had been so good at cultivating his coterie that he was never at a loss for invitations to dine and dine well.

But between the fervent pleas of this monk from America and the urgings of his superiors in Rome, he thought it best that an exception be made. Strange art history finds had come his way over decades and some indeed had merit. At the least, he hoped the meeting would prove amusing. And short enough not to interfere with his lunch date.

Events conspired to make Brocard late for this momentous meeting. First he had to quickly retrieve all the documents and research from Zinka, who could not understand why she herself could not make the presentation and, even more vexing, why he had to rush off, considering how long it had been since they had seen each other. And then, being so very American, when he arrived at the ever crowded main pyramid entrance he did not even consider pushing his way to the head of the line. He did, after all, have an appointment; his name was on a list at the front desk. When he finally made his way down from the courtyard to the lobby below, his nerves were frazzled. And when he was presented to the corpulent and irritated Dr. Rothenberg, his nerves were ready to snap. "Please do excuse me. I deliberately arrived early but the lines..."

"I am so sorry for your inconvenience." It was patently obvious that it was the director who felt put out. "Let us have a look at the documentation you have, shall we?"

Then something remarkable happened. It was as if Father Brocard were seized by a spirit that was not his own. He spoke with the authority and eloquence of someone who had to be reckoned with. As he laid out the infrareds, photographs, and documentation-as he explained with clarity and assurance everything from provenance to condition-Dr. Emil Rothernberg's corpulent body shook with the realization that Saint Agatha belonged to the patrimony of France.

Amazing to say, he didn't mind being late to the table.

94

The premise was absurd and a bit gauche, neither of which bothered Malouf in the slightest. Masterwork dealing had traditionally been a low key, decidedly back room affair. Were Didier, his venerable old partner, still alive, the Poussin would have been dealt by two or three strategic telephone calls. Any more would have burned it, thus lowering forever its desirability. But these were different times which requiring new marketing strategies. The fact was, the old master market was dead in the water. Some of the most respected houses had quietly—because it was always a discrete world even in death—gone belly up. Being an outsider on both sides of the bed, Wilfredo Malouf saw no problem in offending the system. Especially given the possibility of making a profit, which was clearly his expectation that night.

So even though it was in dubious taste to have a black tie opening, complete with color catalogue and an open bar, for an old master painting, he had concluded that, given his potential clientele, tradition be damned. He pinned his hopes on a rather unsophisticated lot: one Taiwanese businessman who was fascinated by the fact that the painting was so old; a couple of aging Brazilians who were impressed by anything French, especially if others were similarly impressed; and a young Hollywood mogul who saw some interesting promotional angles in the "hot," newly discovered painting. The one thing they had in common was that they had ready cash, which was not the case with almost any major institution these days. Except the Getty, which moved far too slowly for his taste.

Malouf had thought of every detail. So as to have time with the clients individually, he had invited them to come half an hour early in the hope that a sale could be finalized before the party began in earnest. And so as to assure that his gallery would look festive, he invited a few empty-headed but voluptuous women, including one he was on the make for, to stand around and sip wine. He even did Dionysius up in a Lagerfeld outfit with a bolero top and extremely tight-fitting leather trousers which, given the visual distractions all around, splendidly displayed his constantly engorged crotch. Something for everyone.

Zinka had talked over her dilemma with (or rather at) Camille for the past two days. Convinced she was the star of the evening, together with little Saint Agatha of course, she did not want to arrive too early, feeling an entrance was in order. Yet, in the off chance that Malouf was up to something sneaky—and he was a worm—she wanted to be there throughout the entire opening so that he couldn't slip anything by her. This conundrum, together with the ongoing problem of what to wear, had assured that both of their nerves were completely frayed by the time they arrived, which was moderately early. Zinka was dressed in an elaborate red Versace borrowed from Camille's mother's closet. As he was one of those designers who makes no concession for breasts, she simply popped off the buttons and wore it dangerously décolleté to the waist. Whatever made her think a size 42 bust would behave itself was beyond any sane person's comprehension.

Zinka recognized Dionysius right away even before she saw his face, and she squished up her face in the fearful expectation that some lingering smell of vomit might waft over to her. To her delight, and the deep satisfaction of Camille who put two and two together upon seeing him, he was locked into a mindless conversation with one of the hired mannequins.

Linking her arm in Camille's, she made her way over to Malouf, who was in the midst of explaining the intricacies of classical French painting to the Taiwanese businessman.

"I can assure you that when the reputation of the painting has been advanced, it will be worth four times the amount." It was clear that the notion of advancing a painting, getting it fully accepted in credible art circles, having it written about and accepted universally, was a concept which completely eluded the businessman.

"How long?" His question was succinct enough and Zinka, who

had snuck up just behind Malouf, felt happy to jump in with an answer. After all, as Professor Mitchum had to return to America for a symposium, she was the reigning Poussin expert at the gallery.

"Historically it is a very long process. Perhaps two years before an article can come out in the *Burlington* magazine and then at least another year before the community has time to assimilate it. It is very helpful that Professor Mitchum has authenticated it and decided to place it in the next addition of his Catalogue Raisonnee but, that too, is only one part of a very elaborate plan which must be put in place."

"Thank you Professoressa Pavlic." Malouf was clearly furious at her intrusion and, were it not for the fact that the businessman was obviously incapable of understanding a word of her Serbian-accented English, would have hauled off and hit her. Instead he decided to take her aside for a moment and tell her the parameters of what she could and couldn't do. But no sooner had he begun then, to both of their astonishment, Otger Aarnack, arrogance personified, entered the gallery together with a rather pasty-looking gentleman whom he introduced as his associate from the Hague. They had no idea of the existence of the document Dionysius had unearthed in Rome and were under the mistaken impression that they were still principles in the painting. Were that all that had gone wrong for Otger it would have been a disappointing but tolerable evening.

No one had yet really taken the time to appreciate Saint Agatha, although she was presented in a beautiful period frame, lit to perfection under meticulously calibrated pin spots, and looked ravishing. Instead Zinka had her claws out for Otger. He in turn was curious about what Dionysius was doing there. While Dionysius's only concern was the fact that he was getting aroused by Camille, whom he had never really noticed before, but who reminded him so very much of the woman he had left behind in Rome. He was beginning to realize he missed her very much indeed. And just at that moment Father Avertanus came in with Hoop Rhutten from Maastrich, converted to the truth and eager to confess to all.

This was the precise moment when Otger realized that something had gone very wrong. How did Avertanus get through to Hoop, and more important still, what had Hoop told Avertanus about the years of rape and plunder? Just as Otger was beginning to make his way to the door, Avertanus turned and extended his hand to a rather ethereal-looking creature draped in black. Sister Apollonia froze in place as she caught sight of the painting of Saint Agatha on the far wall. Tears welled in her eyes as she reached out to take Avertanus's hand and then, as if forgetting herself, she turned to take the hand of an extremely handsome young Italian, her escort Pino, aka ItalStud, who followed her like a well-trained pup. Together the two escorted her over to the painting, where Avertanus left her so that he could confront Otger and his accomplice from the Hague.

"You are surely not planning on going anywhere I trust, Father Aarnack? The party is just beginning." It felt so good to be the heavy, a role he had never been cast in before but always longed to play. "I believe you know many of the guests?" It was then that Bertie rushed in, fearing that Pino was becoming inordinately fond of the nun. He was all set to unburden his soul to Avertanus when he caught sight of Otger and Dionysius.

"Bloody hell, it's a San Redempto alum party! How absolutely appalling!"

Sister Apollonia was as confused by his outburst as she was by the way in which Pino was pressing close to her. Whatever could he mean by breathing on me like that? The thought of physical contact, even of him looking so healthy and assured was decidedly off-putting. She noted how much better he looked on the monitor, blurry and diffuse.

The center of attention that night, if the truth be told, was none of these characters and not even Saint Agatha herself, pretty as she looked. That claim could only be made by Father Brocard Curtis, whose grand entrance alone would have been enough to warrant it.

First the gallery doors flung open to reveal three of the Horsemen of the Apocalypse, those attractive sadists whom Otger had trained so well and Emmanuele had used to his ultimate disadvantage. Brocard had maxed out his credit cards so that they looked appropriately tough and elegant. To Camille's discerning eye, it seemed they had Ferre on the top and Ferragamo on the feet although she wouldn't swear to it.

It was then that Brocard himself made his entrance, looking to all the world like a Jesuit. Button-down shirt and striped tie, hardly overdressed but definitely on target. Bracketing him were two very dapper-looking *gendarmes* who tipped their hats at Zinka, who was relieved to finally see Brocard there.

Brocard walked directly over to Otger, locked eyes with him, and with a low and certain voice which rose from his very depths said one word only: "Checkmate."

Then, turning to the police, he indicated that this was their man.

"Professor Otger Aarnack, charges have been made against you which require that we take you into custody." The lists of charges included larceny, fraud, and murder, and both his accuser and witnesses to his crimes were there to back it up. Thanks to the Napoleonic code, he was guilty until proven innocent. Which meant guilty he would stay, forever.

As gratifying as these events were, they were not the only trick that Brocard had up his sleeve. There was still Saint Agatha, of course, the hapless virgin who precipitated all of this chaos and whose fate was still unsettled. As the horsemen and *gendarmes* circled Otger, space was cleared for the distinguished figure of Dr. Emil Rothenburg.

Zinka recognized him immediately, and overcome with the honor of it all, she nearly wet her pants. Without any prompting from Brocard, the emeritus director of the Louvre went over to the painting to inspect it. The room went silent, except for some low moaning from Dionysius who had no respect for time or place. Rothenburg inspected the painting from a distance, from up close, and then, taking a louche from his pocket, in meticulous detail. Then he demanded it be removed from the wall so he could inspect the back of the painting both the canvas and the stretcher. By now Zinka was drenched in sweat, no, Camille, it couldn't pass for perspiration, and Hoop, whose initial authentication was also on the line, was likewise breathing very deeply.

Only after all this was done did Dr. Rothenburg take the paper he had previously prepared out of his jacket pocket and present it to Malouf. The Painting of *Saint Agatha in Agony* by Nicolas Poussin was designated national patrimony of France and could not for any reason be removed from the country. Furthermore, Rothenburg informed the devastated dealer, negotiations had begun with the Order of Our Lady of Divine Succor, the owner of the painting, for the painting to be purchased over a period of time by the Louvre museum, where all principles agreed it would be best for it to remain. The Galerie Malouf would make a fair and equitable commission.

A series of strange noises followed this remarkable news. To almost all present, it seemed as if Saint Agatha herself had given out a high-pitched and most unladylike yelp. Avertanus alone recognized it as Apollonia's and realized immediately that something had gone awry with her encounter with Pino. Then there was Bertie's strange clucking, that was the only word for it. It was a nasty trait he picked up on the prom in Blackpool years ago and had never been able to shake at times of stress. If asked to explain it he would say it was like the sound a decapitated chicken's head makes as the body goes madly running off. A trying to come to terms with a reality that's hard to take.

However by far the most horrific noise of all was the frightening laugh which came out of Father Otger Aarnack as he was ceremoniously led away to prison. It was a sound which originated somewhere deep in the center of the earth, where the medievals always imagined hell to be. An unearthly and satanic sound overflowing with menace. At the sound of his laugh, it is safe to say, all of Paris was hushed.

The final noise that anyone remembers that evening was Zinka's exuberant cry as she attempted to throw herself into the arms of her hero. How was Brocard to know she was going to lunge in his direction? Missing the mark, the professoressa bounced off the wall and fell flat on her ass directly under the painting. All this was too much for her breasts, which came spilling out for all to see. Especially, it must be noted, Saint Agatha who, despite the felicitous way in which things had turned out, was not at all happy about such a flagrant display of flesh.

95

Dear Father General,

It is quite late here but I cannot even think of sleeping because of the many wondrous things which have happened. Our God is good. First you must know that Dr. Emil Rothenburg of the Louvre has inspected the painting and corroborated the opinions of Professors Mitchum and Pavlic that our painting of Saint Agatha is indeed by Poussin. He took steps to guarantee that the work stay in France as he had provisionally discussed with you recently. Furthermore he will begin the process of accessioning the painting to the Louvre. This means that money will regularly come to the order over the coming years. He has likewise told me that a committee will be set up to evaluate the remaining paintings in the series. Professoressa Zinka Pavlic, who has worked tirelessly on the order's behalf, has graciously agreed to work with the Louvre on this ongoing project.

What this means is that the devious plans of Father Otger to diminish the worth of the painting so as to situate himself in an ownership position have been thwarted. It saddens me, as I know it must you, to have to accuse a brother of such malicious and criminal behavior. I can only assure you, Reverend Father, that I do not make these accusations lightly. It is my hope to be able to talk with you personally about the many charges which have been made against him, some of which go directly to the heart of the dissolution of San Redempto. My plan is to come directly to Rome as soon as I am finished tying up loose ends here. I am sure that you have many questions about all that has been hap-

pening and look forward to answering them to the best of my ability.

Please give my regards to faithful Father Angelus, without whose confidence in my ability and prayers for my success none of these wonderful things would have come to pass.

Yours in Our Lady of Divine Succor,
Father Brocard

96

Even were there no ark to enter and no extinction to be faced, most creatures would choose to march forward by twos. So it was with the majority of the remaining characters of this tale. With Otger's sinister laugh still echoing in their ears, decisions were made which were to affect the remainder of their lives on earth. It is safe to say that, like most of us, they saw their choices as far less significant than they in fact were. Hardly aware of the consequences of our actions, Fate does have a way of beguiling us at times.

The first to break rank and return to his former ways was Dionysius. Ever since he had started to upchuck on Zinka, he sensed that he had made a terrible mistake in leaving his woman and son in Rome. What they lacked in glamour they more than made up for in consistency and patience. Neither of which were character traits in which Wilfredo Malouf set any stock. And even though Dionysius was vauntfully proud of his sexual prowess, he was becoming rather bored with being re-reified. He was, lest he forget, more than an object. So the morning after the opening, he carefully packed his Lagerfeld outfit—at least he had gotten something out of this escapade—ate very lightly, and braced himself for a bumpy flight back to Rome. He had no doubt that his long-suffering woman would be waiting. Dionysius promised himself that he would draw her close and even call her by her name.

Sister Apollonia's separation from Pino was no less decisive. It was not that she didn't want to walk as a couple. Rather, she found the notion of a humanly flawed and emotionally incomprehensible spouse not at all to her liking. She longed for the Spouse who would be there, silently, when she needed Him; who would give her solace and peace in equal measure; and who would not stop suffering, no matter how cheery the day. Pino, she had come to realize, was not such a spouse. Thank God she had found out in time. She knew that if she were to make it back to her hermitage before the ten days expired, she had to leave Paris the following day at the latest. Avertanus had graciously promised to book seats on a train back to Zenderan and escort her safely back over the wall.

From the moment valiant Camille picked up the offending condom with her tweezers, her relationship with Zinka was never in doubt. When one loses one's heart to the likes of the professoressa, only a frame of steel can protect one from ache and pain. And so as others watched in amusement at Zinka's stupendous fall and gapped in wonder at her overflowing tits, Camille Blanchierdarie, a woman of breeding and a friend to the end, whipped off her Hermes scarf and draped it ceremoniously over her lover's breast. The fact that it was too small by far in no way diminished the nobility of her act.

As for Bertie, he quickly realized that Brocard in person had nowhere near the compassion, empathy, and affect of the one he had come to love in cyberspace. While others may have been impressed by Brocard's bravado at the gallery, all Bertie saw was yet another self-assured and slightly priggish cleric. My, my, don't we have all the answers, kept going through his mind as one piece after another fell nicely into place. A man like that held no appeal to Bertie, and as he was quick to note, once the power got to his head, he seemed to have no time for Bertie at all. Not even a little smile. Nothing.

Pino too had learned his lesson, although it hadn't been easy. What at first had seemed like acceptance and openness on Apollonia's part had in reality been little more than projection. Bertie, who loved him more than life itself, had long understood this to be the case. Admittedly this is not how Pino himself would have put it because, as it must be clear by now, his communication skills and powers of introspection were rather limited.

"She was as cold as a statue and didn't even want to touch me."

"Yes, yes, I know." Bertie was glad they had decided to book a private sleeping compartment for the journey back to Rome so that he could comfort his man.

"All she wanted was to pity me. A little pity is very nice but . . ."

"There, there." Pino laid his head in Bertie's lap to have his forehead stroked. Bertie knew that he alone was put in the world to satisfy all of Pino's many needs and appreciate the complexity of worshiping him.

Two by improbable two they walked into the ark.

97

They are beauty itself those pert little breasts. See how lovingly he has modeled each one so that the music of the spheres rings out!" Zinka often mixed her metaphors but on such a glorious day, with lovers strolling and birds singing riotously all around them, neither Camille nor Brocard was about to fault her. The three of them were taking one final stroll in the Tuileries on the morning Brocard was leaving for Rome. The place was of Zinka's choosing not only because of the Maillol statues of women strewn throughout but also because of the grand scale which raised her already soaring spirits even higher.

"Now, carissimo Brocardus, it is time for a little scolding. Why didn't you tell me you were coming to Paris?" For the life of him Brocard could not figure out why she would want to deny having invited him over. Then he remembered the two E-mails he had received from her back to back. "Whatever are you talking about, my precious?"

It took some time for them to figure out that the second E-mail had not come from her at all, that in all likelihood it had come from Otger for nefarious reasons which might never fully come to light. The man was evil, wanted to cause chaos, to rub people's noses in his mess—perhaps that was reason enough. All Brocard knew was that his friend Zinka was mercifully not lusting after him and that those rapidly changing communications were fraught with uncertainty.

"Change is what keeps us all so ravishingly attractive, carissimo!" She squeezed them both tightly to herself. "Oh my little darlings, how wonderful it is to be alive, to have all of these tools at our command. They are ours to exploit, so let's do it!"

Before Zinka got too carried away Brocard asked the two of them where they planned to live now that the professoressa had been appointed a member of the newly formed Louvre research team. It was a subject which they had not yet had a chance to discuss but which had only one answer.

"Rome," they said in unison.

Then Camille more radiant and animated than Zinka had ever seen her, explained why this had to be. "Two such exotic creatures need neutral ground in which to flourish and grow."

"And in which to love, carissima mia, to love!" It always came back to that.

98

My dear friends,

Now that the final chapter in the saga of Saint Agatha has been written, those of us whose lives have been caught up in this web of intrigue and deception have cause to wonder why God chose to draw us individually and corporately into such a fray. This thought consumes me as I write. While the experience is still fresh in our minds I want to offer a few reflections on what has happened and why I believe we had no choice but participate fully. Hopefully these will not be the last words to be said. If I am certain of anything, it is that the lessons we have each learned over this past year will continue to inform our lives, challenge us, and bring us to a deeper understanding of God's ongoing plan for this world.

Consider if you will the magnificent work Saint Agatha has done since being taken down from the ambulatory wall where she had rested for at least two centuries. First she flushed out the petty thieves in our midst, then pointed the finger at the mastermind of it all. Finally, disgusted by the corruption all around, the betrayal of solemn vows, she brought down the walls of the monastery itself. But she was not satisfied with this. No, she moved on to show the deception and greed rife within the art world and would not rest until final justice was done. Throughout it all, she encouraged all of us to focus on what our true needs were. To transform our very selves by searching for that love unique to each of us; for accepting the truth which lies within, no matter how alien that might be to a world in which truth and corruption have so often been mistakenly confused. Each of us in our own way has been

288

driven by demons and angels, by the roles this remarkable virgin martyr has deigned we play. One thought stays fixed in my mind, an aphorism spoken first by that saint and wizard Alberto Magnus: Everyone is capable of magic if they fall into a great excess. *With the ongoing help of the lovely Saint Agatha, may all of you, my brothers and sisters, continue to work magic in your own lives by throwing yourselves into great, luxuriant, and never-ending excess.*

Lovingly yours,
Avertanus

Then, filled with an overwhelming peace, Father Avertanus Deblaer, magus and friend, sent the E-mail out to everyone on his list in the hope that it might encourage them uniquely to embrace the grace of God and the joy-filled struggle of life itself.

99

*o you honestly think recipes would work? Would anyone be interested, really?" It took some time for Pino to convince Bertie that there were many people on the web who would be fascinated to discover the hidden world of mushrooms which he took for granted. When and how to collect them, which are noxious, which nutritious, stewing and stuffing them, munching on them raw, frying porcini like steaks. The list was endless.

"But, Pino, it is you they are interested in when they log on, you they want to see."

It was then that Pino showed himself to be more caring than Bertie had ever imagined. "To know me," he said, looking piercingly into Bertie's eyes, "they must come to know the person who serves my needs." These weren't exactly words of unconditional love, but given Bertie's expectations about life and love, they sounded pretty good to him.

And so the ItalStud Web site developed in tandem with their relationship. No longer did they only take requests, although to keep revenue coming in some of that still had to be factored in. More and more Pino and Bertie shared common Abruzzi wisdom about health and life, like when to plant and when to sow and how the length of a siesta depends on the length of the days. As summer turned into fall, then fall to winter, they learnt how to hibernate in each other, becoming increasingly content to do less and enjoy each other's company more. Given the longing for peace and stability throughout the world it should come as no surprise that their site began to enjoy unprecedented popularity. Several slick agents made a path to their door, a book was planned. One went so far as to envision the Abruzzi taking over from Provence—which admittedly had been done to death—as the refuge of the overworked and overpaid.

Pino continued to express his need to be worshiped and waited on, and Bertie his to be of service and adore. Over the years they didn't really age, the two of them. A few wrinkles, a few less hairs. Pino did develop a slight belly over time which it will not surprise you to learn, Bertie found unbearably becoming.

Epilogue

$\mathcal{I}$t seemed hard to believe that it had been nearly three years since Brocard had been with her, and he could not help but wonder how she had fared with all the notoriety. From her cloistered beginnings to a very controlled introduction into the larger world, there is no way that she was prepared for such unprecedented media success. Life—not just hers but life in general—has always been a curious affair. But without doubt the way it is lived in our scandal-generating globally interconnected time is perverse to the extreme. For these past years Brocard had watched in wonder as a media feeding frenzy broke around her—until now she was all that anyone talked about and all that anyone wanted to see.

The trial of Father Otger Aarnack had rapidly escalated from a Franco-Italian affair to a matter of international interest. Each day he testified brought more banner headlines: San Lorenzo Crypt Nightmare! Torture Chamber Revealed! Throughout it all, the painting which started it all was mentioned.

More than all the excellent scholarship of the professoressa and company, this was the reason that Saint Agatha had become the Mona Lisa of our time, complete with lines of tourists and T-shirt images of her hapless pose. As Brocard paid her a visit, he realized how much she still meant to him and thanked God for the life she brought into his tawdry existence. Finally, he knew that like all good relationships, the struggle had been worth it. Like all true love, they had been good for each other. The game had been worth playing.